A Class on Murder

A RONNIE RAVEN MYSTERY

A CLASS ON MURDER

K. B. GIBSON

FIVE STAR
A part of Gale, Cengage Learning

GALE
CENGAGE Learning·

Detroit • New York • San Francisco • New Haven, Conn • Waterville, Maine • London

GALE
CENGAGE Learning·

Set in 11 pt. Plantin.

LIBRARY OF CONGRESS CATALOGING-IN-PUBLICATION DATA

Gibson, Karen Bush.
 A class on murder / K.B. Gibson. — 1st ed.
  p. cm. — (A Ronnie Raven mystery; 1)
 ISBN 978-1-4328-2593-5 (hardcover) — ISBN 1-4328-2593-3
(hardcover) 1. Women college teachers—Fiction. 2. Murder—
Investigation—Oklahoma—Fiction. I. Title.
PS3607.I2695C57 2012
813'.6—dc23   2011051000

First Edition. First Printing: June 2012.
Published in 2012 in conjunction with Tekno Books and Ed Gorman.

Printed in Mexico
1 2 3 4 5 6 7 16 15 14 13 12

A Class on Murder

CHAPTER ONE

Many people say you should start at the beginning. I'm not one of them. I hate long, drawn-out stories that go on and on until your eyes cross. Just give me the nitty-gritty.

Yet if I told you about the night I died, you might shake your head at what sounds like a bizarre ghost story. But I am no ghost, and this is no ghost story, even with a Cherokee and Irish heritage heavy on other worldly beings like leprechauns and Little People. In this case, Little People aren't a politically correct way of referring to people short in stature. Little People are magical beings—cousins to the leprechauns—according to my Cherokee grandmother. Hidden deep in the hills of eastern Oklahoma, the Little People rarely show themselves to humans. Sometimes they make exceptions for curious children never seen again.

Both grandmothers, Cherokee and Irish, warned me—from the time I started to walk—to never follow flickers of light. Fireflies or lightning bugs, most people called them. Little People, my grandmothers insisted. Although my parents claimed that Little People were just folklore, I received my one and only spanking after I went looking for the Little People at the precocious age of seven. Unsuccessfully, I might add. I'm still waiting to see the Little People.

Modern-day people scoff at the idea of Little People. But the older I get, the more things my grandmothers told me make sense. So why not Little People? I suppose it doesn't really matter, though. Would Little People have anything to do with murder on a college campus?

It all started with spring break. Spring break isn't just for kids. We college professors love it, too. While droves of people headed to the Texas beaches of Padre Island, I scampered off to Breckenridge for a week of skiing with Rick, public defender and occasional boyfriend. I had been looking forward to the muffled silence of Colorado's snow-covered peaks. On the very first day, Rick broke his leg and subsequently expected me to cater to him. He didn't understand my reluctance to act as nursemaid. I didn't understand why more wives didn't kill sick or injured husbands. My mother says that it's this attitude that keeps me single.

If spring break had been more successful, maybe I would have returned protected by that wonderful vacation afterglow instead of going off half-cocked the first Monday back at school. Traffic drives me crazy, and since I only live a few miles from campus, I regularly biked to work, even on blustery March mornings. On that first day back, fierce Oklahoma winds came at me from all directions, whipping already unruly hair into my face and forcing me to blindly wobble down tree-lined streets on my mountain bike.

Much to the surprise of many people I meet (and sometimes myself), I'm a psychology professor. I teach behavioral psychology at Pursley University, better known as PU. Can you imagine? Some people have nothing better to do than to test their creativity by coming up with names like Skunk U.

Spitting hair out of my mouth, I arrived at Rubenstein Hall, better known as Psych. A single rusty bike rack sitting next to the building was swallowed up by a huge . . . I mean *massive* motorcycle—a gleaming black Harley-Davidson with a novelty license plate that read "FREUD".

Sonuvabitch! It wasn't the first time he had done this to me.

He seemed to think he ruled the whole kingdom of PU or at least Psych. And he was just about as unbalanced as the psych building. When they built Rubenstein Hall, the builders started with a classic architectural style of arches and gables. We must have switched university presidents midway into construction because then they decided to go with the sharp lines of a modern design. Now Psych looks like a schizophrenic building that is actively hallucinating. A perfect location for psychologists, especially one who liked to think of himself as another Sigmund Freud, father of psychoanalytic theory and some of the dumbest theories I've ever heard.

Weldon Crutchfield was one of those Freudian throwbacks, the kind who believed *all* women suffered from penis envy. Hell, I figured most women fell down on their knees thanking God they didn't have a penis—especially after meeting Weldon Crutchfield.

The Harley was probably the newest addition to Crutchfield's mid-life crisis, what with his obsession with Freud and having a penis and all. After all, what was a motorcycle but a huge penis between the legs? Before this monstrosity on wheels, Crutchfield had some kind of hair transplant. Not a toupee, he assured me. He even offered to let me touch it, but I refused to touch anything that looked like a dead rodent.

I locked my mountain bike to the nearest tree, a sapling, no great deterrent if thieves wanted the bike that Mom and the nephews gave me for Christmas. I swung my faded denim backpack onto one shoulder before I proceeded to hunt down Crutchfield. He had been making my life hell since I started working at PU three years ago, and I refused to put up with his god complex one minute longer.

I ran up a flight of stairs, my suede sneakers making screeching noises against vinyl floors. I didn't stop to toss my backpack in my office. I didn't want to get sidetracked by the phone or a student. Most of all, I didn't want my anger to dissipate. I wanted to unleash my full fury on Crutchfield.

Our building was shaped like the letter Z (I told you it was schizophrenic; how many buildings are shaped like Z's?) with professor offices on the second floor. My office was the second one from the top of the Z; Crutchfield's was in the center. He liked to refer to his office as "the heart of Psych." More like the "heartburn."

A closed door awaited me when I reached his office. Crutchfield once bit my head off because I had knocked and opened the door without waiting for an engraved invitation. He was a real stickler about privacy and demanded we all knock even when he didn't return the courtesy.

"Crutchfield!" I threw back the door with enough force that the cloudy plastic window in it rattled in unison with the squeak in the hinges. "Who the hell do you think you are? Parking that monstrosity where no one can use the bike racks!"

He sat behind the desk facing the window, the high back of his leather chair shielding his face from view. I wouldn't have known he was there except for the brown polyester sleeve peeking out from the armrest.

"Crutchfield, I'm talking to you!"

Probably staring at some sweet young thing outside his window, which made me want to tear that hairy weasel off his head and stomp on it. I liked to think of myself as a pacifist, but I really hated being ignored. I positioned myself between Crutchfield and the window to force his attention.

Nothing. No leers, no obnoxious retorts. Not even any feebleminded attempts to psychoanalyze my immature behavior. Maybe it had something to do with his bulging eyes and a dark-red—almost black—hole decorating the center of his chest. Body organs may have been floating close to the surface, but since anatomy wasn't my field of expertise, I decided against studying the wound any closer.

Crutchfield didn't bat an eye. His left hand held a gun, small except for the long narrow barrel. A silencer? I knew next to nothing about guns, but what kind of American would I be if I hadn't learned something about guns from television and the movies?

Sallow skin covered round cheeks and a wilting chin that in life had been razor-sharp. His mouth was oddly human—no crooked sneers or lips disappearing with disapproval. If I didn't know better, I would think my friend, Terry, had been here working his makeup magic on Crutchfield's face. As a drama professor, Terry's worst perversion was creating gruesome makeup and special effects. Needless to say, Terry was a hit at Halloween.

My curiosity at viewing a dead body up close won out over the growing queasiness in my gut. Except for eyes that looked ready to pop out of his head, death brought an improvement to Weldon Crutchfield's appearance. And I was pretty sure he was dead. Since the left hand held the gun, I forced myself to reach for his right wrist. Clammy. Like a mannequin but not as solid. No pulse. I quickly dropped his hand, which fell to his lap instead of back on the armrest. And that was where it was going to have to stay. All the chocolate in the world wouldn't convince me to touch his dead arm again. I figured Crutchfield wouldn't mind. After all, he was dead.

Most definitely dead. The realization sent my stomach hurtling toward my chest. I wanted to run from Crutchfield's office screaming, but I felt a perverse sense of responsibility for the body. Finder's keepers, maybe?

I moved to the other side of the desk, reaching for the telephone with shaky hands. I dialed nine-one-one but afterward heard only the silence of an incomplete call. The glossy desk surface revealed my larger-than-normal eyes contrasting against visibly pale skin. I looked up and noticed a hole in the back of Crutchfield's chair, smaller than the hole in his chest but in the same region. I pressed down on the switch hook for a new dial tone. After punching in nine, I was rewarded with an outside line and quickly finished with nine-one-one again. I quickly gave the who, what, and where to the dispatcher on the other end of the phone.

I hung up the phone, intent on looking for the bullet, but instead my eardrums were assaulted. Paula Burke, another professor in the psychology department, stood next to me and poured out a piercing scream. I had no doubt that the scream carried throughout the building. Maybe next door in the English building, too.

My rather loud colleague reminded me of a stuck record, unable to do anything but scream and point at Crutchfield. If the noise hadn't been so bad, I might have found her behavior interesting. Paula Burke, always cool and controlled. I called her the Ice Queen behind her back, but she was anything but that right now.

Paula's screams worked like a siren, bringing everyone in the building running. Students, faculty, and staff filed in to view Crutchfield in all his final glory. A few people adopted an interesting hue of green. The sight of a dead man with a hole in his chest fascinated others. These people worried me the most, the same ones who slowed down at car accidents, craning their necks in hopes of catching sight of blood and gore.

Chaos reigned now, and at a high decibel level, too. After a few feeble attempts to usher everyone out, I decided to concentrate on Paula. Her compact body was almost a head shorter than mine, even with stylish two-inch heels. I'm taller than average, but not enough to qualify as one of those leggy models. Not only because of my height, but I also like to think I have too many curves to pass for an androgynous waif. Although the curves may not be exactly where I want them to be, they are there. If there was a contest on who was stronger—Paula or me—I believe most people would bet on me. And they would lose. This woman was a rock. Finally I got in her line of vision and yelled her name. After a minute of this, she gave me one of those "who the hell are you?" looks. But at least she let herself be steered toward the doorway.

As we pushed our way through the throng of people, a contingent of campus and city police officers arrived. I'm fairly certain that the most serious thing our campus police ever handled was breaking up loud parties. That was one of the things that drew me to a job at a university. Unlike my last job, a research position for one of those mega-conglomerates, a real sense of community inhabited the campus. We maintained our unique identity from the rest of the world. Now violence had invaded our little Utopia.

The scene in Crutchfield's office reminded me of those old *Three Stooges* shows I watched as a kid, and that I still occasionally find when bouts of insomnia send me channel surfing in the middle of the night. Everyone was running this way and that way, bumping into each other. One of the cops even looked a little like Curly. Or was that Shep? I considered looking for Moe when I remembered the hysterical woman in my grasp.

"Let's go to your office, Paula," I yelled in her ear.

We stumbled to the left in what resembled a three-legged race away from Crutchfield's office. By the time I reached for a polished wood door, I could hear only a dull roar from Crutchfield's office. When I entered Paula's office, the white of the walls temporarily blinded me. Gleaming, spotless white walls looked more sterile than any operating room. No hints of color anywhere.

I tried to set my unsteady coworker in her office chair, but finally resorted to a shove. I'm not the best person to be taking care of the emotionally distraught, but I was afraid to leave her. I tried to think of someone I could contact, but couldn't recall ever seeing Paula with someone, either inside or outside of the department. I knew nothing about her or her life. Whether she was married, had children, or who her friends were. It struck me as sad that I could work in such close quarters with someone and know so little about her. I would save contemplating the ins and outs of professional relationships for another time, though.

The woman in the latter stages of middle age sitting before me wore a ghostly mask of shock. Wide streaks of gray overwhelmed her mousy brown hair. And the shakes were bad. Really bad. She shuddered from head to toe, which made walking in heels even more impressive. Put it all together, and she would give the monsters in any horror movie a run for their money.

"Paula, it's me, Ronnie. Ronnie Raven."

"I know who you are," she said. "I haven't lost my mind. Yet."

"I'm sorry. It's just that you don't look too well. I'm worried."

"No need. I'll survive. Obviously, we can't say the same for Weldon, now can we? He had been so depressed lately, but I never thought he would . . . take his own life." Paula leaned forward, her normally crisp clothing taking on a rumpled look. In an almost ritualistic manner, she picked at lint—lint too small for my twenty-twenty vision to see—from the long sleeves of her Victorian-type blouse.

"I didn't realize the two of you were so close." In fact, I didn't recall the two of them ever exchanging words. Crutchfield had a low opinion of female professors and had no use for any woman over the age of thirty, which partially explained my antagonistic relationship with the man.

"Maybe once . . . no, I suppose we were never close. Not

really." Raw pain clouded eyes the color of a foggy day. I looked away, not knowing what to do. I wanted to offer comfort, but she never struck me as a huggable person. I settled for lightly placing my hand over one of hers, almost recoiling from its iciness. I wanted to place her hand between mine and rub some life back into it, but somehow the gesture seemed too intimate.

"Is there anything I can do for you? Maybe call someone?"

She gave me a trembling smile before withdrawing her hand and turning her chair toward a small window sparkling with the morning sun. "I think I just need to be alone, Ronnie. It's a good time to remember."

Remember what, I wanted to say to the back of her chair, but didn't. In grief, the wall surrounding the woman thickened. When I came to PU three years ago, I naturally sought out the only other woman in our male-dominated fortress. But we had never clicked. Maybe Paula was uncomfortable with our age difference. Although probably a couple of years younger than my mother, Paula's rigidly proper behavior made her seem much older. She rarely smiled and never raised her voice, reminding me of a very proper British girls' school matron without the accent.

I looked around Paula's office, the same type of cracker-box design as my own, yet any dust had been beaten into submission. The bookcase matched the desk, both in dark mahogany finish and starkness. No personal mementos adorned any surface. Paula's space was so cold that I shivered.

I started to say the customary "if you need anything," but she was already lost in her own little world—a world I didn't belong in. I hoped she would get a few minutes of peace before the questioning started. The police would surely want to question us since we were the first to find the body.

The body. Just thinking those words sent a shiver down my spine. But that was what I saw as I gently closed Paula's door behind me and turned the corner. A body. Weldon Crutchfield's body draped under a sheet, being pushed on a gurney toward the elevator. White-clothed attendants had trouble maneuvering because the number of onlookers had multiplied in the brief time I had been away. Word traveled fast. I would bet most of the eager faces didn't even have a class in Psych.

A hand dropped from under the sheet. A lifeless, colorless hand adorned with an ornately designed ring. A class ring with a shiny red stone on his right hand. Who would inherit it? Or would it be buried with its owner, never to see the light of day again?

Once Crutchfield's body was successfully loaded onto the elevator, the crowd slowly scattered. Ducking my head down, I swiftly made my way through the remaining onlookers. I headed to my office, needing my own time to process what had happened. And it wasn't even nine A.M., I thought as I approached my door. My locked door. The keys were in my backpack, which was no longer with me. I turned to retrace my steps. Had I taken it into Paula's office?

I stopped in my tracks and groaned. Shit! I had left my backpack in Crutchfield's office.

CHAPTER TWO

My shoes squealed in protest against the scuffed floor as I spun back around toward Crutchfield's office. Winding my way through the remaining gawkers, I received more than a few rude looks. Imagine my surprise when one of my elbows found its way into the side of one young man. And my suede denim-colored sneakers might have made contact with a few toes. Accidentally, of course.

The Boss Man stepped directly in my path before I reached Crutchfield's door. As a person, Zachariah Bent was all right, occasionally demonstrating an interesting sense of humor. But as a department head, he behaved more like a politician than a scholar of psychology. His goal in life was notice from the state regents and a first-name relationship with PU's president. We got off to a bad start when he tried to institute a dress code for professors after I wore jeans to work one day. As if my denims would lead to anarchy. If I were the head of the department, I would be more concerned about male professors with baggy pants heading south.

Zachariah must have been devastated over Crutchfield's death. If Crutchfield had a buddy within our department, it was our illustrious leader. Was it my imagination, or did Zachariah look, well, almost happy as he scurried around managing things. I shrugged. Managing things—and people—was what Zachariah did best.

"Dr. Raven?" He stopped me with a hand to my elbow and

smiled in that plastic manner taught in boss school. Technically, it's a smile because of a slight upward curl at the ends. But teeth were kept under wraps, and the smile never traveled to the eyes. Eyes that now looked as hard as granite. "I need you to take over Dr. Crutchfield's introduction class, starting this afternoon."

"Jesus H. Christ, Zachariah, the body isn't even cold yet."

His hand dropped from my arm, and I was rewarded with a look of barely concealed rage. Even his plastered-down salt-and-pepper hair looked ready to pop up. "The students shouldn't have to suffer for the unfortunate actions of a troubled man. And I can't think of anyone better suited to teach an introduction class than you."

I knew that teaching Introduction to Psychology was a fate worse than death. And he knew I knew. Teaching 300 to 400 freshman students only the most general and trivial of psychology required the patience of a saint. I knew this, as I was already teaching one section of Intro and was nowhere near sainthood. But my momma didn't raise no fool. I knew this was one battle I hadn't a chance in hell of winning. And, frankly, I didn't care. First on my to-do list for today was to burrow in my office until I could make sense of this morning's events. I put on my best saccharine smile. "Why, thank you so much, Dr. Bent. I can't think of anything more enjoyable than teaching another section of Intro."

Zachariah narrowed his gaze before sharply turning away and taking long strides down the hallway. Another suit approached him before he got very far. Before I had taken a single breath, Zachariah changed his posture from one draped with anger to one of concern. I couldn't hear what the two suits were saying, but Zachariah gave a sympathetic nod before steering the obviously distraught man upstairs.

My next opponent stood guard at Crutchfield's door. A

campus police officer in an ugly beige uniform. Like a Boy Scout, patches and pins gave the shirt its only color. He even looked a little like a Boy Scout, with a face so smooth that it probably required only a weekly shave. With a mop of black hair and a neatly crisp uniform, he looked like a kid playing dress up for Halloween.

"I'm sorry, you can't go in there, ma'am."

I hated being called ma'am. It shriveled up that "young at heart" attitude I tried so hard to cultivate. "Can't hear you. Left my hearing aid at home."

The kid looked at me like I was a possible loon he might have to cart off to the state hospital. I sighed. Time to play by the rules. "Look, Officer . . ."

"Lieutenant."

"Lieutenant? Really?"

He shrugged his shoulders before nodding. Obviously, I wasn't the first to comment on his youthful appearance.

"Sorry. Let's try again, shall we?" I took a deep breath, willing myself to relax. "I'm Ronnie Raven. I'm a psychology professor here at Rubenstein Hall."

The cop's eyes sparkled. "Psychology professor? Really?"

I grinned. The truth was that I probably looked as much like a university professor as the kid looked like a cop. Khakis replaced my usual jeans, and I wore an oversized long sleeved T-shirt in a muted rust color. Makeup was minimal, which was normal, and my reddish-brown hair had been styled by gusty Oklahoma winds.

"You got me. Look, I need my backpack. My keys are in it. Without my keys, I can't get into my office. For that matter, I'm locked out of my home as well." I didn't mention my emergency entrance through a window that refused to lock over the kitchen sink.

Was it my imagination or had his smile cooled significantly?

He pushed open Crutchfield's squeaky door. "Detective Melvin? She's here."

What was going on? Before I could ask, I was ushered in. Unfortunately, I was greeted by the sight of a protruding belly hanging over a belt, and rapidly thinning hair attached to a face that looked anything but happy to see me. Which made it mutual. The protruding belly was rifling through my backpack.

"What the hell are you doing in my backpack?"

"Right now it looks like evidence, missy."

"Missy? *Missy?*"

"Excuse me." He flipped open my billfold to look at my driver's license. "Veronica Raven?"

"Ronnie Raven."

"It says Veronica."

"I prefer Ronnie." I turned to see the young cop standing behind me. No doubt blocking my escape.

"All right, *Ve-ron-i-ca,*" Detective Melvin said. "Why don't you tell us what your backpack is doing in this office?"

"I must have dropped it when I found the body, *Mel-vin.*"

"That's Detective Melvin," he said stiffly.

"And I will answer to either Professor or Dr. Raven," I answered with even more attitude. I usually didn't go for that formality stuff, but this guy was asking for it.

"Um, Professor Raven, are you saying that you were the first to find the victim?" a decidedly less hostile voice said behind me.

"Yes, Lieutenant, I was," I said, keeping my eye on Melvin. He was someone I didn't feel comfortable turning my back on. "I called nine-one-one."

Melvin snorted. Not a pretty sight.

"You can check it out. I gave my name when I reported it."

"What phone did you use?"

"This one, of course." I pointed to the black desk phone sitting on the desk.

"Is it your habit to tamper with a crime scene?" Melvin said.

"What crime scene? And how do my fingerprints on the phone at the scene of a suicide tamper with anything?"

I was answered with silence. Turning my head, I saw the young cop staring at his glossy shoes, shiny enough to give off a reflection. I jerked back at Melvin, who had suddenly found the ceiling interesting. Turning back to Crutchfield's desk, I looked again at the hole in back of the chair, the leather pushing inward. Unless he was a contortionist . . .

"It wasn't a suicide, was it? Someone killed Crutchfield," I said.

"And just what would you be knowing about that?" Melvin said.

I looked up at Melvin. Watching me. Sneering. But he had done nothing else since I entered, so I couldn't be sure what he was thinking. "Nothing, but then it certainly didn't make sense for Crutchfield to kill himself, either."

"Then you're saying someone killed him. You maybe?"

My first impulse was to laugh. *Me? Kill someone?* But Melvin didn't look like much of a joker. "Don't be ridiculous. Of course I didn't kill him!"

Melvin pulled out a small spiral notebook and a pen from his suit pocket. "Then why were you in the victim's office?"

"Because the *victim* left his stupid motorcycle parked in front of the bicycle racks. I couldn't park my bike in a secure location, so I came in to tell him to move the damned motorcycle."

"Have you always felt such animosity toward this man?"

The detective chose that exact moment to spit tobacco juice from his mouth into a paper cup. Although I had survived the sight of a dead body and an overlarge detective in an undersized cheap suit, my stomach churned with the sight of muddy juice dripping into a paper cup. I stumbled backwards . . . needing some distance between us before my Cheerios blanketed the dull wood floor. I inhaled deeply through my nose, unfortunately catching a whiff of sickly sweet chewing tobacco. I turned away and pressed my hand to my stomach, willing it to cooperate.

"I repeat, why did you hate the victim?"

"I don't believe this! I didn't hate the victim. I was just angry because I couldn't park my stupid bicycle." Exhaustion fell on my shoulders, almost knocking me down in its intensity. All because of parking a bicycle. Why hadn't I walked to school today? I looked at Crutchfield's window. Like a spider web with hundreds of tiny cracks spreading outward, it reminded me of the time a logging truck had thrown a pebble into my car windshield. The crack had started small, but kept growing until I had to get my windshield replaced. Funny, I hadn't noticed the broken glass earlier. Now the glare of the sun made it impossible to miss.

"Did that happen often?" Melvin said.

I turned back to Melvin's harsh gaze, aimed like a gun—at me. I sighed. "Did what happen often?"

"Your becoming irate at the victim . . . or others?"

"Only when he behaved like a Freudian jackass or called me 'Missy.' "

I thought I heard a snicker behind me. However, when I turned to glare at the lieutenant, his face was wiped clean of any expression, amused or otherwise. Instead, he had his own questions. "Professor Raven, did you hear a gun shot? Any loud noise?"

I shook my head.

"See anything? Anybody coming out of this office before you came in, or even somebody in the hall?"

Although I appreciated the reasonable questions, I had seen no one nor heard anything unusual. "You might want to check with Paula. She came in soon after I did."

"She the screamer we heard about?" Melvin drawled.

I turned back around. "Yes, Paula Burke. She was quite upset. Most people are upset at the sight of a dead body."

"But not a tough broad like yourself, huh? You're free to go now," Melvin said stiffly. "But don't leave town."

I waited for him to crack a smile. I mean, surely, real cops never used "don't leave town." But no smile, no joke. What did I expect from a man who used words like *broad* and *missy?*

"I can't go anywhere until you return my backpack to me."

Melvin dropped my faded canvas pack on the vinyl couch, causing the contents to spill out. Moving to the desk, he plopped his large backside on it to watch me. Although my first impulse was to shove my things back in and get the hell out of Dodge, I deliberately took my time. I wasn't going to let any spitting redneck detective chase me away. I scooped up the loose change, a dangling hoop earring without a mate, and assorted gum wrappers.

"I didn't steal anything!"

"I just want to make sure I have everything, *Detective.*" I swooped up my beaded turquoise key chain and stomped toward the door.

I passed the young man still standing by the door. His dark eyes sparkled with amusement, making him look even more like a kid. Lieutenant Kiddie Cop.

Normally I found humor in any situation. It's what has left me in relatively good mental health after thirty-eight years on a not-so-sane Earth. But my encounter with the police left only one thought swimming around my muddled brain. Crutchfield might have been holding the gun, but this was no suicide. Somebody had murdered Weldon Crutchfield.

Now if there's anything I hate more than teaching Introduction to Psychology, it was teaching *two* Introduction to Psychology classes. There was nothing to do but lecture since the size of the classroom was roughly equivalent to the size of a football stadium with rows and rows of chairs designed to keep students anonymous. Professors had two choices. One was to be boring. The other was to make a fool of yourself trying to gain the attention of your audience.

The other downfall to teaching in such humongous classrooms was the amplified noises. Worst were the snorers. The lecturer soon loses the attention of the awake students who try to search out the snorer. Once the one-man sleeping chainsaw was located, everyone pointed and giggled until he woke up. Sometimes for a little variety, someone sent a stack of books crashing to the floor instead. And we all jumped to what sounded like a cannon being fired.

Sometimes my ego wished the sleepers would stay home, but who was I to talk? I did some of my best sleeping during my own undergrad classes. Besides, if you took all the sleepers out, you were left with a few too many *patients*.

The *patient* was a type of student in psychology classes convinced that something was terribly wrong with him or her other than teenage angst. Maybe their id murdered their superego. Or they suffered from schizophrenia. Would Pavlov's behavior modification experiments with dogs help them with their own problems with food, sex, or calling home more often? More than information, the patients wanted confirmation that they were normal. Most beginning college students still lived with the high-school mindset that to be different was wrong.

Zachariah Bent required every faculty member to teach an introduction section. He said it built character. Thanks to Crutchfield's death, I was going to have character coming out the wazoo. With visions of leaving very sharp tacks in Zachariah's desk chair, I marched off to teach my newest class totally unprepared.

Although I arrived on time, students continued trickling in. It would be a special challenge to capture the attention of students who had just swum in from a sunny Texas beach. Maybe I had judged the boyfriend with the broken leg too harshly. Taking care of him would have been a breeze compared to the day I was having.

I looked up to a vaguely familiar face floating in front of me. He was a study in monochromatic with chestnut brown skin, clothing, and eyes. Shyness clung to him far tighter than his baggy clothing and closely cropped hair. Wire-rimmed glasses rested on an average-sized nose with lenses he must have borrowed from Mr. Magoo. An awkwardly placed bandage covered his right hand.

I suspected that if I didn't say anything, he would remain silent, not doing anything to call attention to himself. "Yes?" I finally said.

"I'm Trevor McKinley."

"Hi, Trevor, I'm Ronnie Raven." A moment of awkward silence followed. "Is there something I can help you with, Trevor?"

"I'm . . . I'm . . . I'm your assistant. Graduate student. I'm working for, or rather I worked for . . . for Dr. Crutchfield."

"Oh." Crutchfield probably chewed this young man up and spat him out for sport. "Well, I'm very glad to meet you, Trevor. Since Crutchfield's office is blocked off, I can't get in, and I don't have the slightest idea what's . . ."

"Excuse me, ma'am?"

We were interrupted by a husky body as blond as Trevor was brown. Looked like football material. Probably popular with everyone except to women whom he called ma'am. Two ma'ams in one day was my limit. If it happened a third time, I was going home with a carton of Rocky Road.

"We were just wondering if y'all were going to be having class today since Dr. Crutchfield isn't here, you know," he said with a twang that hurt my ears.

I walked over to the podium and turned the microphone on. "Neither rain, nor snow, nor gloom over the end of spring break will keep this faithful psych class from being held. We'll start in about five minutes, folks, as soon as I figure out what the hell I'm doing."

A couple of snickers answered back. Young freshmen might cuss like workers on an oil rig, but get one in a college classroom, and he finds it hilarious that a professor uses the occasional swear word.

As I moved away from the microphone, the football player grumbled and left for his seat amid a bevy of tanned beauties. I really didn't think the class would be too much of a hardship for Mr. Football Player.

"Okay, Trevor. What's the game plan?"

"Excuse me, Dr. Raven?"

"Ronnie. Tell me what's going on in this class."

"Uh, well, they turned in midterm papers before spring break. Dr. Crutchfield was going to hand them back today."

"And where was he on the course outline?"

"He was going to start lecturing about psychopathology today."

I groaned. Talk about patients coming out of the woodwork. Just my luck. I glanced at Trevor. "Have you lectured yet?"

If it had been possible for Trevor to swallow his tongue, I think he would have done so at that moment. "Me? No! No, Dr. Raven!"

"Call me Ronnie. Never?"

"No, R . . . R . . . Ronnie."

"Exactly how did you assist Crutchfield, then?"

"I graded tests. Typed up lecture notes . . ."

A secretary. Crutchfield was training this young man to be

his secretary. "Trevor, what do you want to do when you graduate?"

Trevor looked down at his feet, covered in a pair of brown-and-white Adidas, worn from age, not use. His gaze never left them, even when I thought I heard him say, over the growing roar of students behind us, "Teach."

"Let's talk after class," I said before turning to face my audience. In the minutes it took everyone to settle down, I made a decision. The only psychopathology I wanted to deal with today was my own.

"My name is Ronnie Raven. I'll be your psychology professor for the rest of the semester. In case you just flew in from outer space, let me be the first to inform you that Dr. Crutchfield was found dead this morning. Questions? Comments?"

It was the most silent five seconds the room had ever known. No gasps or cries. No reaction. Just complete, utter silence. Either everybody had already heard about Crutchfield or nobody cared. But how could they not have any questions when I had too many swimming around in an already overcrowded brain? Perhaps it was a class project to kill the professor?

I shrugged my shoulders, took a deep breath, and began. "Well, all right, then. As I'm sure most of you know, there are various branches of psychology. Psychologists, especially professors of psychology, all have different theories about how the human brain works. And because of this, a behaviorist like myself approaches the subject of psychology a little differently than the traditional psychoanalytic view of someone like Dr. Crutchfield.

"Behaviorism is a theory that explains the psychology of all of humankind. There are no distinctions based on what part of the world you live in or your financial situation. These factors— geography and economics—have little to do with the mind. The focus of behaviorism is the overt behavior of each individual."

I saw some students with their pencils poised, trying to pick out what was noteworthy. Others looked like they were trying to take down every word I said. More than a few looked like they didn't own a pen or pencil. I shifted into automatic with my standard first class lecture about how fascinating the human mind was. An unknown territory compared to the human body. I equated mind and body as an exploration of sorts. The human body was Earth. There were fascinating places on Earth, but basically every inch had been discovered.

The human mind, however, was space. Lots of theories and conjecture, but there was still so much we didn't know. We memorized the distance from Earth to other planets in the solar system, but we still struggled with how many moons belonged to the outer planets.

If I had been more disciplined, I might have tried to be an astronaut instead of a behavioral psychologist. At a very young age, I spent several summer days indoors watching men walk on the moon. My whole family did. It was one of the most amazing things I had ever seen; and for a year, I had incredibly vivid dreams of walking on the moon.

It was the same feeling. Astronomy. Psychology. So much to discover and understand. Even if I devoted every waking moment to the study of the human mind, I would still only understand a fraction of it by the time I died. The vastness of the mind, like space, left me in awe.

I paused in my lecture to take in a familiar sight. Many students had retreated to doodling on their notebooks or taking catnaps. A few thought they were fooling everyone by "reading" their psychology text. One of these days, I promised myself I would sneak up on one of them and pull out the *Penthouse* hidden inside the book.

But, as always, a few students sat with minds thirsting for knowledge. Not unlike the truly religious on the verge of a spiritual experience, their eyes glowed and their bodies were poised to exclaim hallelujah. These were the kids with a special gift for learning, maybe even a talent for psychology. Myself, I didn't experience the feeling until midway through graduate school, so it fascinated me that there were eighteen- and nineteen-year-olds who could feel such passion for something besides rock and roll. Not that rock music wasn't something to be passionate about.

Out of the corner of my eye, I saw a slightly more animated Trevor. How had a withdrawn male graduate student ended up assisting Weldon Crutchfield, the prince of psychoanalytic pop psychology? Crutchfield, with his booming voice and reputation as an aging lothario, was a user. He was only interested in what others could do for him, which left me with a burning question. What had Trevor McKinley done for Crutchfield? Or perhaps to him?

The lecture passed swiftly with no mishaps. I dismissed class without making a reading assignment, despite a young man's attempt to remind me. I chose not to hear him, which was to his benefit. Just asking had earned his head a couple of paper-wad missiles.

I turned to where Trevor had been sitting, not too surprised to find that he had disappeared. It was probably just as well. Zachariah Bent had scheduled a faculty meeting, his regular mid-semester "let's be clear on why we're here" meeting. Which, by my calculations, would start in three minutes.

I would catch Trevor later, if only to define his role in relation to this class. But I had another reason to talk with Trevor McKinley. If anyone could shed some light on Weldon Crutchfield, just maybe it was his painfully shy assistant.

Although class had more or less cleared out, a young woman with reddish-blonde hair—strawberry blonde, I think it's called—sat in the front row. Obviously taking her time. And unless I missed my guess, I was her target. While I debated making a run for it, she placed herself directly in my path.

"Yes?"

"Dr. Raven, I want to check my mid-semester grade." The reed-thin waif spoke so quickly that it took a moment to decipher her words.

"And your name is?"

Her body swayed back and forth, looking like the stem from a grandfather clock on speed. "Alvarez. Desiree Alvarez."

Deep blue eyes never wavered from mine. Contacts. No one had eyes that blue. "Well, Desiree. Are you aware your professor was found dead this morning?"

Something flickered in her eyes. Sparks of hostility mixed with something else. Fear? "I'm sorry if I sound insensitive. It's just that I had a conference yesterday with Dr. Crutchfield about my midterm paper. He agreed the paper was worth an A, but I don't know if . . ."

"If he got around to entering your grade?"

"Yes."

"Well, Desiree, I really can't say. Your professor's office is off limits for the time being while the police do their investigation," I said. "Unless you know something I don't, I believe that includes grades for this class."

"I hadn't thought of that."

"If you want to get back with me in about a week or two, I'm sure everything will have died down by then." I was about to excuse the unintentional pun, but she didn't seem to notice. The A was the only thing that mattered.

"But what happens if he didn't change my grade?"

"What was your grade before the paper?"

"It was a B," she said in the same voice used to announce the presence of a skunk.

"B's aren't bad." I tried to sound like I felt sympathy for her plight. In fact, I was still trying to decide if she was for real.

"But I've never made a B!"

"What do you mean, never? Like, since you started college?"

Desiree stood silently, chewing on her lower lip.

"Never, as in not in high school?"

"Never, as in never in my life."

"Why? Do you get a thousand bucks for every A or something?"

She jutted out her chin, looking for all the world like a defiant toddler. "Grades are important to me."

One B after thirteen or fourteen years of A's might be a hard blow, but it might lead to a healthier young woman. But the clock was ticking, and I needed be on the other side of the building. "Look, if your grade hasn't been changed to an A, I'll take a look at your paper."

"But I wrote it for Dr. Crutchfield!" Her already high-pitched voice went up two octaves as panic registered.

"I'm sorry, Desiree, I don't get your point."

"I mean I wrote it the way Dr. Crutchfield wanted it. I said things he wanted to hear, the way he wanted to hear them!"

"And I'm not Dr. Crutchfield?"

She nodded, her eyes wide and shiny.

"Your paper should be a reflection of your thoughts and ideas, not what you think a professor wants to read."

Her mouth quivered. Oh, hell. I did not want to have to console a perfectionist freshman who, for all I knew, hadn't even written a paper. "Desiree? Why did you meet with Crutchfield yesterday? Most kids were just getting back from spring break."

Her gaze darted to her hands, and again her body began rocking back and forth. First her body shifted onto her left foot, then her right foot. Left foot. Right foot. Left foot. Right foot. I put out a hand to steady her before she spun off her axis. "Okay, I'll look at your paper and pretend I'm Crutchfield."

"You can do that?"

"I played a dead person in a high-school production of *Our Town,* so I think I can do Weldon Crutchfield. I'm willing to try, anyway." I ran a hand through my hair, moving it away from my eyes.

A brilliant smile lit up her face, and she hugged me. I squelched the desire to pat her on the back. "Now I'm late to what is sure to be a boring faculty meeting, but one that I will be in a great deal of trouble for missing. So . . ."

"Thanks, Dr. Raven."

I watched Desiree Alvarez walk away; arms wrapped so tightly around her books that her hands almost met behind her back, giving the appearance that she was hugging herself. I glanced down at the scratched face of my ten-year-old Timex and groaned. I was now late enough to earn a *look* from Zachariah, maybe even a scathing comment. I hurried through the vacant halls, my footsteps echoing around me.

CHAPTER THREE

I arrived at the faculty meeting breathing heavier than I should have after two flights of stairs. Time to start exercising—again. I always started with good intentions, but inevitably, something better came along. This morning, I had noticed James Dean was looking a little jiggly around the middle, too, so he could join me.

Everyone looked my way as I entered. After shrugging apologetically to Zachariah, I took a seat at the far end of the table next to Paula Burke. She seemed to be the only person in the room not giving me the once-over; in fact, she ignored me. After our strange bonding experience that morning, I had expected a nod of recognition. But the Ice Queen returneth, leaving no signs of the hysterical, rumpled woman I had escorted out of Crutchfield's office hours ago. Her beige suit, different from this morning's outfit, was as starched as she was.

The windowless room, spacious by university standards, still left me gulping a little more air. *Don't think about the fact that there are no windows,* I told myself. *Concentrate on something else.* Fluorescent lights buzzed like insects over our heads. I looked around the table at the lifeless faces of my colleagues and wished I had skipped the meeting altogether. At the very least, I regretted not stopping for a Diet Pepsi, my only vice when I was being good. One of many when I wasn't. Keeping my behind glued to the hard plastic contours of my seat, I tried to suppress my craving. But you know how when you want something and can't have it, that urge grows and grows until it's so overwhelming that it threatens to consume you? That's what my need for a Diet Pepsi was doing to me at that moment.

"And on to my next point. Punctuality," announced Zachariah from the head of the table with eight full and associate professors paying court from either side. He paused, tapping his fingers against the hardwood grain and looking around the table.

No way was I apologizing. As thoughts of being assigned another of Crutchfield's sections danced in my head, I relented at explaining myself. "Dr. Bent, I was counseling a student. After all, isn't that what we're here for?" I saw a few heads nod, but otherwise received no support from my peers, which wasn't unusual.

"I appreciate your concern for your students, Dr. Raven. But I continue to believe that punctuality is the cornerstone to successful academia. This means punctuality to classes." Zachariah's eyes bored into Justin. Justin, whose last name I conveniently blocked. The newest addition to the faculty and the only other professor close to my age. We suffered through a single date about six months ago, but there had been no click— personally or professionally.

"And punctuality to meetings," Zachariah added, turning his deadly gaze on me. I told myself I was immune to such devices. I was an adult, not a child to be chastised. I met his gaze, and we had a duel of wills until help arrived from an unexpected quarter.

"Dr. Bent, you know yourself how difficult it is to get away from some of the more determined students. Why, they practically dig their teeth into you," Paula said from my right.

Zachariah nodded at Paula. If my designated role at these little family get-togethers was "the rebellious child," Paula's was "the peacemaker." Both of us fulfilled our roles quite well, if I did say so myself.

"Ah, well, I do see your point, Dr. Burke." Zachariah turned a softened expression my way. "And I suppose this was a student from the class you just came from . . . Crutchfield's introduction class?"

I nodded. Truthfully, I would have been late had any student from any class needed to talk with me. Particularly when faced with a faculty meeting. But volunteering that information seemed utterly stupid.

"I suppose everyone is aware that Dr. Raven found Weldon Crutchfield dead in his office this morning," Zachariah announced. "I'm afraid he took his own life."

"That's ridiculous!"

"Excuse me, Dr. Raven?"

"Zachariah, did you see his office? Where the bullet wound was? He was murdered!"

Zachariah's voice thundered over the collective gasps in the room. "Are you moonlighting as a detective, Dr. Raven?"

"Of course not, it's just common sense . . ."

"Then I suggest we allow the police to do their jobs without any fanciful theories from you."

I hoped Paula might confirm my suspicions. But how much had she actually seen? I didn't know. A few hours ago, all her energy had been focused on screaming. Now she sat rigidly beside me, refusing to meet my gaze. She clenched her hands in front of her on the table. Tiny blood vessels stood up and created valleys of loose skin. A band of purple deepening into black surrounded the wrist of the hand closest to me. It was a strange bruise, as if her wrist had been caught in a vise. Before I could take a closer look, Paula tugged her sleeve down to cover her wrist.

"We shall, of course, all miss Weldon Crutchfield. He was a great man and a great professor," said Zachariah. "A memorial service is pending. You will all be notified and expected to attend. You may also inform your students that they may attend if they wish to do so. That will be all."

I was shocked that more discussion wasn't taking place. A man was dead. He might have been an asshole, but his death was horrific. I heard murmurs of "poor Weldon" as other professors rose from the table. I could just see the headlines now:

Beloved College Professor Commits Suicide
Students and Faculty Mourn a Great Man

I wish someone would please tell me how you shoot yourself in the back! I shook my head. Impossible. Next to me, Paula stood up slowly. Poor woman. I knew what it was like to lose someone you cared about. And for better or for worse, she had obviously cared for Weldon Crutchfield. I put a hand on her shoulder, feeling her flinch underneath my touch.

"How are you feeling, Paula?"

"I'm fine, Dr. Ra . . . Ronnie," she said in a voice not much louder than a whisper and looking everywhere but at my face.

"It's been a difficult day for you. I'm sure Zachariah wouldn't object if you needed to take some personal time." At that moment, she looked me in the eyes and I felt her icy demeanor slip away, for a moment, anyway. "I'm sorry if I upset you with what I just said about how Crutchfield died."

Paula's chest rose with a deep breath before the mask of ice slipped back in place. "I don't like all this talk of death. I wish we could forget Weldon Crutchfield and go back to our normal lives."

And with that, she picked up a half-full coffee cup and a handful of pink message slips, and she walked away. Any thoughts I had that we were beginning to connect on an emotional level fell away. Paula had been hysterical about Crutchfield's death just hours earlier. Now she wanted to pretend he never existed? For that matter, she wasn't the only one in a hurry to forget Crutchfield. The fact that Zachariah had me stepping in for Crutchfield's intro class on the day of his death hadn't missed my notice, either.

The room emptied, leaving only Zachariah's haggard face, looking older than its years, and me. Eyes dulled with fatigue were made more prominent by the lines bordering them. "Zachariah? Are you feeling all right?"

"Fake concern doesn't become you, Ronnie," he answered, finally dropping the formal "doctor" reserved for public appearances.

Ouch! I slid down the table to sit next to him. The truth was that I liked Zachariah. I wouldn't work for him if I didn't. I rebelled against his bureaucratic ways sometimes, but that was just me. After many years of rebelling against the establishment, I'd finally come to the realization that someone had to be the bureaucracy, and as long as it wasn't me, I could live with it.

"It's just that I don't think I've ever seen you look like this before."

"It's called stress. Not all of us have your *'que sera'* philosophy," Zachariah said.

"My what?"

"You know, Doris Day. *Que sera, sera,* whatever will be, will be. It's all in the hands of fate, ad nauseam." As Zachariah stood up, his voice regained its booming authoritative sound. "My job is to present an A-one academic department to the regents. A task that's not easy when I'm dealing with idiots, rebels, and suicidal professors." He pounded his fist on the table, a reverberating sound that made me jump even though I saw it coming.

"Zachariah, you don't really think Crutchfield killed himself, do you?"

Worry returned to his eyes, zapping his strength. "I don't know. What do you think makes worse press? A psychology professor committing suicide or being murdered?"

"Surely, you can't be blamed for either happening. You don't have control over people's lives."

Zachariah seemed amused. "Why not? The regents blamed me for Weldon's upcoming book."

"What book?"

"One of those pop-psychology things that invariably find their way up the best-seller lists."

"Really? Crutchfield was going to be published?" I was flabbergasted. What did he have to say that was publishable in the mainstream press? All I had ever heard him spout was regurgitated Freudianism.

Zachariah sighed, shaking his head at me.

"What? What did I do now?" I said.

"If you ever came to faculty meetings like you're supposed to . . ." He gritted his teeth and clenched his jaw. "You would have heard Crutchfield discussing the hundred-thousand-dollar advance for his book, *The Myth of Fidelity*, or something like that. It hasn't been published yet. I believe Weldon was supposed to have turned in the manuscript to his publisher sometime this semester. I wonder what the chances are that he died before he could finish that awful book . . ."

"I usually tuned Crutchfield out as soon as he opened his mouth. A hundred thousand, huh?" I shook my head. "But what's the big deal? I thought you wanted us to be published?"

"In respectable academic journals. Not sensationalist crap that theorizes that marriage and fidelity have outlived their usefulness. Something the Oklahoma regents wouldn't understand. If that . . . that travesty were published, they would crucify me."

The regents were a group of good old boys. Conservative with a capital C. Always promoting family values. Not that family values were bad. It was just their concept of family values that I disagreed with. A vote for family values was a vote for fundamentalism.

"Maybe one of the regents killed Crutchfield to keep the book from being published." I meant to say that to myself. Unfortunately, I said it out loud. Speaking what played in my brain was a bad habit that I couldn't seem to shake, even though it sometimes got me into jams.

Zachariah's face looked even more strained before he turned away from me. "I really doubt the regents murdered Weldon, Ronnie."

"Hey, you never know. Remember how upset they were last year when the football team got beat by everyone but Missouri? I thought they would eat that last coach alive instead of just firing him."

"Give it a rest, Ronnie," he sighed. "Just do your job. You're actually pretty good at it."

"Why, thank you, Zachariah." The compliment took me by surprise.

"But quit cursing during your lectures," Zachariah added.

"Jesus H. Christ, Zachariah. It's not like my lectures need to be rated R or X."

"No, just PG-thirteen. Remember *Doctor* Raven, this is the Bible Belt, not one of those liberal let-it-all-hang-out places of yours. The code of conduct is different. Act accordingly."

With that, I was apparently dismissed, as Zachariah turned from me and walked out. Who the hell did Zachariah think he was? He was from Michigan or Minnesota—one of those "M" states up north. I was the born-and-bred Okie here. Hell, my BA in psychology came from PU.

I should have stayed in Colorado and played nursemaid to the attorney. Even being snowed in at the Denver airport would have been a picnic compared to this. Although I had just returned from spring break, I already found myself counting the days to the end of the semester. Of course, I would have to go see Mom and the boys, but after that, I imagined traveling to New Mexico. Taos. My favorite place on earth.

I quickly flew down a flight of stairs to the second floor that professors shared with a few small classrooms and a room of cubicles that the graduate teaching assistants shared.

With my office door closed, I could see the print of my father's wonderful painting of the Taos Pueblo. It wasn't one of his most popular paintings, but it was my favorite. Maybe because he had taken a fourteen-year-old with an unbearable attitude with him to Taos when he painted it. We had left Mom and my brother, Steven, home for those two weeks. Soon afterwards, Dad died. It had been almost twenty-five years since his death, but I still missed him.

"Dad, where are you when I need you?" I sighed. Closing my eyes, I rubbed my temples with my forefingers.

Somebody murdered Crutchfield, I was sure of it. Although it was understandable that an almost middle-aged female professor wouldn't be fond of him, I was surprised that his students may have felt the same way. Yet that was how it appeared. They showed a definite lack of compassion and interest when I mentioned Crutchfield's death. I would have received more of a reaction if I had told them it was raining outside. Although I had jokingly wondered about a class project to kill the professor, maybe it wasn't unrealistic to consider that a student had murdered him. Or a graduate assistant sorely abused by his boss? What about a department head who didn't want a book to see publication?

I turned to look out my window. One of the best things about my office was the window overlooking the oval. The majority of classes were held in the buildings bordering the oval. Some of the buildings had been here for the more than one hundred years that the university had been in existence.

Early-morning clouds had vanished, leaving the sky bluer than any painting or photograph could ever reproduce. From this vantage point, I couldn't see if my bike was still present and accounted for. Zachariah would see quite a tantrum if my bike had been ripped off.

The grassy area next to the building was roped off, the grass still brown from winter. A single person stood to the extreme right of me. I had to push open my rusty window and lean out to see who it was. Lieutenant Kiddie Cop closely examined the grass at his feet, as still as a statue for several minutes. Impressive. Absolute stillness was a skill I gave up on developing a long time ago.

Lieutenant Kiddie Cop finally knelt and picked up something. When he stood up again, he was studying a small object between his fingers. Although my window was too far away to see clearly, the glint of the object suggested that Kiddie Cop had found the bullet that killed Weldon Crutchfield.

CHAPTER FOUR

Weldon Crutchfield's memorial service was scheduled in the Elias P. Woodruff Auditorium, located on the lower level of the Student Union. It was the nicest of the three campus auditoriums, although with a seating capacity of only a hundred, it was too small for most groups. In fact, the only times I had ever stepped foot inside the Woodruff were for the occasional avant-garde movies offered by the Alternative Film Club. And more often than not, the audience held my interest more than the movie, particularly when subtitles were involved. Ruby-colored carpet matched the shabby, yet still-elegant upholstery of the chairs. Lights fashioned to resemble antique lanterns lined the walls, sloping down toward a small stage. Today, the stage was bare except for a lean podium with a microphone perched on top.

I supposed it was as good a place as any to hold Weldon Crutchfield's memorial service. Rumor had it that a distant cousin in Arkansas would take charge of Crutchfield's body—as long as the college paid the shipping costs. How much did the post office charge for shipping dead bodies these days? Probably had to use Priority Mail, although perhaps FedEx was the way to go.

I crossed the threshold into the auditorium, quite uncomfortable in a navy dress that had seen better days. With fashion's quickly changing skirt lengths, the slightly-above-the-knee dress seemed a safe bet for most functions requiring a dress. Actually, it wasn't the dress that bugged me as much as the damned pantyhose. Besides making my legs sweat, pantyhose made me feel as if every inch of leg was being squeezed. When I walked. When I sat. When I stood.

As I entered the memorial service, the first person I recognized was the young campus lieutenant, standing in uniform inside the auditorium door, his gaze clearly focused on my legs. I had long passed the stage of getting offended if a man stared at some part of my body. We all check out each other's bodies anyway. Men do it. Women do it. Some do it with more class than others, but we all do it.

After getting his fill, Lieutenant Kiddie Cop looked up and let an apologetic grin cross his face. "Hello, Professor Raven."

"Lieutenant," I nodded. "Are you an usher today?"

"No," he replied hesitantly, looking around the room. "Uh, I don't think there are any."

"You're standing where an usher usually stands, but I suppose you really just want to see who comes to pay their respects to Weldon Crutchfield. I wonder why."

An unmistakable clearing of the throat emanated behind me. I turned. Another campus cop, older but with less decoration on his uniform. Unless I missed my guess, the clearing of the throat was for me because he had business with the leg-staring non-usher.

I nodded at Lieutenant Kiddie Cop and slowly walked down the center aisle, taking an inside seat in the middle, careful not to sit too close to anyone. I didn't come here to socialize. Attending Crutchfield's service was an order from Zachariah, whom I spotted at the front, shaking the hands of expensively clothed elderly men. The regents. Sitting next to them was the college president, W.B. Smith, Oklahoma's next governor, according to people in the know.

"Good afternoon, ladies and gentlemen, let's go ahead and

get started," Zachariah announced from the stage. "First, we'll start with some comforting words from our university chaplain. Chaplain?"

A balding man with a gentle round face slowly walked over to the podium and began delivering a generic memorial address through a static-filled microphone. I doubted the chaplain had ever made the acquaintance of the deceased, a fact that seemed likely when he repeatedly stumbled over the name of Weldon Crutchfield.

Lots of empty seats stood between me and the stage. People sat alone or grouped in twos, except for the front row of dignitaries. One was the apprehensive man who had appealed to Zachariah outside Crutchfield's office the day of his death. Because of his seating position, I had to assume this man was one of the regents. He looked like one today, dressed in somber charcoal gray, and more solemn than previously when he had tugged at Zachariah's sleeve in agitation.

Everyone at the service looked vaguely familiar, so I had to assume the distant cousin hadn't made the trip. A few students were scattered here and there, including the girl so concerned about her grades in Crutchfield's intro class. She was hard to miss, dressed in a fuchsia color designed more for a celebration than a memorial. I caught her eye, but she looked quickly away. I swear it looked like she was rocking in her seat. Was that girl never still?

Psychology department faculty made up the majority of the audience. Zachariah had followed up the staff meeting with a memo inviting the faculty to come. The underlying message was that if you didn't make an appearance, you were destined to a lifetime of serving as the department's safety-committee representative.

"And now if anyone would like to say a few words about Feldon—I mean Weldon, Weldon Crutchfield?" the chaplain announced.

I felt a brief moment of panic. Surely, Zachariah didn't expect us to get up and say nice things about Crutchfield? But I needn't have worried. President Smith rose, and I knew he would talk for a while. It was ironic. Although I hadn't known Crutchfield well, I think he would have liked having the college president talking about him as if they were buddies.

Crutchfield had always struck me as a man who thought he was more important than he was. He always had to have the last word in any conversation. Once last year, I did a little experiment in a faculty meeting. Every time Crutchfield said anything, I responded. Sometimes my response had nothing to do with what he said, but that didn't matter. The point was that he couldn't let anyone else have the last word, especially me, a mere female.

My eyes passed over the group in front of me. The few who weren't fidgeting had adopted a glazed look that said they were somewhere else. Except for one. Paula. She sat at the far end of the row in front of me, so I had a side view of the mournful professor. Her back remained rigidly at attention in a way that looked painful. I don't know how long I watched her, waiting for some slight movement. But nothing. No, wait. A tear. Traveling down a worn path of her face. She didn't wipe the tear away, even when it settled precariously along the jawline.

My attention was drawn from Paula to the movement around me. People standing, stretching, yawning. Relief evident on their faces. The memorial service was over. People gathered in groups to talk about poor Weldon Crutchfield. I spotted Justin, playing head of the family, going from group to group, patting men on the back. What a kiss-up.

I debated joining one of the groups before realizing the young hyperactive grade-obsessed student was no longer in the auditorium. Her brightly colored ensemble was nowhere in sight. I turned toward to the entry doors. I didn't see her, but I did see a familiar blur of brown rush out the door.

Now why was Trevor hurrying off? He certainly had a right to be at a memorial service for Weldon Crutchfield. After all, he had worked for the man.

I hurried after Trevor, but when I reached the door, he was nowhere in sight. I decided to take a left in hopes that he was just around the corner. As I neared the corner, I did hear voices, but neither belonged to Trevor.

"What do you have?" said a gruff voice.

"Forty-four caliber. Registered to Weldon Crutchfield. Silencer, homemade by the looks of it. It's not sold in the gun shops around here. Bullet found outside, below the victim's office. Matches the gun and the holes in the victim. We've sent it to ballistics just to be sure."

I was sure the second voice was Kiddie Cop. But I couldn't quite place the first voice. I leaned against the wall, close to the corner, no longer interested in tracking down Trevor.

"Prints on the gun?" the first voice said.

"Only the victim's."

"Which would support the theory of suicide even though there wasn't a note."

"No, the bullet entered the back of the chair and went through the victim and then went through a plate-glass window," said Lieutenant Kiddie Cop. "There's no way that could be a self-inflicted wound. Besides, there's something else."

"What's that?" said the first voice.

"The victim was right-handed. The gun was found in his left hand."

Of course! Something had nagged at me ever since I had left Crutchfield's office. Something hadn't quite fit. Someone had to have placed the gun in the wrong hand!

"Pretty sloppy," the first voice said. "I thought that highfalu-tin women's-libber professor was smarter than that."

"Detective Melvin," said the young cop. "I really don't think . . ."

Their voices quickly faded as they walked away. I was tempted to follow, but couldn't think of a way to do so without being seen. I envisioned a bad spy movie as I dodged from doorway to doorway. Instead, I returned to the auditorium.

The scene before me was much as I had left it. Small groups of people chatted. Justin was still thanking people for coming, but Paula wasn't anywhere in sight. It looked like none of the other psych professors had felt the need to stick around. No, wait. Zachariah was there in the middle of a group that included the regents, but he was staring at me. *What had I done wrong this time?*

I turned to leave, intending to take the long way back to the office. I had a lot to think about. No doubt I was the highfalu-tin professor that Melvin had referred to. Although an ass, Melvin was right about one thing. Sloppy. It certainly didn't sound like the killer had planned things very well. Everything pointed to a spur-of-the-moment killing. Something emotional, out of control. Definitely unplanned.

"So, how did it go at Mama's during spring break?" I asked Terry as we carried our lunch trays from the cafeteria line. I surveyed the sea of tables in front of me, finding a lone one by the wall. It might be a little crowded, a two-seater table for me and Terry, a mountain of a man. But there weren't any other vacancies unless we shared a table with others. Prior experience with Terry's high jinks had taught me of that danger. The last time we sat with a group of other people, he introduced me as the campus stripper!

"Never. Never again will I agree to meet the parents of

someone I'm dating. From now on, it's orphans," Terry announced with his usual flair for the dramatic.

"Meeting Mama didn't go well, I take it?"

"Luv, I told that woman I was from Illinois. She must think we don't have food up there." Terry shuddered. "Grits, chitlins, greens, fried everything, biscuits and gravy . . ."

"Ooooh," I practically drooled. "I love biscuits and gravy. I can't make gravy worth a damn, which is probably a good thing or I would eat biscuits and gravy. All the time. My granny, she does it all from scratch."

Terry looked at me with a mock horrified look.

"Sorry."

Terry nodded warily. "Then Daddy asked me what my intentions were toward his little girl."

I chuckled, not at all affected by Terry's glower. "Well, what did the love of your life do during this drama?"

"She took a trip back in time to when she was sixteen years old. This is a woman who runs her own business. An intelligent, sophisticated woman who has traveled throughout the world. Suddenly she was giggling and blushing about how Daddy was so silly. It was one of the most disgusting things I have ever seen. And I've seen a lot of disgusting things. This lunch for instance."

"I take it that means it's over."

"Orphans, Ronnie. From now on, I'm only dating orphans." Terry stabbed a piece of mystery meat and carefully placed it in his mouth and grimaced. "Ah, I'm home now."

I shook my head. "I don't know how you can eat something you can't identify."

"Well, let's diagnose your lunch, then. A salad. Eating healthy today?"

"I always eat healthy."

"Yeah, right, and I'm John Wayne."

"Maybe around the nose."

Terry's answer was to throw a roll at me.

I enjoyed bantering with Terry. The day I hooked up with him at a new professor tea was the day I found a friend for life. I enjoyed his flamboyant personality that fit perfectly to life as a drama professor. I'm not sure what he saw in me. Maybe it was my knocking the teapot over onto the lap of the president's wife. Regardless, we both shared a view of the world as a rather skewed place with lots of potential for laughs.

"Uh-oh. Want to tell your pal Terry about it?"

"What are you talking about?"

"Life is not all hunky-dory for you, darling. You're eating salad, which means your jeans are too tight. But you're having really mixed feelings about your life right now, because you also have practically a whole box of crackers. And you're guzzling Diet Pepsi like you've been stranded in the desert for a month."

"I'm thirsty."

"Let's see. All didn't go well with your ski hunk, but you're not too terribly torn up about it. Basically you've forgotten him."

I leaned back in my chair with a smirk. "Do you see anything else in my lettuce leaves, oh wise one?"

"Yeah, a new man in town."

"Well, that's where you're wrong. I am completely manless for the time being, and I'm considering making it a permanent state. Men, in the romance department, are too much damned trouble. Who needs them?"

"You do, for that voracious sexual appetite of yours."

His comment was loud enough to draw stares from nearby tables. I shot Terry a look that meant he better check behind doors for a while. I turned my attention back to my salad. Wilted lettuce and brown carrots.

Terry pushed his half-eaten plate of food away. "I'm not meeting you here for lunch anymore. We eat off campus or bring our lunches, but not this place anymore."

I was inclined to agree. "Sorry, I just have too much work to do. Not only do I have my regular load of classes, but now I have to teach one of Crutchfield's classes, too. Plus this morning was the memorial service."

"I heard about the excitement at your building," Terry said. "Was Crutchfield the one with the bow ties or that rodent-type animal?"

"A mole. But Crutchfield was neither."

"Ah, then he must have been the sexist asshole. Details, Ronnie. Let's hear details. Why did your professor hang himself?"

"Hang himself? Is that what people are saying?"

Terry nodded. "Yep. All because the love he felt for a graduate student, a male graduate student, was rejected."

Having just taken a bite of food, I had to cover my mouth with a napkin to keep it from spilling back out because of the laughter. Gossip—the greatest comedy and the greatest tragedy of all.

"I take it the gossip mongers have it slightly wrong? C'mon, Ronnie. Inquiring minds want to know." Terry put his hands together in a pleading gesture.

"Well, I guess I'd better start with sexual preferences. While I wouldn't want to deny probable homophobia in Crutchfield, it was still deeply hidden within the recesses of his sordid mind. Actually, he was quite partial to young, pretty, *female* students. He probably diddled students."

"Did he ever try to diddle you, my dear?"

"Of course not. I'm too old, *and* I have a brain. A combination Crutchfield couldn't abide. Anyway, I'm the unfortunate one who found him."

"Really? Oh, this is exciting. My best friend involved in a suicide."

"Crutchfield was shot in the back, and yours truly may be a suspect in a homicide . . ."

Terry waited for the punch line. When none was forthcoming, he turned ashen. "No shit?"

"No shit. A Detective Red-Neck has decided I have the perfect motive for murder since I hate men. I entered Crutchfield's office for the express purpose of giving him the riot act for parking his damned motorcycle in bicycle parking, so apparently it's not too much of a stretch that I would shoot him in the back for it." I tried my best to sound flippant about the whole thing, like being involved in a murder was an everyday happening for Ronnie Raven.

Obviously, I didn't pull it off because Terry's eyebrows furrowed until they joined in the middle. I thought he might blow a gasket or something. "Look, Terry, it's not a big deal. I didn't kill the asshole. The police will figure that out."

"It's not that. I've been your friend, your best friend, for three goddamn years, and this is how I find out that you hate men?"

He used his mask of rage so well that it took a minute to compute. But then the laughter gushed all over me. I laughed so hard that tears came to my eyes, and I worried about peeing in my pants. Out of the corner of my eye, I saw a lean figure approach us, but dismissed the person as one of Terry's drama groupies. But while I wiped my eyes with a coarse paper napkin, I discovered that the "student" was none other than the mop-top campus cop.

"Sounds like you're having a good time," he said in a soft, deep voice that made me second guess the nickname Kiddie Cop. No . . . still had that young, clean-shaven look and shaggy black hair. The guy should really look into another career. He looked nothing like a cop.

"As a matter of fact, I am." I didn't feel inclined to let him in on the joke. For one thing, jokes always lose something in the translation. And for another thing, it wasn't any of his business.

"Lieutenant, this is Terry Panetta. Terry, this is Lieutenant . . ." I waited for Kiddie Cop to jump in with his name, but he was busy studying Terry.

Terry adopted an amused little smirk. Then a shrieking beep sounded from the cop's pants. Pulling out a beeper, he pushed a button and was gone. Because I knew what was coming, I developed a renewed interest in my salad.

"So, that's the new man," Terry commented.

I looked up to Terry's broad smile. A smile that couldn't be stopped by an eighteen-wheeler heading straight for it.

"Don't be ridiculous. He's just one of the campus cops investigating Crutchfield's death."

"He didn't seem to be treating you like a suspect, my dear."

"Maybe he has enough brains to know I didn't do it."

"And what else?"

"What do you mean?"

"Ronnie, the coy act doesn't work with you. But I'll play. One, your cop made a point of coming over here for purely social reasons and to check me out. And, two, you practically glowed when you looked at him."

"I don't glow!" I tossed my napkin on the table. "This is insane. In case you hadn't noticed, he's younger than I am. Not just a year or two, but noticeably younger than me."

Terry shook his head. "Ronnie, Ronnie, Ronnie. Did I ever tell you that one of the best relationships I ever had, sexually and intellectually, was with a woman ten years older than me?"

Still hungry after that pitiful salad I had for lunch, I made a side trip to the vending machines for another Diet Pepsi and a healthy dose of chocolate. I ripped open the Three Musketeers as soon as I entered my office and took a bite. For the bezillionth time I thought about getting a refrigerator for my office. One of those little square jobs that would hold a six-pack of Diet Pepsi. While deciding where to put a refrigerator—electrical outlets were in as limited supply as space—I missed the opportunity to close my office door. That's how the jock and his coach ended up in my office.

When the two men appeared at my door, I tucked the remainder of the candy bar in my top desk drawer with more than a little regret. "Can I help you?"

"Ronnie Raven?" said the older man whose muscled arms contrasted with the protruding beer gut covered by a green-and-gold university T-shirt.

When I nodded, he proceeded into some kind of oration about the stress football players feel in living up to the school's expectations. Blah, blah, blah. I glanced over at the pretty boy who had sunk his hulky body into my brown leather chair. I hoped all that muscle wouldn't damage it. The chair might be a garage-sale reject, but it was one of my best finds. Leather smoothed by age and use made the chair so comfortable that students immediately relaxed when they sat down.

The kid looked relaxed as he studied his fingernails with bored interest. I was fairly certain that he was the one from Crutchfield's Monday psych class. The one who had asked about class being canceled. But I wasn't positive. Most jocks looked alike to me—bulky body, hair cropped so short you weren't sure of the color, and the "I'm hot shit" attitude.

Finally, I interrupted the older man since he showed no signs of slowing down on his own. "Excuse me, but who are you?"

That stopped him cold. His mouth flapped a couple more times but nothing came out. Instinct told me not to laugh.

"I'm the football coach!" he finally said with indignation.

I waited for a name to follow. The kid even dropped the pretense of looking at his fingernails.

"Henderson. Harry Henderson."

Well, you would have to be a hermit to have not heard of the infamous Coach Henderson. Reputed to have gang connections, he was a man both feared and admired by anyone who enjoyed football. That meant ninety-nine percent of Oklahoma. Still, I thought it was awfully egotistical to think you could go through life never having to introduce yourself to anyone.

"I guess you want to be called Coach Henderson, then," I said to his continued look of amazement. "It's nice to meet you. And I assume this is one of your players?"

The coach shot me a look of pure suspicion. The kid adopted a subtly insolent look—a look that could easily be misconstrued. And he knew it. If I confronted him, he would adopt the innocent look and be believed. I might not have known his name, but I knew his game. Manipulation. I think I disliked him on sight.

The kid jumped to attention and grinned a cheesy smile. "Joe Bob Wayne, ma'am."

I nodded, not willing to waste any more time with formalities. "Coach Henderson, what can I do for you and Joe Bob today?"

"As I was saying, my players are all under stress. Joe Bob, our fullback, particularly."

"That's too bad."

"Well, now, Dr. Raven, I'm glad to hear you say that. You see, we're worried about his classes. We don't want any bad grades sneaking in and making our boy ineligible to play next season. He is in that Crutchfield's class, the one you took over."

"I don't see a problem with his psychology grade." Both men breathed sighs of relief. "As long as Joe Bob turns in average or better work." Judging by the looks on their faces, that must have been easier said than done.

"I don't think you understand," Henderson stammered. "We need your help to ensure that he gets a good grade."

"I would be glad to arrange for a tutor."

Henderson became red in the face. "Do you realize that if Joe Bob fails this psychology course, the very future of the PU football team is threatened?"

"Like I said, I would be glad to arrange for a tutor . . ."

"What kind of commie pinko are you?"

To say I was flabbergasted would be an understatement. While I may have leftist leanings now and then, I have always considered myself as patriotic as an American can be despite the numerous attempts to annihilate the Native American people.

The star of the conversation sat cool as you please. Must have thought he was invincible because he was a football star or something. All I know was his smug grin made me snap. I rose to my full height, which rivaled that of Coach Asshole.

"I don't believe tutors are a Communist plot to overthrow American football, Henderson," I said, gripping my desk to keep from strangling him. "I still don't have Dr. Crutchfield's grade book. When I do, I will be able to give you more information about this . . . this student's grade. Meanwhile, for the remainder of the semester, he has a new professor. Me. I expect Mr. Football Star to come to class, every class. He is also to complete his assignments. His final grade depends on his performance in my classroom, just like every other student in there. Is that clear?"

It was tempting to jab my finger into Henderson's chest, but the thought of touching him made me recoil. My stance and demeanor must have done the trick though, because he backed away.

"I'll have him switched to another professor," Henderson threatened.

"No dice. You need my written permission to do that. And if you go over my head on this, I will be vocal—make that very vocal—that the reason behind the switch is that I wouldn't hand your boy here an A on a silver platter. I'll bet the NCAA would love to hear about that. I'd venture a guess that you could even tell me who I would need to talk to about that."

His answer was a look of such pure hatred that I knew I had made an enemy for life. Gee, no football coaches in my future. But it was still somewhat disconcerting to have someone look at me with eyes narrowed in such absolute hostility. Henderson turned and stalked out, his heavy footsteps echoing down the hall.

Still in my comfy chair, a chair I now considered sterilizing, was Joe Bob. The hot-shit look faded, momentarily leaving a confused boy. Probably for the first time since Joe Bob started playing sports, Coach hadn't made everything all right. I would have felt sorry for him, but I knew the greatest service I could do this kid was make him realize he needed more than football to get through life.

"Do you have any questions?"

"Are you going to flunk me?"

"That depends on you, Joe Bob. Do the work. Pass the tests." He gnawed on a fingernail. "Do you need a tutor?"

He jumped up, quickly dwarfing me. "Hey, lady, I'm no dummy. I'll pass your stupid class."

"Good, then we don't have a problem."

I walked back behind my desk thinking that maybe I could finally eat my candy bar in peace. If there was ever a day meant for chocolate, today was the day. But with growing irritation, I realized Super Jock was still standing in my office.

"Is there something else?"

"You know, I thought things would be better with Crutch-field out of the way, but you're worse than he was."

He turned, almost running down the student receptionist from the main office. Not that she seemed to mind. You would have thought she had just seen Tom Cruise, or whoever young females drooled over these days.

"That . . . that was Joe Bob Wayne," she said breathlessly.

Oh, for heaven's sake. She wasn't going to faint or anything, was she? "Did you need something?"

"What?"

I raised my voice. "Was there a reason you came to my office?" Really, these people didn't know what they were dealing with by keeping me from my chocolate.

Unfortunately, she still looked lost in space.

"You were supposed to tell me something?"

"Dr. Bent said to give you this." She handed over a black book. "He said it was Dr. Crutchfield's grade book."

She left as I ripped the candy wrapper to shreds, but stuck her head back in the door. "Oh, yeah. Dr. Bent also said for you to take the cans for recycling ASAP."

I had insisted on the recycling box last year. And while other profs made use of the box, the job of taking the cans for recycling still fell to me.

"Right. Will you please close the door on your way out?" I asked as sweetly as possible. No point in attacking the messenger.

Jesus H. Christ, my head was swimming. I quickly finished my candy bar without really enjoying it. Too much anticipation, I guess. I could feel a binge coming on. I glanced at Crutch-field's black book. Somehow, a black book didn't surprise me, although I would have thought any black book of Crutchfield's would hold names like Wanda Wiggles and different types of grades. This was a standard grade book. Heaven forbid he should use a computer.

I checked through the names. Everything seemed in order. Except . . . no mid-semester grade for Desiree Alvarez. For some reason, three stars stood next to her name. The girl who had been so worried about her grade. Everyone else had a grade. No wait, here was one more. Joe Bob Wayne. No grade for him either. Strange. Why would neither of those students have a grade? Desiree told me she turned in a paper. Joe Bob? Well, I wouldn't be surprised if he hadn't turned in a paper, but wouldn't Crutchfield still have marked a grade, even an *I* for incomplete?

What had Joe Bob said before leaving my office? Something about Crutchfield being out of the way? Out of the way. Football was important to some of these guys, but important enough that a star fullback might kill a professor who kept him benched? I tried to dismiss the idea. Ludicrous, really. But an uneasy feeling had grabbed hold of me, remaining with me for the rest of the day.

CHAPTER FIVE

Placing a sneakered foot against the weathered brick of my drafty fireplace, I stretched in preparation for jogging. Terry would be so proud. He was always after me about stretching and how one day I would pull a ligament or something if I didn't stretch. Never had. But it had been a while since I last ran. It wouldn't hurt to stretch my muscles.

Stiff muscles. I rolled my shoulders forward, then backward. I supposed I had a reason to feel tense. After all, it wasn't every week I discovered a dead body. Hopefully, running would clear my mind. For some reason, the discovery that the gun had been planted in the wrong hand hadn't stopped the nagging feeling that something else was off about the murder scene.

I forced myself to relive bursting into Crutchfield's office to yell at a dead body. I played the scene over and over in my head. Nothing had seemed disturbed in the office. It was as if he had just been sitting quietly while someone sent a bullet through his back. A bullet that exploded out through his chest. The sight of the bloody wound still made me shudder. Wouldn't most people panic at the sight of a gun? Try to get away? But he was shot from the back, so maybe he didn't see it. Didn't expect it. I remembered Kiddie Cop saying that the gun was registered to Crutchfield. Would Crutchfield have been careless with his own gun? I couldn't see it. He was a control freak.

What was I missing? But the more I tried to recall what it was, the blanker my mind became. Experience told me it would have to come in its own time. Although there was no love lost between Crutchfield and me, I couldn't help but wonder who killed him. I mean, sure, he had been a pain in the ass, but murder? Even the limping attorney boyfriend abandoned in Colorado hadn't deserved murder.

A Labrador retriever, his black coat wavy and shiny, blocked my path to the front door. A barely audible whine accompanied soulful eyes. Smart dog. Knew subtlety was the key. "Do you want to go for a run, James Dean?"

An enthusiastic tail wagging answered me. How could anyone doubt that dogs understood what people said?

I was barely able to get his leash off the hook by the front door when James Dean pounced on me. All seventy-five pounds of him. I laughed as I stumbled back a step with the impact. "Okay, boy. Be still for a minute so I can get you hooked up."

No sooner did I have his leash on than James Dean pulled me out the door and down the tree-lined street. Soon, it was no longer clear who was leading whom. But just as suddenly as he started, James Dean abruptly stopped, requiring quick footwork on my part not to fall on top of him. My dog became victim to the wondrous smells of the world, and soon I was dragging him from prime sniffing places.

The trees on my street formed a canopy where only wisps of sunlight escaped. When James Dean and I took the next left, it felt at least ten degrees warmer without the shade of the canopy. I picked up the pace a little as I passed Oak Lane, nicknamed "Greek Street" for its abundance of fraternities and sororities.

In no time, I passed under the arches that identified the beginning of the university at the North Oval. I jogged down the oval past Psych, dark except for some windows on the top floor. Zachariah burning the midnight oil? Whoever it was had my sympathy. The early evening was truly gorgeous.

The sun was beginning to go down, but there was still plenty of light. The temperature was just right for my gray sweatpants and Hard Rock T-shirt that my wandering brother had given me last Christmas. The fact that my brother realized it was Christmas had been the first surprise. And I knew Hard Rock shirts didn't come cheaply. God knows I wouldn't pay over twenty dollars for a T-shirt. Still, it had been a nice-enough shirt until the washing machine decided to decorate it with bleach spots. I, of course, had nothing to do with that laundry mishap. The Hard Rock shirt had to join my growing supply of laundry-impaired shirts that were only useful purpose was for painting walls or sweating in.

My goal was the south end of the campus near the Student Union, a little over two miles. A nice easy jog, I thought, for a five-mile-a-day runner. Well, okay, the last time I did five miles was last fall. Still, it surprised me to be heavily panting by the time I reached the student dorms. Great. What better place to have a heart attack than in front of the student population?

I stopped. My burning lungs gave me no other choice. James Dean quickly watered the nearby tulips with a look of sheer ecstasy. What had I done? A mile? As my breathing slowed, I felt far older than my thirty-eight years. I turned to lumber home, creaky bones and all, allowing James Dean more time to investigate all the interesting odors the world had to offer.

And explore he did. We must have stopped at every tree, bush, and fire hydrant. With all the landscaping the last university president had done, this meant a lot of greenery. When James Dean took a strong interest in some juniper, I examined the student dormitories in front of us. Because the student dorms were designed to house as many kids as the fire code would allow, the buildings were probably the least attractive buildings on campus. Cars circled the dorms at all hours in hopes of landing a prime parking place in front. In spite of the efforts of dedicated groundskeepers, fast-food sacks and beer cans still popped up at an alarming rate.

Still, you couldn't deny the energy that emanated from the student residences. Alive with the hopes and dreams for the future. I had to admit to being a little envious. Of course I hadn't realized how great life was when I was eighteen; I was in too big of a hurry to grow up. I couldn't remember what I had been in such a hurry for. Work? Romance? Not likely. Since I was fifteen years old, I went out of my way to be different. The other girls graduating from college were planning great careers or marriages, not me. I wanted adventure. And I had it—for a while. Yet eventually a constant dose of adventure gets old.

When my brother, Steven, dumped his sons with Mom and disappeared, it seemed like a good time to come home. But small-town Oklahoma didn't have much for a behavioral psychologist to do. I certainly wasn't about to put out a shingle and start seeing all the nuts. After all, I grew up with those nuts.

James Dean pulled me from my reverie by getting tangled up around a "bicycles only" sign. Once I untangled him, it seemed like a good time to head home. The sun was going down fast.

A vaguely familiar figure left the dorms in front of me, his head aimed at his feet. Crutchfield's vanishing graduate student, Trevor. I tried unsuccessfully to wave him over when I thought he might be looking my way. Maybe his Coke-bottle glasses made distances difficult. A stitch in my side introduced itself when I tried to quicken my pace to catch Trevor. I soon gave up and hobbled home feeling utterly miserable. Whoever said exercise is supposed to make you feel better was full of it.

I was so wrapped up in feeling sorry for myself that it took a distinct growl from my companion to alert me to the thug casing the outside of my home, a home constructed of a hodgepodge of stones with ivy climbing up the uneven walls. I began leasing it last year after falling in love with the fairy-tale exterior.

It had to be love, because it took six months for me to see that it was falling apart inside. In comparison, it usually only took two dates to see when guys were falling apart. Fortunately, my landlord gave me a certain amount of latitude in painting and decorating as long as I paid the rent on time. And now some punk thought he was going to destroy my home, my castle? To quote Terry: not bloody likely.

I watched the back of a head peer in my windows. Wait a minute. The black hair over the collar was familiar. And the lean frame, too. "You didn't tell me you had a second career as a Peeping Tom, Lieutenant."

Lieutenant Kiddie Cop had the decency to look embarrassed. His sheepish grin continued even after the color faded from his face. He still wore that very unflattering uniform. Actually, he didn't look that bad in it. It was just the color. I obviously had beige issues.

He took careful steps out of my flowerbed, not damaging any crocuses that I could tell. For that, I would let him live, at least long enough for an explanation.

James Dean strained at the leash. Probably wanted to lick the intruder to death. But since he didn't know that, the campus cop showed good judgment by approaching warily. "Sorry. I really wasn't peeping, though. I was looking for you, Dr. Raven."

"Call me Ronnie. Did you try the doorbell?"

"It didn't work, Ronnie."

"Oh." The latest of many things to break down. I would call the landlord in the morning since I hadn't taken Doorbell Repair 101 yet. "Well, there's an earlier invention. Quite simple, really. It's called knocking."

"Did that. Since I didn't get an answer, I thought I'd look around. Just in case you couldn't hear my knock. I guess you don't live with anybody?"

"I live with James Dean."

"James Dean? I think he died before I was born," he said.

"Figures," I sneered.

"And you were how old?"

"Look, Kiddie Cop . . ."

"*What?*"

"Jeez, please tell me I didn't say that out loud." But one look at eyes wide with surprise told me I had done it again. "Look, I'm really sorry . . . looked so young . . . well, I don't know your real name! I had to call you something."

"How about Mick? Mick LeGrand."

"Mick, huh? Is that short for Michael or something?"

It was kind of cute watching him shuffle his feet and mumble. And if I had been any kind of sensitive person, I might have let him get by with it. "I'm sorry, what did you say?"

"I said no, Mick is not short for Michael or anything," he said, speaking through gritted teeth.

"The only Mick I ever heard of was Mick Jagger." At his heightened face color, I knew I had scored. "You're named after Mick Jagger? Really? I've heard of lots of people named Dylan, even Jimi. But I've never met anyone named after Mick Jagger." I took my jogging necklace from around my neck—a piece of hot-pink-plastic-covered wire that held my key while I ran.

"My mother was a fan."

"Then your mother and I have something in common. My goal in life when I was nineteen years old was to have sex with Mick Jagger."

"Did you?"

I moved to the door, recently painted a bold red, and concentrated on inserting the key in the lock. "So you know who James Dean is, huh?"

LeGrand didn't wait for an invitation, but followed the dog and me into the living room. "James Dean? *Rebel Without a*

64

Cause? Saved my life when I saw it as a misunderstood sixteen-year-old."

"For me it was *Catcher in the Rye*," I murmured, grinning when he nodded.

Most guys I knew were into war or horror movies, the bloodier and gorier the better. And let's not even talk about reading a book. How many guys did I personally know who had even a passing acquaintance with *Catcher in the Rye* or *Rebel Without a Cause?* Much less affected by them? Maybe Lieutenant Mick LeGrand was all right after all.

"That's James Dean the Second moaning with pleasure in your arms," I said. My lab—the one I rescued from the animal shelter last year—and this was how he paid me back. Nuzzling a cop that he just met. What an ungrateful mutt!

I tugged at the leash. James Dean granted me a quick second to unhook his leash before turning back to waiting hands. At that moment I believe James Dean would have left me for Lieutenant Kiddie . . . no, Lieutenant LeGrand. The lieutenant petted and scratched, leaving no place untouched. Some watchdog. And even more irritating was that Mick LeGrand looked right at home sitting on my secondhand couch being baptized by James Dean's tongue.

"Did you have another reason for looking in my windows other than coming to pet my dog?"

"So much for social talk, huh?"

"I wasn't aware this was a social visit."

"It could be."

I would have given him hell for flirting with me if I had been sure that was what he was doing. Young guy named after a rock star, who looked more like a rock star than a cop, interested in a quickly aging woman who was sweating through every pore in her body? Right now, I could feel the sweat spreading from my armpits. I sat down in the oak rocking chair as far from the couch as I could get while remaining in the same room, keeping my arms tightly clenched to my sides. I'll bet *he* could run five miles without taking an extra breath.

LeGrand grinned again. A nice smile really. Not too much, not too little, before reaching into his back pocket and pulling out a small spiral notebook. James Dean sighed, laying his head on LeGrand's thigh. "What did you think of the memorial service this morning?"

I shrugged, averting my gaze and wondering if he knew I had listened in on his conversation with Melvin. "I guess it was okay as far as memorial services go."

"Not much of a turnout."

"No, I guess not." Sudden irritation overtook manners. "Look, why don't you get to the point of this visit so I can go take a shower."

LeGrand nodded, but still took his time before speaking. "I wonder, do you remember anything else about the morning you found Crutchfield's body?"

I snorted. "You mean the suicide?"

"You sound like you don't believe it was a suicide," he said.

"I don't."

"Care to elaborate as to why?"

Because I overheard you saying as much, I thought, but decided that wouldn't be a wise move. Nor would I mention that the gun had been placed in the wrong hand. "Well, I'm the first to admit that I know diddly-squat about guns. But unless Crutchfield had some hidden talent as a contortionist, he couldn't have shot himself in the back."

"How do you know he was shot in the back?"

"Wait a minute," I said, suddenly uncomfortable with the questions. "Am I a suspect or something?"

"Officially, everyone's a suspect. Personally, no, I don't think you're a suspect."

"But Detective Melvin does."

Mick LeGrand's lack of an answer and refusal to look me in the eye told me what I already knew.

"Let me guess. 'That women's-libber bitch did it all right. She just hates men. You can see it in her eyes,' " I said, trying out my best impression of Melvin.

LeGrand proved to be an appreciative audience by silently laughing with his entire body. "So you hate men?"

"Hate is rather a strong word. I do dislike self-centered, sexist men like Melvin and Crutchfield. Otherwise, I happen to love the male species."

"Love is a strong word, too."

Across the room, eyes dark as midnight connected with mine, sending a charge through me that I felt in my toes. "I suppose you're right."

LeGrand cleared his throat. "Anyway, it's not unusual to remember things later. Especially in a crime. Something suddenly clicks that you didn't remember when you were first questioned. It's fairly common to recheck with witnesses. But I have to admit I am curious how you know Crutchfield was shot in the back."

As my heart calmed to a barely audible beat, I tried to regain as much self-assurance as I could with damp clothes sticking to my body. "The hole in the chair. I saw it when I dialed nine-one-one. The leather goes inward as if an object had been forced through the chair. The front of Crutchfield had everything spilling out." I silently retched at the graphic memory.

"Good observation."

"And when I went back for my backpack, I noticed the broken window. Something small and hard coming from inside broke that window. I'm guessing a bullet."

LeGrand nodded. "Do you remember anything else? Are you sure you didn't hear or see anyone come from his office?"

I shook my head. "After I found him and called you guys, Paula came in and started screaming."

"Paula? Paula Burke?"

"Have you talked with her?"

He nodded. "I'm afraid she wasn't much help. Just looked at me with those steely eyes and gave me one-word answers."

"I think Paula is from the old school where you don't talk about distasteful matters. She was awfully upset. She might not have seen much. Any ideas about who did it?"

"I don't know. The man seemed to have more enemies than friends. But nothing very specific."

I agreed. "He wasn't a nice man."

"Other professors? Students? Can you think of anyone who would have a reason to murder him?"

I mentally checked off the faculty in my head. Out of all of us, I was the most passionate in my dislike of Crutchfield. Everyone else played the game better than I did. When I don't like someone, there is no question about it.

"I can't think of anyone on the faculty. That means it must be a student, right?"

"Not necessarily, but since no one saw anything out of the ordinary, it's possible it was someone who belonged in Ruben-stein Hall."

"Like a student or faculty member. God, I hope it's not a student in his introduction class who has a thing for killing professors." I laughed, but the cop frowned at my joke.

"What do you mean?"

"Zachariah—he's the department head—he assigned Crutch-field's introduction class to me. I taught the first one Monday."

"Wasn't that kind of soon? Crutchfield was just killed that morning," LeGrand said.

"That's what I thought. I would have cancelled classes myself, but Zachariah's a real stickler for sticking to a schedule."

Out of loyalty to Zachariah, I tried to keep my usual anti-authority sarcasm out of my voice, but I could see LeGrand scribbling in the notebook.

"Is that Zachariah Bent?"

"Yes, but you can't suspect him. He's against anything that makes the department look bad. Murdering one of your professors makes a department look bad." I laughed at the absurdity of it all. "Besides, if Zachariah went after anybody, it would be me."

"Ronnie." LeGrand leaned toward me. "It's no joke. Somebody murdered Crutchfield, and it's possible the murderer is someone you know."

An icy shock ran over me. He had a point. I probably did know the person, at least as a nodding acquaintance. The fact that I knew a murderer was unsettling, to say the least. "What about the time of death?"

"They're having trouble pinpointing the exact time of death," he said. "Crutchfield's alcohol level was pretty high, so the coroner is having a hard time getting an accurate temperature reading from the liver."

"Then he was drunk?" I said.

"He was a big man. It probably took a lot to get him drunk," LeGrand explained. "But he definitely had imbibed quite a bit before his death. There was even a flask, an empty flask, inside his jacket pocket."

"That's odd." I stood up and moved over to the couch. "I would never have suspected Crutchfield as a drinking man."

"Why is that?"

"He was such a control freak. And for most people, alcohol leads to a loss of control." I silently wondered if a drunken Crutchfield was better than a sober one. "Is there no other way of finding out the time of death?"

LeGrand closed his notebook. "The coroner is doing some

other tests that aren't as accurate. Right now, he's guessing around eight A.M., maybe a little earlier, from the degree of rigor mortis."

"I came in around eight-fifteen." I swallowed. "That means I just missed his being murdered. If I had been a little earlier, I could have stopped it."

"Or been killed yourself."

I studied the young cop before me. He had laid his pen and pad down on the couch to resume scratching James Dean behind the ears. My rational self said LeGrand was on my side. Nothing wrong with that. My irrational side wanted to know *why* he was on my side. Did he know something or did he feel the need to take care of me? Well, I didn't need anyone to take care of me. I had been taking care of myself for a long time now, thank you very much.

"Look, why don't you think I did it, like your pal Detective Melvin? Obviously I was there close to the time of death."

"I don't always see exactly eye-to-eye with Detective Melvin." LeGrand grimaced. Obviously, he didn't dish out crap on a fellow officer, even one who worked on a different police force. Melvin was the city cop, LeGrand a campus cop. Who had jurisdiction here? And did LeGrand have the authority to be questioning me?

"Then why didn't I do it?" I pushed. If Mick LeGrand was trying to trick me, I wanted to know. Right now.

"Too easy. Besides, you're not the type who kills a guy, even an asshole, just because he parked his motorcycle in the wrong place," LeGrand said.

"Excuse me, but we just met. How do you know what kind of person I am?"

LeGrand unfolded his body and stood, shoving the pad back in his pants pocket. He gave James Dean one last pat on the head and walked to the door. I followed, caring more about an answer than staying downwind any longer.

He turned toward me, his face inches from mine. "Because everything you think, everything you feel, is written all over your face. Your hazel eyes, especially. When you're angry, emotional, they turn a brilliant shade of green."

"And when I'm not?"

"Brownish, I think. It's hard to tell. Whenever I see you, your eyes are green."

"Maybe I'm angry at you." I crossed my arms and leaned against the doorway.

"Maybe."

He looked at me again. Even at close range, I couldn't identify the color of his eyes. They were so incredibly dark. Black? Deep blue? Maybe a dark brown framed by indecently long eyelashes.

"Ronnie. Be careful. Not only do we not know who killed Crutchfield, we also don't know why."

"I'm betting on an unbalanced freshman systematically murdering all his teachers so he can get out of going to class. Either that or a fraternity initiation."

LeGrand rolled his eyes. "It's nothing to joke about."

"It's better than the alternative. Being so paranoid that I'm tied up in knots." Enough. I wanted a shower. Then dinner. To be followed by bed. No more murder. No more grinning young cops, no matter how sexy they might be. But before I could close the door, he called my name again.

"How come you prefer to be called Ronnie rather than Veronica?"

I grinned at what was usually a third-date question. "Two reasons, I guess. First, my dad always called me Ronnie."

"And the other?"

"Because of the Archies."

LeGrand looked blank.

"You know, the Archies? Archie, Veronica, Betty, and Jughead?

'Sugar, Sugar'?"

I closed the door on his perplexed expression. How could you possibly take a guy seriously when he didn't know who the Archies were?

CHAPTER SIX

My vintage Mustang easily maneuvered the sharp turn needed to pull into the parking place that had sneaked up on me. The Mustang threatened to disintegrate if pushed past fifty miles an hour, but like my fairy-tale home, I ignored its flaws. It, too, had character. And to make sure everyone else knew, I'd painted her green. Not a "yuck, I think I'm going to throw-up" retro-fluorescent green. No, my car was the color of the tallest pines of the Ouachita Forest. A rich evergreen unlike any other green in the world. Next to James Dean, the car had been my pride and joy for the past ten years. I once made it a rule never to own more possessions than could fit in my Mustang. It certainly made moving easy over the years.

I was a little embarrassed about driving Evelina (don't ask) the short distance to campus, but my muscles had rebelled big time from last night's jog. Just getting out of bed resulted in a cussing James Dean hadn't heard the likes of for quite some time. I remained in the shower as long as the hot water held out, and while it loosened my muscles, each step became a testament to my rapidly aging body.

With all the stop signs, pedestrians, and cyclists between my house and campus, it took longer to drive and locate a parking place than to ride the distance on my mountain bike. Yet soreness aside, my bicycle had brought nothing but trouble this week.

Now that I had unearthed my parking card from under the

passenger seat, I had options. Without that little piece of plastic, I would have to park in the commuter lot three miles from campus in order to ride the shuttle bus, defeating the purpose of driving in the first place.

I eyed the elevator on the first floor. *No way. Never.* My pride refused to take a one-floor elevator trip. Bracing the chipped black paint of the metal handrail, I took a deep breath and began my assent. Several students walked around me. Most ignored me. A few even threw sympathetic glances my way, including that girl from Crutchfield's class. Divinity? Dionysus? Desiree! Speeding up the stairs like a demon. Did she take anything slow?

Desiree's Introduction to Psychology class—now with me—met Mondays, Wednesdays, and Fridays. Today was Thursday. No student was allowed to take another psychology section until he or she completed Introduction, so where was she flying to? By the time I reached the top of the stairs—feeling as if I had climbed Mount Everest—Desiree had disappeared.

My office door resisted opening, but that was normal. Something about the high humidity warped doors with as much frequency as six-packs jumping off the shelves at the local convenience store. Luckily, no dead bodies or evidence of the third-floor toilet leaking through the ceiling again awaited me. Except for sore muscles, I started to believe it might be a good day after all. Even the soreness was growing tolerable. Traveling another flight of stairs to the cola machine in the faculty lounge was definitely doable. I dropped my backpack on top of the cluttered desk and took the next flight of stairs at a near-normal pace.

Seconds away from treating my cola fix, a hurricane in the form of Paula Burke came bursting into the faculty lounge. She didn't see me, so intent was she at pacing the far side of the room with clenched fists, glancing up briefly when the Diet

Pepsi came bounding out. I quickly drained half the can, sighing with the appreciation that only the first cola of the morning can bring.

I glanced back toward an obviously distraught Paula, struggling with whether to approach her or not. I'd like to say my decision was based on altruism, but it wasn't. I was curious. "You look upset, Paula. Is there something I can do?"

"Only if you can get rid of all these prehistoric *male* professors who wouldn't know progress if it bit them in the ass!"

Whoa. Where had that come from? I was shocked to hear such anger and language coming from Ms. Ladylike's mouth, and it stirred my curiosity. "What happened?"

Paula eyed me warily. After a moment of sizing me up, she spoke slowly, as if carefully weighing each word before letting it out of her mouth. "I made some suggestions to Dr. Bent about introducing some new classes next school term. He wouldn't even hear me out. Just said that we couldn't."

"Did he say why?"

"Something about the budget. But I bet my bottom dollar if one of his young, male protégés recommended a course on Psychology of Marriage and Family, Bent would think it's a brilliant idea."

"Marriage and family? That is a good idea."

"He just couldn't accept that it was my idea. That I might be successful at something besides teaching brain-numbing fodder like Statistics or Analysis of Classic Psychological Theories."

I thought she might be overreacting a bit. Zachariah might be a lot of things, but he never struck me as sexist. He required all of us to work our butts off equally. "Well, the budget has been tight lately. Jesus H. Christ, they even ration the toilet paper . . ."

Paula gave me a hard stare. "I thought you might be different. I should have known you would be on *his* side."

"Look, Paula, it's not about being on sides . . ."

"Hello, ladies," said Zachariah from the doorway. Not waiting for a reply from either of us, he slipped a few quarters in the juice machine.

"Paula," I whispered while Zachariah was waiting for the can to come bundling down. "Why don't you try talking to Zachariah again? Surely he'll listen . . ."

Before I could complete my sentence, a look of cold terror passed over her face before she ran from the room. She had been on fire a few minutes ago, and I had to admit I enjoyed seeing that side of her, as I never found much in common with the prim and proper, buttoned down "lady professor."

Night and day. Even her language. Paula used very proper language and wouldn't be caught dead uttering words like "bottom dollar." The only thing that had changed was Zachariah entering the room. He might be boring, but frightening? Zachariah? Why would she be scared of him? Not only that, but he seemed totally oblivious to the reaction his presence brought.

"Ronnie, Ronnie." Zachariah shook his head like a disappointed parent as he eyed the mountain of aluminum cans I didn't want to hear about.

"Have you heard anything about the investigation, Zachariah?"

"What investigation?"

"Crutchfield's death?"

Zachariah's face tightened and lines popped up. Obviously, this was not his conversation of choice. "I understand the police are questioning everyone in the building. Why, I don't know. They found the gun in his hand. It was obviously suicide."

"Are they questioning everyone? Even the students?"

"I should hope not!"

I was a little taken back by his response; after all, the students were looking like better suspects than the staff right now. If I were a betting woman, I would look at a football player or a teaching assistant. "Why don't you want the students questioned?"

"All we need is one of these rich little brats running home and telling Daddy all about being questioned in a homicide investigation." Zachariah actually shuddered.

"Have you been questioned?" I interrupted.

"I have met with Detective Melvin to discuss the case, Ronnie, but he didn't question me."

"Really? One of the campus cops came by my house to question me yesterday. I got the impression that they were looking at all of us as possible suspects."

I had hoped that by sharing the information that I too had been questioned, Zachariah might be willing to do a little sharing, too. Instead, he looked deeply troubled.

"Zachariah, is there anything . . ."

"Ronnie, I've scheduled a faculty meeting. First thing tomorrow morning, eight A.M. Be there. And be on time!" Zachariah ordered before leaving the faculty lounge.

I groaned. Just what I needed. Another mind-numbing meeting where everyone sits around for too long discussing nothing of importance and taking no worthwhile action. What a great way to start a day.

After draining the remainder of my drink, I tossed the can toward the recyclable box. The can tumbled down from the mountain of cans heaped in the overflowing box. I walked over and picked up the can, wedging it in, hoping it wouldn't send all the cans clattering to the floor.

I debated hauling the box to my office with me, but decided against it. Not only would the cans take up half my office space, but also I feared what little six- and eight-legged creatures might decide to take up residence. These old buildings bred cockroaches that you could ride. And the fumigation smell was even worse than the bugs themselves. I would have to remember to return for the recycling box later in the day.

For some reason, I took the other staircase, the one at the far side of the building from my office. Maybe I wanted to delay work for the day, or maybe I just needed variety in my life. Either way, my alternative route took me past Crutchfield's office, where glow-in-the-dark police tape still decorated the door. I was startled when the door screeched opened for Justin to limbo himself underneath the yellow tape.

Justin still hadn't realized I was there as he reached through an opening in the tape to pull the doorknob toward him. Removing his hand became more of a challenge when the police tape affixed to his watch. A series of twists and turns only made the matter worse.

"Damned tape," I heard him mutter, pulling at the tape.

"I'm no expert at sticky situations, but maybe if you slipped the watch off your arm first, it might be easier," I said.

Justin glanced over his left shoulder, then his right, finally locating me with a look that said he wished I would disappear. Like I would leave such an amusing situation. Besides, I wanted to hear his explanation for being where he obviously didn't belong.

After pulling the shiny gold-and-silver watch off his arm, it required only seconds to disengage it from the tape and slip it back on his wrist. Justin then brushed off his sports coat before looking back at me.

"I suppose you're wondering what I was doing in there," he said.

"The thought crossed my mind."

"I, um, well, I left something in Crutchfield's office last week."

"Last week was spring break, Justin."

"Then it must have been the week before that. I'm not sure." I nodded, but said nothing.

"Oh, all right." Justin sighed. "The truth is I wanted to check the size of Crutchfield's office." Justin paused for a couple of nervous twitches. "Well, I am in that little cramped corner office, you know."

That cramped office next door to mine. The same size as mine. "Lucky for you Crutchfield went and died, I guess," I said as I headed to my own office space.

My lecture on stimulus and response the next day ended with a few students still awake. Early-afternoon classes should come with a warning:

Caution: This class is held after lunchtime. It has been clinically proven that concentration skills are at a low in the early-afternoon hours due to full stomachs.

Trevor hadn't bothered to make an appearance or get in touch with me since our first and only conversation. Was he always this lax in his job duties, or was it me he had a problem with? Personally, I thought I would be a breeze after working with Crutchfield.

"So, for every action or stimulus in our lives, you can expect a reaction or response," I told the hundred-plus students in the auditorium. "Seeing a pizza commercial on TV is a stimulus. Your hunger, your cravings are a response to that stimulus."

Since I wasn't getting much response for my audience, I decided to give them a little stimulus. "When I give you homework, you groan. Homework is the stimulus and groaning is the response. And for today's homework, you are to find ten examples of stimulus and response in your lives."

I smiled as I heard the chorus of groans. Wait until they found out that this wasn't a homework assignment that I planned on picking up, much less grading. Any sane professor assigned homework very carefully in a class of this size. But the assignment would get them thinking about stimulus and response, and maybe a few brave souls would be willing to share their examples out loud during the next class.

"I know some of you are probably wondering about your midterm grades. I just received Professor Crutchfield's grade book. Unfortunately, it doesn't seem to be complete. But I do plan to have all grades posted by tomorrow morning. Look at the usual bulletin board on the first floor."

My comments affected two students. One, a panicked, jittery young woman, looked like her world was coming to an end. The other, a star football player, responded with a frown. I watched both leave the auditorium with worry etched on their faces.

With plans for grabbing a beer with Terry after work, I also left. Just as I passed through the same doors as the students, I jumped a mile when Jim Joe Bob, or whatever his name was, tapped me on the shoulder. I think Mr. Football Player planned it, and that was why he was lurking behind the door. And why he grinned when I jumped and squealed.

"Yes?" I tried with a deeper, more dignified tone.

"The midterm grades. What about mine?" Joe Bob said, looking down at me.

"You are one of the students whose grade report isn't complete. Did you turn in a midterm paper?"

"Of course I did."

His eyes glittered with indignation. It was a good performance, but I didn't buy it. "Well, I'll have to see if I can find it, because Professor Crutchfield's grade book has no grade for you."

I turned to walk away when he shouted.

"It was a B!"

Well, I had to turn around at that, didn't I? "And how would you happen to know that?"

"I saw Crutchfield, that Sunday before he died. He told me." I studied Joe Bob, slouched with his thumbs hanging out of his front jeans pockets. Insolent, yes, and maybe a little bit scared.

"Why did you see Crutchfield on Sunday?"

"We . . . we had an appointment."

"On Sunday? The last Sunday of spring break?"

Joe Bob gave a jerky nod. Desiree had also said that she had met with Crutchfield on Sunday.

"Did you happen to see any other students either before or after your meeting with Crutchfield?" I said.

"No, ma'am. I don't think anyone was in the building."

Which would make the meeting awfully hard to prove. "I'll get back to you, Joe Bob. But I'm not giving you any grade without confirmation of it, or unless I see your work myself."

I left Joe Bob and took the stairs to the second floor by myself. While walking back to my office, I saw Detective Melvin coming out of Justin's office. I'm ashamed to say that I ducked into the bathroom. Good thing, too. I heard knocking. And since my office was next to Justin's, it was a good bet Detective Redneck was beating on my door.

I slowly turned the latch inside the door, praying for its silence. Once the lock engaged, I leaned against the door and exhaled. I didn't want to take any chances on Melvin entering to relieve himself. *God, what an awful thought.*

I sighed. Reduced to hiding out in bathrooms, and the fumes from this frequently used bathroom were already getting a little noxious. Since only faculty resided on the second floor, we were unfortunate enough to share this little one-toilet unisex bathroom. I wasn't sure how often it got cleaned, but if you considered that nine of us probably used it several times a day, it wasn't enough. Correction. All of us but Crutchfield. Part of the appeal of his office, in addition to its larger size, was that it had a personal bathroom adjoining it.

Had the police bothered to check Crutchfield's bathroom? An idea was beginning to form. What if the killer had still been in Crutchfield's office when I came in? Hiding out in the bathroom? That would explain why I hadn't seen anyone leaving Crutchfield's office. LeGrand said I had probably arrived soon after Crutchfield was shot. And when the crowd gathered in Crutchfield's office, it would have been a simple matter to slip out and become part of the crowd. I struggled to remember the faces, but no one stood out in my memory. Had Trevor been in Crutchfield's office that morning? Justin? The football player?

I wasn't sure what kind of clue might have been left in a bathroom, but knowing Melvin's single-mindedness, it was possible the police hadn't bothered to check the bathroom for clues. Somebody should check, just in case, I told myself. And what better time than this evening? The building would be more or less empty. I could also search for the mysterious midterm papers at the same time. Satisfied with my plan, I opened the door and peered out. Detective Melvin was nowhere to be seen.

On my way to my office, I glanced in Justin's office in time to see him punch one of his desk drawers. It had to hurt. The desk looked similar to mine, surely made of a hard wood. If the wood didn't give, his hand surely would.

One last punch did it. To his hand. He gritted his teeth, but a loud moan escaped anyway. I hurried on to my office, certain that Justin wouldn't want me watching his tantrum. But what had upset the normally easygoing professor?

CHAPTER SEVEN

Naturally an early riser, I rarely set an alarm clock, preferring instead the peacefulness that came from waking up naturally in the morning. I never overslept . . . except on rainy days.

Snuggling deep into my cocoon, I heard a rumble of thunder and eventually became aware of the steady pounding on my roof. I worried briefly about my roof leaking, but the last guy swore he patched it so it wouldn't leak again. Yeah, like I hadn't heard that one before.

Oklahoma has some of the best rain I've ever seen. Not that light misty rain with drops so fine it's practically invisible, but good, strong rains that wash the grime from our cars and our psyches. When the rain ends, usually the same day, a sparkling new world awaits with brighter colors and sweeter smells.

When I'm in a funk, there's nothing better than walking in the rain and getting drenched. However, my favorite part is afterwards when I wrap myself in my beloved, tattered robe. Actually, it's my only robe, a gaudy purple terry-cloth thing that I've had forever. With a blanket and a cup of hot chocolate, I plant myself on the couch with a murder mystery. Wryly, it occurred to me that I had my own real-life murder mystery to solve. It wasn't near as much fun as curling up with a book.

Curiosity eventually drove me to search for the time on the clock radio, but I was pinned by a furry coward. Storms accompanied by thunder drove James Dean—usually possessed of an adventurous soul—to quaking under the covers. My guess was that in randier days before James Dean's potential for fatherhood was removed from him, the gun-toting owner of a female dog must have taken some shots at him.

After lots of twisting and turning and trying to move an immovable object, I managed to look over my defender to see the digital clock. Eight-fifteen. In the morning. I hadn't slept that late since . . . Oh, shit. It was a work day. And not only that. Zachariah had delivered an ultimatum late yesterday about an emergency faculty meeting . . . at eight this morning.

I pulled on the nearest clothes I could find—jeans and a T-shirt—while I brushed my teeth. I tossed a tube of mascara in my purse, the extent of my usual makeup routine. Dear Zachariah and the rest of the faculty, however, would get to see the real me.

I tossed my purse strap around my neck and gathered keys in one hand and a brush in another. The traffic gods were with me. Either that or everyone else was lucky enough to be able to stay in bed. I hated the lazy bums, even if their absence allowed me to make it to Rubenstein Hall in record time. After one last flick with the hairbrush, I tossed the brush into the car and slammed the door shut.

Of course, the clouds above me chose that exact moment I got out of the car to drop huge buckets of rain on my head. I had never seen the necessity of owning an umbrella. You couldn't find them half the time anyway. Besides, the worse that could happen was that you got wet. And if you got wet, you would eventually dry.

As I splashed my way inside, I quickly ducked into the downstairs bathroom. One glance in the mirror confirmed my suspicions that I looked like a drowned rat. Paper towels and the hand dryer didn't help much, but at least I didn't leave any more puddles wherever I stepped.

Zachariah's compulsive need to schedule every minute of

every day made me wonder what the impromptu meeting held in store for us. Probably something about late paperwork, but for some reason I couldn't chase away a nagging feeling of anxiety.

I tried taking the stairs three at a time, but almost broke my neck and had to settle for two at a time. After flying around the corner, I put on my brakes to catch my breath. How about that? I'd had my morning workout without even planning it. I entered a half-empty room (or was it half full?) where Zachariah had the gall to look me up and down before shaking his head in disgust. Like his narrow, pasty face was any prize.

"At least I'm here," I replied.

"Since we're still waiting for half the staff, you could have taken a few more minutes with your, er, your appearance," he said.

I sat down next to Professor Szalkowski, whom I nicknamed Bow Tie, as I could feel my itchy middle finger fighting to get the better of me. It had nothing to do with Zachariah's authority. I just didn't want him shooting one of those "how juvenile" looks that I hated so much. When I received them, I typically responded by acting more juvenile.

"And before I forget, Dr. Raven." Zachariah cleared his throat. "Those cans of yours need to be toted off immediately."

"My cans?"

"I believe it was at your insistence that we save aluminum cans so that you could save the earth. Am I correct in that assumption, Dr. Raven?" Zachariah sneered.

"And for this I got out of bed?" I muttered to myself after nodding to Zachariah.

That business completed, he turned to his brown organizer in front of him, while the other professors talked in low voices or sat like zombies with cups of coffee in their hands.

Paula, of course, was there in full costume and makeup. She

must sleep like that. Always where she was supposed to be and, of course, looking quite professional in her standard Victorian pastel blouse covering her neck and arms. She looked my way, and then turned away quickly. Still angry with me for "siding with the enemy"? But then she turned toward me again and nodded a hesitant greeting. Hmmm. Which Paula would I see today? Prim and proper or hostile and unpredictable?

"I'm glad everyone could make it to this morning's meeting," Zachariah announced loudly, signaling everyone to quiet down. "Even if we are starting forty-five minutes late. Thank you, Dr. Burke, for being the only one on time."

Before Zachariah could comment further, my favorite redneck cop entered, sporting an all-knowing smirk that I wished would fall into that dreadful paper cup in his hand.

"Everyone, this is Detective Melvin. He is in charge of the investigation into Professor Crutchfield's death. I don't have to remind everyone to cooperate with Detective Melvin," Zachariah announced before looking at me.

"Morning, folks," Melvin said after spitting in his cup. He sat the cup down and placed both hands squarely on the table, his bulky frame eclipsing the light from the window behind him. "Our preliminary investigation shows that your professor was murdered."

"But . . . but he was holding the gun in his hand, wasn't he?" Zachariah stuttered.

"He was holding *a* gun, Professor. Interestingly enough, it wasn't the gun that killed Weldon Crutchfield. The ballistics test shows that the gun found in his hand had not been fired recently."

"But how can that be?" said Bow Tie.

"For some reason, somebody wanted to make us think that your professor killed himself. No doubt to throw suspicion away from the killer."

Most of the staff wore bored expressions on their faces, as if they heard this kind of thing every day. Too much TV. It desensitized people. Only three people reacted. Justin frowned, but the expression could just as likely have been directed at a spot on his tie he was rubbing at. Paula's lips quivered, leaving little doubt about her feelings for Crutchfield. Zachariah surprised me most of all. His usual composure was in danger of unraveling as I watched fingers lightly drum the table while beads of sweat congregated on his upper lip.

"No one indicates seeing anybody or anything out of the ordinary. Therefore, it's obvious that the murderer is someone who spends a lot of time in this building. Maybe even somebody in this room."

At this revelation, whom do you think Melvin's hard-ass stare focused on? Yours truly, of course. I returned it and tried to appear unconcerned about where the present conversation was leading.

"Can any of you tell me of anyone who might have had a reason to wish Professor Crutchfield dead?" Before the silence became noticeable, he fired another question. "Professor Raven," he said as if he had bitten down on something sour. "Perhaps you would know why anyone would wish Professor Crutchfield dead?"

Wide-eyed stares focused on me. "Detective, nobody liked the man, but I don't know anyone, including me, who wished him dead," I said calmly to both the detective and my department, who seemed all too willing to let me become the sacrificial lamb.

"Detective?" said Justin. "I didn't see anything, but I may have heard something."

Melvin swung his gaze to Justin's sandy head.

"I was here early that morning, about seven-thirty, preparing for the day's lectures." Justin looked at Zachariah, obviously wanting to make sure the boss heard about his dedication. I struggled to keep from snorting. I couldn't remember the last time Justin had stepped foot inside Psych before noon.

"I heard arguing coming from inside Weldon's office. I had intended to ask if I could borrow one of his texts. Needless to say, when I heard arguing, I decided to come back later," Justin explained.

"Did you recognize the voice?" Melvin thundered.

"I'm afraid not. I can tell you that it was female . . ." Justin looked apologetically at me. Melvin adopted a seedy grin before turning back to me.

"Professor Raven, you admitted going to the victim's office in a fit of anger. Maybe that anger got the best of you . . ."

"You've got to be kidding, that is so . . ."

"And, in fact, you have a history of hostility toward men in positions of power?"

Before I could think of an appropriate answer, I heard Melvin being summoned.

"Later, LeGrand." Melvin turned his sneer back to me, like a pit bull poised for attack.

"Detective Melvin . . ."

"Look, LeGrand, I already know your opinion about this particular suspect and . . ."

"Detective Melvin." LeGrand's voice was low, but hard as granite. The campus cop I had dismissed as a flirtatious kid suddenly sounded like a dangerous man to cross. "Some additional evidence has come to light that I think you should know about. Now."

I could tell Melvin didn't want to stop haranguing me, but continuing at this point would have made him look ridiculous, and he knew it. "We'll be talking to each of you again. Everyone remains available until further notice," he growled. "And that means everyone."

I tried to catch LeGrand's eye to smile my thanks at his timely rescue, but instead he grimly followed the stalking detective out of the faculty room.

Our department head then turned sad eyes toward me and shook his head. Zachariah cleared his throat. "Well, I guess that concludes our meeting for today. I expect everyone to cooperate with the authorities. The sooner they solve this . . . this situation, the sooner the spotlight will be off the department."

I didn't bother with after-meeting chitchat. I figured that if anyone looked at me like I was a murderer, I might make it come true. Instead, I quickly retrieved my breakfast of a Diet Pepsi and bag of Fritos from the vending machines and escaped to my office.

After firmly closing the door behind me, I sat down behind my desk, resting my feet on a partially open drawer while I crunched on Fritos and meditated on the Taos print. Muted colors swirled around a figure with faint features, clothed in traditional tribal garb. I had always suspected that the figure was meant to represent my father.

I look around and see myself within the Taos pueblo, the adobe buildings contrasting brilliantly with the blue sky and the Sangre de Cristo Mountains. As I try to draw the mountain air deep into my soul, two Pueblo children race by, squealing in delight. I see the figure from the painting, the one I suspect is my father, heading to an easel. I hasten to reach him. When I reach out to touch his shoulder, he turns and I see an elder instead. I let my arm fall and return his greeting in Tiwa. I turn away, marveling that I remember Tiwa words forgotten long ago. A woman and I silently greet each other, not daring to speak for the benefit of the rude tourists who have come to the pueblo. Although the tourists have received instructions in polite behavior within the pueblo, they forget easily and shove their fancy cameras in our faces. But wait . . . I look down at the hard ground and see that I'm dressed as the other woman, in a skirt with a shawl . . .

I shook my head, feeling as if I had awakened from a trance or one incredible daydream. As a child, I took trips like the one I just had . . . often. Usually in school, which led to the nice teachers saying that my head was in the clouds; the mean ones sent me to the office for not paying attention in class.

I took one last look at Dad's painting, a puzzle with many facets. If I could just figure out how to tie the pieces together, the painting would tell me things. There was a certain similarity to the situation with Crutchfield's death—lots of pieces of a puzzle, but I had no idea how to tie them together.

I had been in lots of jams throughout the years, many of my own making, but to be accused of murder was definitely a first. It would be laughable if it weren't for the fact that Melvin had already decided I was guilty. Then there was Zachariah, wanting things wrapped up quickly to limit adverse publicity for the psychology department. And he didn't seem to mind if he lost another professor in the process.

The only way to prove my innocence was to figure out who the killer was. I pulled a legal pad from underneath a pile of papers that had been steadily multiplying since January. On the first clean page, I wrote WHO KILLED CRUTCHFIELD? at the top.

Melvin said the killer was probably someone frequently in the building. Grudgingly, I admitted this made sense. So, staff and students. I drew a line down the middle of the page for two columns.

What did I have? Crutchfield's murder was not a random killing. It was personal, probably committed by someone who had never killed before. Personal . . . someone angry with Crutchfield. A moment of passion? Maybe Crutchfield threatened someone, pushed him over the edge. In my mind, I saw a faceless person trying to reason with Crutchfield while Crutch-field laughed. The other person lost it and killed him. It could happen.

Staff. Well, Zachariah did look uncomfortable in the meeting. Zachariah didn't strike me as a murderer, but it wasn't as if I personally knew any murderers. One thing behavioral psychology had taught me was that anything was possible under the right circumstances.

I wrote down "Zachariah." He had mentioned Crutchfield's book not seeing publication now that he was dead. Next to Zachariah's name, I wrote "Crutchfield's book?" as a possible motive. Then there was Justin. Justin, who wanted Crutchfield's office space. That wasn't much of a reason, but what if Justin believed that with Crutchfield out of the way, his own career would advance? I added "Justin" with "career" next to his name.

Had he really heard Crutchfield arguing with a female, or was that his way of throwing any suspicions off of himself? The only other female in the department was Paula.

I hesitated to put down Paula's name. After all, she had been positively devastated when Crutchfield died. But why? What was their relationship? I added Paula's name with question marks. Maybe unrequited love on her part?

That was all the staff I could think of who might have a motive. Now, students. A knock at the door stopped further introspection. I answered, "Come in," while flipping to the previous page of the legal pad. Time to be a professor again. But instead of a student, I was greeted by the welcome sight of Mick LeGrand.

"Hi."

"Hello. Would you like to sit down?"

He sat down in the leather chair and grinned. "Nice chair."

"Thanks. I guess I should also say thanks for the save a while ago. Melvin seems intent on crucifying me."

"Yeah, sorry about that. I thought it might help if I found a witness corroborating your story."

I sat up taller and leaned forward on my elbows. "You mean there really is evidence? What is it?"

"Ronnie, this is an investigation. I'm not supposed to release any information . . ."

"But you said it's a witness for me? Who?"

LeGrand pulled a memo pad out of his shirt pocket and flipped several pages. "Trevor McKinley, a graduate student. Do you know him?"

"How is he a witness for me?"

"Says he saw you enter the psych building at eight-fifteen A.M. when he was on his way to the library."

"I don't understand. How does that help me?"

"You walk so fast that it probably only took you two minutes to get to Crutchfield's office. You made the nine-one-one call at eight-nineteen. Even if you make a habit of carrying a gun around with you, the body temperature was too low by the time we got there for you to have killed him in the minute before you called. Besides, no one reported hearing a gunshot."

"That's great! That means I'm not a suspect anymore!"

LeGrand rose from the chair and walked around the desk to stand behind me, his gaze focused out the window. I turned my chair and studied his profile. Lines marred his face, lines that shouldn't have been there.

"What is it?"

He turned and leaned against the windowsill. Although I could see more of his face, he still wasn't looking at me.

"LeGrand? You're scaring me."

"Sorry." He smiled. "Don't mean to. Apparently, even though there's a witness who can corroborate when you entered the building, it still doesn't prove you weren't in the building earlier."

"Let's see if I understand this. I kill Crutchfield, leave the building for an hour, give or take, return and find him? That's ridiculous."

LeGrand nodded, frowning. Ridiculous or not, I was still a suspect. Somehow, it didn't surprise me. What surprised me was LeGrand's making a point to come and tell me. He didn't have to.

"Ronnie, I hate to do this, but I have to search your office. We're searching the entire building. We need to find the gun that was used to kill Crutchfield."

To say I was speechless was an understatement. LeGrand avoided looking me in the eye.

"You have every right to demand a warrant, Ronnie. The only thing is, uh . . ."

"What?" I whispered, close to tears.

"Melvin will be the one to request the warrant, and if so, he'll probably be the one to conduct the search."

Oh, God. The idea of Melvin touching every inch of my office—my space—was too much to take. "Do it. Now."

LeGrand nodded and started at the window. He was very methodical. His hands and eyes touched every inch of space as he examined the perimeter. He made quick work of the bookshelves before stopping in front of Dad's painting.

"Hey, I know this painting. *The Spirit,* right?" LeGrand approached the print at an angle.

I moved to the front of the desk and leaned against it, watching him. I'd seen this kind of behavior before. I just didn't expect to see it in a campus cop who was my only defender against a murder charge.

"Let me guess. Art major?"

LeGrand nodded. "Painting doesn't pay the bills, though. I've always loved this painting. It was one of the last things painted by . . . by Wes Raven!"

I nodded.

"Uncle? Cousin?"

"Father."

"Oh, wow, that's so cool."

At that point, I wouldn't have been surprised to hear "dude" come out of his mouth. In fact, if I hadn't met LeGrand in another capacity, I might have run from the expression on his face. The art-groupie look. It used to bother me when people paid attention to me only because I was the daughter of Cherokee artist Wes Raven.

LeGrand treated Dad's painting reverently, and it was at this point that I had trouble seeing two feet in front of me. I took a deep, slow breath in to pull myself together while LeGrand made quick work of my desk.

Before I knew it, the campus cop stood before me and blanketed my right hand between both of his, surprising me with their size. I had long hands for a woman. Actually, it was my fingers that were long. Just right for playing the piano, my mother used to say. Unfortunately, long fingers didn't magically translate into musical talent. But his hands more than over-lapped mine. They were warm, a little callused, but I had to admit, they felt nice.

"Melvin is so certain I did it that he's not even looking at anyone else, is he?"

LeGrand finally looked at me, his expression telling me what I wanted to know.

"Well, then, I guess it really is up to me to find out who the killer is," I said out loud, but more for my own benefit than LeGrand's.

"Ronnie, I don't think that's such a good idea. This person is almost certainly someone you know. If he killed once, he might kill again to protect himself."

LeGrand's expression was so earnest. And he was right, of

course. The panic that led to killing Crutchfield might reappear if the killer felt threatened. And I was certain of one thing. There had been something personal between Crutchfield and his killer, something that led to panic and ultimately to Crutchfield's death. I would just have to be careful. "If I don't, I'm looking at being prosecuted for a crime I didn't commit," I whispered.

LeGrand sighed. "It's going to be over soon. But it makes much more sense for me to nose around than you. It is my job, you know."

It took me a minute to recover from the shift in the conversation. It was as if the tenderness had never occurred. I jerked my hand from his grasp and reached inside my backpack on top of my desk. I pulled out my keys and quickly disengaged the most accessible one, my house key.

"Here, you'll need this to search my home. I would prefer you don't go crashing through doors. They're the original doors."

"I don't need to check your house—yet. But Ronnie, we're not playing games." LeGrand lingered in front of me. "This person has killed one professor—a psychology professor. When are you going to get it through that thick head of yours that your life could be in danger?"

I wanted to yell at him for taking such an authoritarian attitude with me, but his closeness disconcerted me, leaving me whispering. "It's exactly because my life is in danger that I have to do something."

His dark eyes reached inside me in the same way that his hands had transferred warmth to me. I waited in anticipation for what was to come next, forgetting about Crutchfield's murder. Forgetting that Mick LeGrand was so much younger than I was. All I could think about was the very kissable mouth coming closer to mine.

My body was so taut that when the knock sounded at the door, I nearly jumped out of my skin. A flash of irritation passed over LeGrand's face before he retreated a careful distance away. "Come . . . come in," I said, hoping I could be heard over the roar of my beating heart.

Trevor McKinley hesitantly opened my door with a look of apology already settled on his face. When he saw LeGrand, he took a step back.

"I'm sorry. Should I come back later?"

LeGrand looked at me for a minute, perhaps wanting a signal from me for him to stay. But I couldn't give it. There were too many things to sort out before I trusted myself to be alone with him again. As if the age difference weren't enough, now there was the additional problem of his being a struggling artist. I had made a resolution at age twenty—no more artists. It was the only resolution I had ever kept.

"No, that's all right, Trevor," I said. "Come in. We're finished."

"For now, at any rate. I'll see you later, Ronnie," LeGrand promised.

When the door closed, I gestured for Trevor to sit down. He did, accompanied by wringing hands. He reminded me of a frightened animal frozen by headlights.

"Trevor, do you always act like this, or do I do something that upsets you?"

"The police were here. I thought . . . I thought they would stop thinking you killed Professor Crutchfield after I talked to them."

There was something in his manner. If possible, he was more anxious than before. "You didn't really see me, did you, Trevor?"

He shook his head.

"Then, why? Why did you lie to the cops on my behalf?"

Trevor spoke in a clear, determined voice. "Because I know you didn't kill Professor Crutchfield."

I wasn't sure if I wanted to know why Trevor was so certain of my innocence, especially since my first thought was that the only person beside me who knew without a doubt that I wasn't the killer was—the killer. The bait was there. Did I want to take it? Trevor stood between the door and me, but I felt as if, in my panicked state, I could mow him down.

"Did you know that I requested to be Dr. Crutchfield's intern?" Trevor began pacing in front of my desk, about four strides across for his long, skinny legs. Unlike his previous behavior, he was a coiled-up bundle of energy, and I watched for signs that he might strike.

"His reputation in the field of psychoanalytic theory was excellent. I thought I could learn something to, to . . ."

"To help others?"

"Yeah, I guess so. I mean, I thought I wanted to be a therapist, maybe a professor. But Dr. Crutchfield said that was just a sham, and that I was the one who really needed help. I don't know. Maybe he was right." Trevor pulled off his glasses and rubbed at his eyes.

I studied the young man standing in front of me. Worry lines etched a face that should have been a smooth canvas of youth. But it was the eyes that really got me. He clutched his glasses— held together with more than a few pieces of tape—in his right hand. Without the thick lenses, I saw so much emotion wrapped up in his caramel-colored eyes—fear, sadness, and hopelessness.

I could approach this conversation in one of two different ways. I could redirect him back to Crutchfield's murder or I could be empathetic and try to uncover what troubled him. The latter option might turn me into the boy's therapist, a process that overstepped the ethical boundaries of our current professional relationship . . .

"Did Crutchfield see you for therapy?" Trevor didn't answer, but I suspected that I had hit on something. "How often, Trevor?

How often did you see Crutchfield for therapy?"

"Twice a week."

I didn't know what to say. I wanted to jump up and down and swear about what a shit Crutchfield was, but I didn't want to send Trevor scurrying off like a frightened rabbit.

"I hated him!" Trevor said with such venom that he even seemed to surprise himself. "But I didn't kill him! I swear I didn't!"

"Okay, Trevor. It's okay. You didn't kill Crutchfield. But why are you so sure I didn't kill him?"

Trevor looked down toward his feet, wrestling with unknown demons. "I . . ." His voice faltered before he brought his gaze even with mine. "I've seen what Dr. Crutchfield does to people—did to people, I mean. Lots of people hated him. Wanted him dead. They argued with him, pleaded with him. You never had anything to do with him. In fact, you stayed out of his way."

I laughed with delight. "You are a genius, Trevor! With all the so-called psychology and criminal experts roaming these halls, you are the only one who has said anything that remotely makes sense." I hesitated before blurting out that even Mick's faith in my innocence was based on intuition—or physical attraction.

Trevor let a tentative smile escape as he put his glasses back on.

My joy was short lived. Trevor's deduction wouldn't hold water with Melvin. To get Melvin off my back, I was going to have to find another suspect. Someone who had a stronger reason for wanting Crutchfield dead than where he parked his Harley.

"Trevor, you said lots of people hated Crutchfield. Who do you think had a reason to kill Crutchfield?"

His eyes darted to every segment of my office. Everywhere, that is, except for my face. In a flash, Trevor bolted for the door.

"I've got to go."

"No, please wait. I really need to know . . ." The last of my words hung in the air as Trevor disappeared. I considered chasing him down, but what would I do if I caught him? Badger him like Crutchfield did?

I let out a deep breath and stood, taking Trevor's place pacing in front of my desk. Was Trevor telling the truth? I had little doubt about Crutchfield seeing his graduate assistant for therapy. It was just the kind of unethical practice that I had often suspected him capable of doing. Trevor hadn't denied hating Crutchfield, either. But the rest? Being under Crutchfield's thumb like that, well, it was conceivable that Trevor might have snapped and killed Crutchfield. But he denied killing Crutchfield, and I think he believed that. Could Trevor have murdered Crutchfield but blocked it out?

I placed my hands on top of my head, hoping to send an energy surge to my brain. Trevor. Did he or didn't he? Only his hairdresser knows for sure.

A quick twirl of my Rolodex ended when I came to the name of Charles Anderson, a calm nonthreatening therapist who, as luck would have it, also happened to be a man. Perfect for an anxious graduate assistant recently at the mercy of Crutchfield. I quickly wrote down the phone number on a sticky note and held it in my mouth while I gathered materials for my Advanced Applications of Behavioral Psychology section.

I stopped by the faculty lounge to slip the note about Anderson into Trevor's box. It might be days before Trevor decided to show his face again. I could only hope he checked his box with more regularity than he checked in with me. As I turned to leave, I saw Zachariah. He saw me, too, and did an about-face into his office, closing the door. While I found myself releasing pent-up breath in relief, I couldn't have explained why, even to myself.

CHAPTER EIGHT

When I arrived at Emilio's for dinner, I found my dinner partner flirting with the waitress. Things must have been going well because Terry didn't harangue me for being late.

Emilio's was a little hole in the wall right smack in the midst of the campus shops east of campus. The Tex-Mex institution was one of the few holdouts that had managed to remain in business since my college days. You had to wonder how it stayed open, though. Even now, at the height of the dinner hour, there were just a handful of us in the dimly lit restaurant. I had to believe that places like Emilio's would continue to exist because they inspired loyalty in a clientele looking for great food without all the noise of those cookie-cutter places that lined the interstates.

While savoring the spicy smells, I could ignore the shabby, mismatched chairs and tables that held their share of dents underneath a pound of wax. I took another deep breath, but unfortunately got a whiff of cigarettes from the group at the bar watching college basketball. Sure, Emilio's had a nonsmoking section. Unfortunately, it was right next to the smoking section.

"Margarita, on the rocks," I told our diminutive waitress.

"I'll have another Tecaté, Maggie."

Terry's gaze followed Maggie until she was out of view.

"Nice. Is she an orphan?"

"If only. Single mom."

Interestingly, Terry looked anything but upset about Maggie's status. However, he also didn't invite further discussion. He buried his receding hairline behind a menu yellowing and curling with age. I grinned. Terry talked little about relationships until they were over.

"I think I'll have the enchilada platter. How about you?" Terry said.

Without even looking, I knew what I wanted. "Chile relleno."

"Ronnie, you always get that. Try something else for a change. Be adventurous."

"No thanks, I've had quite enough adventure in my life lately. I'm not even sure my delicate psyche can handle the excitement of eating Tex-Mex."

"I shouldn't wonder, what with killing your fellow professors and all."

"Very funny."

Terry's clear blue eyes shone with uncharacteristic seriousness. "Actually it's not, Ronnie. I think it's time for some legal advice. I know someone who is pretty good." He pushed a slip of paper toward me. Amid all the doodling was the name of an attorney I had never heard of. Probably a good sign. If I had heard of her, it meant she advertised on late-night television.

"I don't know. Somehow hiring an attorney seems like I'm admitting guilt, like I have something to hide," I said.

I hesitated telling Terry that I had given Lieutenant Mick LeGrand permission to search my office. I probably should have received some legal advice before doing so. I had been acting out of fear of Melvin putting his swollen, clammy hands on my stuff. A fear that the campus lieutenant exploited. The jerk.

"Actually, I think it's time to figure out who killed Crutchfield so all this nonsense can stop." I reached for a tortilla chip.

"Any ideas?"

I dipped the chip in salsa with the philosophy that chips and salsa were a great brain food. The other was making its way to our table right now. Maggie placed a two-handed margarita in front of me. I ran my finger along the salty rim of the glass while we ordered. Maggie walked away after leaving a shy smile with Terry.

"The cops say it was probably someone who frequents Psych, otherwise someone would have noticed." I took a rather large sip of my margarita, shivering at the lip-puckering tang.

"That makes sense," Terry said. "Like a professor or someone on staff?"

"Or a student."

Terry leaned back in his chair with a stunned look. "You're kidding, right? A student? Why would a student kill a professor? For assigning too much homework? No, how about because a test was too hard?"

I didn't laugh, briefly recalling Desiree and her panic over her grades. Who knew why someone felt compelled to murder another person?

"Okay, tell Uncle Terry what you have so far."

"There's his graduate student, who was probably an emotional punching bag for Crutchfield. If I were this kid, I probably would have killed Crutchfield, but I just can't see this guy doing it."

"Any other prospects?"

"An obsessive college freshman who has never received any grade other than A."

"Definite nutcase," Terry commented.

"Then there's this really creepy football player, Joe Bob Billy Joe Justin somebody . . ."

"Joe Bob Wayne, the fullback? He's in your class?" Terry's eyes opened wide with delight.

"Well, he is now. He was in Crutchfield's class." I inhaled half of my margarita, trying to ignore how silly my suspicions were sounding when I voiced them to another human being.

"He's great. They're predicting he'll turn pro his junior year."

"Are you done fawning over this guy, Mr. Football Fiend?" I said with more than a little irritation. What if this kid really did it? Terry was my friend, and if he found it hard to believe that Joe Bob Wayne killed Crutchfield, what chance did I have that anyone else would believe me?

"Sorry, luv. I don't get many football players taking drama, although with all the athletes turned actors, maybe they should," Terry grinned, probably waiting for a smart-aleck comment from me. But my heart just wasn't in it, so Terry quickly assumed a more sober expression. "Why do you think Joe Bob did it?"

"I don't know that he did it, Terry. I'm just looking at people who might have had a motive." At that second, I was ready to chuck it all. Who needed a career as a university professor? It was too mainstream for me anyway. Who needed friends? I could up and leave. Go live in some isolated Rocky Mountain oasis and never see another human being again.

Terry watched. I couldn't stand pitiful looks aimed in my direction right now. Or hand holding or patting me on the shoulder.

"If you're going to say something, just say it, damn it!"

"I wondered how long it would take before you let the truth out," my friend said softly.

"What truth is that?"

"That you're scared shitless."

The understatement of the century. Part of me truly wanted to believe in our system of justice. To know I wouldn't be convicted of a crime I didn't commit. But I knew the system was faulty. With holes big enough to let people like Leonard Peltier spend most of his life in prison for a crime he didn't commit.

Even if I didn't get convicted, what would the publicity of an arrest and trial do to my career? If I gave up teaching, I wanted it to be my decision, not that of some two-bit detective stinking of chewing tobacco. But perhaps I worried most about the publicity impacting my family. My brother's alcoholism would fade next to newspaper headlines like: "Famous Artist Wes Raven's Daughter Charged with Murder." I groaned, unable to conjure up the appropriate TV news sound bites for such a situation.

"Ronnie, it's okay to be scared. Anyone would be." He gave me a big wink. "Hell, they'd have to find me. I'd hide my ass in Mexico. Maybe turn myself into a senorita."

I blinked back tears, knowing that if I started, I might not be able to stop. I couldn't even remember the last time I had a good cry. Yes, I did. When my father died. Too long ago.

Luckily, our food arrived at that moment and salivary glands overpowered my tear ducts.

"Another margarita?" Maggie said.

Terry answered "yes" at the same time as my "no," leaving Maggie suspended.

"You need to relax. Have another drink," Terry said.

"Have to check on midterm papers after this. That will be hard enough to do with one giant margarita sloshing around inside me."

"I don't have anything to do after dinner," Terry said. "Let me have another beer, would ya?"

"Sure thing, Terry."

After a couple of bites of gastronomical bliss, I tried my best nonchalant voice. "So, you think she got the hint?"

"Who?" His face was all innocence. He would have made a great actor if he had been willing to relocate to Los Angeles or New York. Fortunately for me, Terry believed both locations were heavily overpopulated with nuts.

"When does she get off work?"

"About half an hour."

"That should be just about when we're through eating our dinner."

Terry grunted before taking a huge bite of chicken enchilada. For a few minutes, we ate in companionable silence until both of us were forced to slow down by rapidly filling stomachs.

"So, how are things going with your cop?"

I looked at Terry blankly. Two could play this game. But Terry never gave up.

"What was his name again? Dick? Stick?"

"Mick." I stuck out my tongue at him.

"You're so dignified, Ronnie." Terry grinned. "So, have you seen Mick since our lunch the other day?"

"Actually, I saw him earlier today." I ignored Terry's smirk. "He's investigating a homicide in the building where I work, in case you've forgotten."

"So everything's business?"

"He seems concerned about, well, about my well-being. Keeps warning me to be careful. But isn't that part of his job?"

"Could be. What do you think?"

"I don't know. Sometimes I think he's flirting with me, but that seems too ridiculous. Maybe I'm reading him all wrong." I ran my fingers through my hair, pushing the unruly mop from my face, and leaned back in my chair with my arms folded.

"I don't remember you having trouble reading the signs before." Terry paused. "In fact, remember that time right after we met when I thought about making a move on you? You told me to quit acting like a goofus before I even tried or said anything."

"That's because you were looking at me silly."

"How does Mick look at you?"

"Like I'm a margarita, and he's a very thirsty man."

Terry didn't say anything. He didn't have to.

"The question is, what am I going to do about it?"

I left Evelina at Emilio's and strolled west to the campus to clear my head from margaritas and murder. The sun was staying out longer, even though we hadn't yet gone through the April ritual of springing time forward.

In the early-evening light, I could make out the vibrant color of jonquils like yellow suns in a young child's painting. The buds on the oak trees trailed behind the ornamental pear trees that were already flashing colorful foliage. It was impossible not to see new life sprouting. Although autumn was my favorite season, there was still something intoxicating about early spring in Oklahoma. Barring the tornadoes, it was heaven on earth.

The air. I couldn't get enough of it. It was like the overwhelming craving a new ex-smoker feels for a cigarette. I would do anything for it. I had a theory that the air was responsible for spring fever, a phenomenon I'm certain exists, even though there's little proof. Zachariah was always berating me for not being more scientific. But you have to believe in things you can't prove, whether it's spring fever, religion, full moons, or the Little People.

Students strolled hand in hand around me. Enjoying the outdoors was more special when you were with someone you liked. This of course brought my thoughts back to Mick. Being alone never bothered me before, never led to the loneliness that drove so many people to be with the wrong person, so long as they were with *someone*. But now . . . maybe spring fever was trying to claim another victim this year. If the summer humidity didn't arrive soon, I might start acting like a love-starved idiot, too.

Even with mixed-up feelings claiming my attention, Psych appeared before me all too soon and ended my walk. A few people loitered on the first floor, probably from one of the weekly evening classes, if the more mature appearance of the students was any sign. Maturity didn't seem to affect their vocal cords. If anything this group was louder than a room full of eighteen-year-old freshmen. But as I took to the stairs, the noise of evening students evaporated behind thick walls and floors.

Although the yellow police tape was gone, I still hesitated before opening Crutchfield's door. The picture of him with a bullet through his chest remained vivid in my mind. The old door emitted an eerie squeal as I pushed it open to a dim office. I ran my hand along the walls feeling for a light switch. Unsuccessful, I searched for the lamp I knew sat on the desk. I finally located it and held my breath as I turned on the light. Illumination didn't reveal any dead bodies or ghosts of professors past.

"Jeez, Raven, what the hell is wrong with you?" I muttered.

I checked the bathroom first, flooding it with the overhead florescent light and instantly feeling safer. You just don't think of ghosts haunting bathrooms. I opened the cabinets below the sink, not really expecting to find anything. And outside of three rolls of toilet paper and a scrub brush that had seen better days, I didn't. If anything were in the bathroom, it would have been left by accident, not hidden in a cabinet.

So, down on hands and knees I went, peering closely at every inch of the floor. It was over by the toilet, its shiny brass color contrasting with the dull white porcelain. I picked it up, turning it over in my hand. A class ring. The ruby-colored stone twinkled at me, but the writing surrounding it was faded with age. It was obviously old. Not many people wore class rings anymore unless they were getting ready to graduate. I couldn't even recall where mine was. I knew for a fact that this wasn't a PU class ring.

But wait. Hadn't I seen a ring like this one recently? I tapped the tarnished treasure against my hand. Crutchfield! When they were wheeling his body away, I saw a ring much like this one.

Obviously, I wasn't holding Crutchfield's ring. So who did this one belong to?

I stood, tucking the ring in one of the front pockets of my jeans. Maybe someone would ask about the ring. I couldn't even be sure the ring belonged to the killer. For all I knew, it had been lying there for years, just waiting for me to come along and rescue it. I shook my head. Time for the rest of my mission.

My gaze fell to the desk chair. The chair in which Weldon Crutchfield died. I knew it was silly, but I couldn't sit in the chair. Not when the last thing to sit on its smooth leather was Crutchfield's dead ass. The hole in the middle of the back was big enough to push my finger through. I sent the chair across the room with my foot and decided on a hard molded-plastic chair. At least it would keep me from falling asleep.

Not having the slightest idea where Crutchfield would put midterm papers, the only thing I could do was begin a systematic search, starting with his desk. The thin center drawer held the usual—pens, pencils, paper clips, and rubber bands.

The drawers on the left contained treasures like telephone books, legal pads, and envelopes. Somehow, I thought Crutchfield would have a more interesting desk. But these contents could belong to anyone. A quick glance at the walls made me wonder why there was nothing personal in his office. No pictures or letters. Not even mounted diplomas.

The drawers on the right side of the desk held more office paraphernalia. I looked beneath a pile of *Journal of Consulting and Clinical Psychology* to see if anything else was in the bottom drawer, but there wasn't.

I sighed. Better straighten the professional journals. I didn't know who would be taking care of Crutchfield's things, but I didn't want anyone thinking I had ransacked his office. Actually, I wasn't sure I wanted anyone to know I had even been here, although looking for midterm papers was certainly a legitimate excuse. It was while straightening up the journals that a breast slipped from the pages. A picture of a breast, I mean, and quite a large one, too. I couldn't think of a single reason that the American Psychological Association would be showing breasts within its hallowed pages, so I opened the journal.

Surprise, surprise. *Hustler.* Tucked into an academic journal. How about that? I guess that was personal, sort of. Out of professional curiosity, I checked to see if other journals had the same material tucked in. Not really. The others had *Beaver, XXX,* and of course, what collection would be complete without *Skin*? Those college freshman boys didn't have anything over their professor, did they?

The shrill ring of Crutchfield's telephone sent a couple of those magazines, not to mention me, three feet in the air. I stared at the intruder for another ring before gently picking up the receiver. My heart was beating wildly. "Hello?"

"Weldon Crutchfield, please," an impatient voice demanded.

"Who's calling?"

"I'm Weldon's publisher, Ben Calvin, Brothers Publishing." I sensed drumming fingers across a desktop, maybe a steering wheel.

"Mr. Calvin, this is Ronnie Raven, I'm a colleague of Weldon's . . ."

"Where is that lazy, lying son-of-a-bitch?"

"Excuse me?"

"Weldon's the one who needs excusing." The publisher's voice rose to such a level that I had to hold the phone a couple of inches from my ear. "I've given him extension after extension, and I still don't have more than three chapters on my desk. I'm sorry I took that bastard on as a client. Now, where the hell is he?"

"Dead."

The first response was blissful silence. "What is that, Okie humor?" The irritation was still present, but now tempered with wariness.

"No, we only joke about dead lawyers and publishers." Okay, maybe I should have left out the part about dead publishers. "Mr. Calvin, Weldon was found dead in his office four days ago. The police are investigating it as a homicide."

"Murdered? I . . . I can't believe it," the publisher stuttered. "I thought people were only murdered in New York City and here in California. Not in Oklahoma." Typical outsider observations. He probably saw Oklahoma as a land where the tumbleweeds roared across the plains with non-English-speaking Indians in full regalia and war paint, riding horses bareback.

"Unfortunately, Mr. Calvin, we have murder in Oklahoma, too."

"Pretty dumb thing to say, huh? You handling the estate?"

I looked at pictures of various body parts strewn about the desk. Pictures I could have gone a lifetime without seeing. "Me? No."

"Who is?"

"I'm not really sure. There's a cousin . . ."

"Look, could you leave a message for whoever it is I need to talk to?"

"About the book?"

"Yeah, I talked with Weldon on Friday afternoon. He promised to send the rest of the manuscript over the weekend, FedEx, but I haven't received anything."

"Well, I, uh . . ." I wasn't sure how to answer. But the conversation was giving me some new ideas to explore. I found a notepad and wrote down "Motive: who would benefit from Crutchfield's death? Heirs? Life-insurance beneficiary?" And maybe more importantly, had someone taken Crutchfield's manuscript? Was there someone in addition to Zachariah who didn't want this book published? Enough to kill for it?

"We had a contract, and he was paid an advance. It's all legal. You can have one of your dead Oklahoma lawyers check it out."

Nothing wins me over more than a sense of humor. "I'll see what I can do, Mr. Calvin. Give me your number."

"Call me Ben." He gave three different phone numbers. Home, office, and cell. I wrote them down on another sheet of paper, tucking both it and my questions about motives into my front jeans pocket. "You said your name was Ronnie?"

"Yes."

"You've got a nice voice, Ronnie."

"Thanks, Ben. You, too. We'll be talking to you." I hung up the phone and collected the girlie magazines, stuffing them back in the drawer. They were out of order now, but who would know? I had more important things on my mind. Like locating midterm papers and, now, a manuscript. I pulled open the drawer where I had seen the phone book and quickly thumbed through it.

"FedEx," was the answer on the other end.

"Yes, I'm trying to track down a package I believe was sent through your service from Weldon Crutchfield."

"Are you Weldon Crutchfield?"

Did I sound like a Weldon Crutchfield? Would the voice believe me if I answered affirmatively? No, I couldn't risk it. "I'm his secretary. Mr. Crutchfield is out of town, and we just received a call from the other party saying they haven't received the package."

The FedEx man took down all the information and put me on hold to listen to an acoustical version of *Muskrat Love*. Like the original wasn't bad enough. Surveying the room, I saw a file cabinet behind me in the corner and a bookcase not far from that. They looked like the only places left to search.

"Ma'am. We don't have any record of the package. He must have used another mail service."

Bloody unlikely, I thought, feeling a little like Sherlock Holmes in my investigating. "Well, thank you for your help."

Pulling the to-do list from my pocket, I now added "check post office and other mail services" to it, before putting it back in my jeans.

I perused the bookshelf first. Typical texts. *Statistical Analysis in Psychology. Experimental Psychology. The Standard Edition of the Complete Psychological Works of Sigmund Freud.* No reference to behaviorism. But then Crutchfield had once told me that human behavior had nothing to do with the mind.

That left the file cabinet. Not a task I relished. But to my delight, everything was organized and labeled. Nothing like my own files. I found class work dating back ten years, but nothing for this past midterm or anything even remotely resembling a book manuscript. He could have worked on the book at his home, which would explain why there was no trace of it. Would he have taken the midterms home, too? It was the only other possibility. Trevor had said Crutchfield planned on handing them back the first day after spring break.

I reached to turn off the lamp. It was then that I noticed a discrepancy in the paneling near the door. Like someone had cut through the paneling. A secret hiding place? Crutchfield might have just been paranoid enough for something like this, at least for his manuscript. There wasn't a handle or knob to pull on, so I hammered at the paneling with my fist in a few strategic places until it came open.

A closet. At least that's what Crutchfield used it for. A jacket and umbrella hung on hooks. I knelt by a cardboard box sitting at the bottom of the three-foot-by-three-foot space. I tried to lift the box, but it threatened to rip under the weight. Since it was too dark in the closet to see what weighed down the box, I dragged it out of the closet, twisting it from side to side until the soft glow of the desk lamp captured it.

I settled myself comfortably on the floor, cross-legged, in front of the box, intent on finding three things. Midterm papers for Desiree and Joe Bob, and if I was lucky, a manuscript. Maybe something to shed some light on Crutchfield's murder. Excited, I reached into the box.

And that's the last thing I remember before darkness fell.

CHAPTER NINE

Mumbling. Distant mumbling growing louder . . . and annoying . . . like a fly buzzing inside my ear. The mumbling refused to leave me to the darkness, leaving me no alternative but to listen to words impossible to ignore.

"Oh my God, she's dead, isn't she? Just like Crutchfield. I knew it; we shouldn't be here. Let's just get out of here." A feminine voice, skirting around hysteria, rambled.

"It's okay, she's not dead," said another voice, familiar, yet unfamiliar at the same time. "Look, she's breathing."

"What do you think happened?"

"Calm down, Desiree. I don't see any blood. I'm guessing she fainted or . . ."

"What? *What?*"

"Somebody employed extreme force to the medulla region."

"You mean somebody hit her over the head? Why would they do that?"

My thoughts exactly, as a moan escaped my lips.

"We've got to do something, Trevor. Call the police or something."

Trevor. Desiree and Trevor? The Desiree and Trevor I knew didn't compute, forcing me to open my eyes to see if it was the Desiree and Trevor I knew. It was.

Trevor smiled. "Hi, Ronnie. I'm guessing you're not the type to pass out. Am I right?"

I tried to answer "of course not, you dolt," but words

wouldn't come. Instead, I nodded and almost cried from the pain.

"We need to get you looked at. Do you want me to call an ambulance or can you walk?"

I answered by sitting up, which caused unbelievable pain to radiate from the back of my head. My body weaved back and forth as Desiree and Trevor each took a side and eased me to my feet.

"Oh, shit. Oh, jeezus! Oh, shit." The pain emanating from my head made any sore muscles from jogging as insignificant as a chipped fingernail.

Luckily, the kids led me because I had no idea where to go. At that moment, my only goal in life was to keep my head as steady as possible in order to contain the pain. When we got to the service elevator, they leaned me against the wall while Trevor dug in his pockets for his copy of the elevator key. I tried to focus on Trevor. Something different. He seemed larger than usual. More confidence. Something missing. I felt myself sliding down the wall, unable to make my voice ask for help. Although they caught me before I hit the floor, tugging at me didn't do much for the pain.

If I had thought movement was bad so far, it was nothing compared to riding the elevator. Never one of my favorite ways to get someplace, this particular elevator ride shot my brain to my stomach, leaving me in danger of upchucking them both. My first clear thought since losing consciousness came. I was going to find out who killed Weldon Crutchfield, no matter what. Because just as sure as a Baptist preacher preaches hell and damnation, my bashed-in head had something to do with Weldon Crutchfield's murder.

What can I say about the car ride? I couldn't focus on much about Trevor's car. It was old, that much I could tell. And it definitely needed a new muffler . . . and shocks. Definitely needed new shocks. Quite simply, the drive to the campus clinic less than two miles away was one of the worst experiences of my life. A stomach flu during a ten-hour plane ride couldn't compare with that five-minute car ride. If I had been Catholic, I would have given up riding in cars for Lent.

As we burst through the automatic doors, Trevor on one side of me and Desiree on the other, a blast of fluorescent lighting broadsided me. I closed my eyes, but the light still invaded the inside of my head. I couldn't escape it. That was the problem with this world. Too much fluorescent lighting.

An older woman with circles under her eyes and wide hips greeted us at the desk of the neon structure known as the campus clinic. The place looked deserted, and she appeared quite delighted to see me. She soon gave up on the challenge of getting my eyes fully opened and instead tried to coordinate my hand and brain to fill out forms.

Trevor explained that I was a psych professor, but I don't think she believed him. Luckily, all the proof she needed was in my social security number. As many times in a lifetime that we have to recite our social security numbers, it is the one number that we can recite even when we're half-dead. Her computer told her that I was indeed Ronnie Raven, psych professor, when my appearance didn't offer a clue.

"Drugs. I need drugs to stop the pain," I said, not certain how loud I spoke, but my voice sounded like shouting in my head.

"You have to talk to the doctor about that. Let's get you into a room."

She led me into another fluorescent-radiated room that sent waves of agony through my head. "The lights. Turn off the damned lights."

"You got a migraine, honey?"

I started to shake my head before realizing it would be less painful to talk. "Hit . . . on . . . head."

Apparently, this qualified under the "all right to turn off lights" category because she did just that after laying me on the exam table. Working by a dim bulb near the sink, she asked the usual name, rank, serial number, and allergy questions before leaving me in blissful peace.

I think I might have slipped out of consciousness at that point. The next thing I knew, a tiny penlight was shining in my face, and I didn't have the energy to knock it away.

"Ronnie? I'm Dr. Thomasina," said a soothing voice that received high marks in the bedside-manner department. "I need to check your pupils."

I let the good doctor struggle with eyelids that had a will of their own under the best of circumstances. After a couple *mmm-hmms*, he started his questions.

"Full name?"

"Ronnie Raven."

"Do you know where you are?"

"Campus clinic."

"Date?"

"March something." After a moment of silence, I shrugged. "Look, I have trouble remembering the date even when my head hasn't been bashed in."

Dr. Thomasina chuckled. "Swallow this."

I gratefully tossed capsules to the back of my throat, washing them down with lukewarm water from a flimsy cone-shaped cup. "What did you give me? Demerol? Morphine? Heroin?"

"Acetaminophen."

"Tylenol? What's that supposed to do? Stop my little finger from hurting?"

"Hopefully, it will give you some relief during the next twenty-four hours. You can't have anything else until we determine what kind of trauma you've suffered."

The doctor turned from me to talk to the wall. "She appears to be suffering from a mild concussion. Check her orientation every two hours or so. If she becomes disoriented or her speech becomes slurred, take her to the city emergency room immediately."

Trevor and Desiree. I tried to tell the doctor that Trevor and Desiree wouldn't be staying with me, but the good doctor had closed the door behind him before I could form the first word.

"How are you feeling, Ronnie?"

"What are you doing here?"

"Officially, I'm making a report," LeGrand said. "Unofficially, I'm your nurse for the next twenty-four hours."

When pigs fly, I decided. Unfortunately, I also chose that moment to hop off the exam table as if nothing were wrong with me. And promptly fell into his arms.

"Look, just get me to a phone. I'll call a friend to stay with me."

LeGrand looked at me doubtfully. Whether he had doubts about my ability to dial a phone or have friends wasn't clear. And I didn't care.

He showed good sense by keeping quiet as he walked me out to the waiting room phone. I tried not to lean on him much, but the truth was that, without his solid frame supporting me, I most certainly would have fallen flat on my face.

"Trevor and Desiree?"

"The two kids? I sent them home after they answered some questions. Need a phone book?"

"I already know Terry's number, thank you."

"Terry. The guy you were having lunch with the other day?"

Talking took too much energy. Instead, I turned to support myself on the counter and dialed. I shouldn't have been surprised when the machine picked up. After all, he and Maggie were exchanging lovey-dovey looks the last time I saw them. My only hope was that they took their horniness back to his place.

After wincing at the answering machine beep, I pleaded. "Terry? If you're there, pick up." No response. "Terry, it's an emergency." Still nothing, not even a pissed-off voice threatening me. If I found out he was there and not picking up . . .

I handed the receiver to LeGrand who quietly replaced it. I quickly racked my brain for someone else to call. I could call my mother, but it would take her four hours to get to my place and that would be after loading up my nephews. Besides, I really didn't want Mom fussing over me. Or in the middle of this mess. She had a reputation for turning into a mother lion when one of her pack was hurt. I needed to think. Figure out what . . .

"Ready to go?"

I looked up, irritated with LeGrand for interrupting thoughts that were proving hard to form into some kind of coherent logic. And I decided he had done it on purpose. He didn't want me thinking.

"Look, LeGrand, I appreciate your concern. Really I do, but I'm sure I'll be all right on my own."

"Yeah, you did great on your own tonight, didn't you?" He took hold of my arm, leaving me no choice but to go with him. "Somebody needs to stay with you for two reasons."

"Two reasons?"

"One. Somebody needs to wake you every couple of hours throughout the night and check your responses. I don't think James Dean is capable of that."

I ignored his sarcasm and high-handed manner. For now. "And two?"

"Somebody hit you over the head on purpose tonight. Unless you can tell me otherwise, I'm going to assume it has something to do with Crutchfield's murder, and that you could be in danger. Maybe it's better to have a cop hanging around than risk your boyfriend's neck, even if he's nowhere to be found at one o'clock in the morning!"

Then he just about threw me into a campus police car and shut the door behind me. When he got in, he jerked his seat belt around him and narrowed his eyes at me. I reached where I thought my seat belt should be. Of course, it wasn't. A hand, his hand, came around me, pulling my seat belt into a snug harness binding me in. The back of his hand lingered at my front until I grabbed the seat belt from him and clicked it shut.

The soothing night air was a little on the chilly side, but it served to inject a little logic into my addled brain. I resigned myself to LeGrand's nursing skills. Why should I be nervous about his staying with me tonight? He was a cop, for God's sakes.

Yet when I glanced over at him, I noticed he was out of uniform. Jeans. Denim shirt. Gorgeous. Maybe it was a good thing that I had a concussion.

LeGrand's hands gripped the steering wheel, his knuckles white against the black leather. Angry? Had my accident interrupted his own romantic evening? I certainly didn't want him to feel obligated to stay with me.

I hated to admit it, but the Tylenol seemed to be working. I still hurt, but my brain seemed to jump-start itself, and LeGrand's last words began to penetrate the fog.

"What boyfriend were you referring to?

"Huh?"

"Back at the clinic, you said something about my boyfriend not being able to stay with me. What boyfriend did you mean?"

"There's more than one?"

I should have let him believe there were hundreds, but I wasn't feeling particularly smart at the moment. "Actually, as of five days ago, zero boyfriends."

LeGrand frowned, giving me a quick glance, before turning

onto my street. "You broke up with Terry?"

"No, I broke up with Rick during spring break. Things . . . well, things just didn't work out. To be honest, he was a self-centered old fogy with no sense of humor and no sense of adventure. And how would you like to spend your spring break waiting on him and his broken leg?"

LeGrand pulled to a stop underneath the massive oak tree in my yard. "Then what about Terry?"

"What about him?" I couldn't follow the confusing thread of conversation, and from the look of LeGrand, it had nothing to do with the bump on my head. He was having trouble, too.

"You broke up with Rick, but you're still seeing Terry?"

"Well, of course I still see Terry; he's . . . wait a minute." The light bulb went off, dim, but it did finally go off. "You mean seeing Terry as in a dating kind of thing?"

I began laughing, but had to cut it short because of my head. "The only thing I see Terry for is friendship."

"Just friends?"

"He's my best friend."

Mick looked at me for a minute longer, boring his dark gaze into the cobwebs of my mind. I didn't especially want him wandering around in there, so I reached for the door handle. Before I could get the door all the way open, my knight in shining armor stood in front of me and reached for my hand.

His fingers touched my palm, and there it was again. A jolt surging through my body. I pulled away, rushing for the door. I stopped to dig the key from a pocket in jeans that were a little too snug.

After a couple of tries, the key connected with the keyhole, but before I could open the door, Mick shoved me aside. So much for knights in shining armor. He kept a hand behind him as if to keep me at bay. In my own house!

"What the hell . . ."

"Shhhh."

If this wasn't so out of character from the Mick I thought I knew, I would have told him what warm place he could pay a visit to and push him out of the way. Instead, I watched him check behind doors, curtains, and in closets. I felt like I was watching a police drama badly in need of an action scene. Served him right to see my home in all its glory. Clothes strewn about and more than one empty Diet Pepsi can decorated the living room. Then he came to *the closet.* In the hallway, to the right of the living room was a hall closet for coats and things. My purpose for the closet was a little more creative. I threw anything in there that I couldn't find an immediate place for. Usually I tossed in an item and quickly shut the door before I could actually see the closet. I wasn't afraid that the desire to clean would overcome me. I was only afraid that something would fall on me.

When Mick quickly swung open the door, he had to take a step back to dodge a flying shoe. So that's where my old jogging shoes went! Carefully, Mick lifted various piles with his foot.

"Careful, you might disturb Jimmy Hoffa." Even his exasperated look couldn't stifle my giggle.

Reluctantly he closed the door. "Excuse me for trying to make sure your house is safe."

I pointed to the sleeping canine on the couch. "If someone were hiding, do you really think my dog would be sound asleep in a place he's not even supposed to be?" I had thought I was the reason for the sagging left end of the worn blue couch because I usually sat in that spot. Now I began to wonder whether James Dean might share responsibility for the sagging.

"Probably not," he conceded. "He probably would have licked him to death. But you could hide a whole army of bad guys in that closet and never know."

"That's the beauty of it. I don't want to know." I walked to the kitchen. "Do you want some tea?"

"Sure, but why don't you let me make it?"

I shook my head. Making tea in my own kitchen was a way to gain back some of the control I had abruptly lost when someone hit me over the head. No one wants to give up control, especially not me. In minutes, I nuked some hot water in the microwave and dropped tea bags into two cups—one a souvenir cup from Mesa Verde National Park where I spent a summer exploring the ruins. The other made reference to being proud to be a bitch. I kept the bitch cup for myself.

We sat adjacent to each other at the dining table, probably the nicest piece of furniture in my rental home due to a lack of use. I'm a habitual "eat while standing in front of the kitchen sink" kind of person, although for variety I'll take a meal to the living room to eat in front of the TV.

Mick and I silently concentrated on dipping tea bags in the steaming mugs. Mick finally took a sip and screwed up his face. "What is this?"

"Tea. Chamomile. It helps you relax."

"Herbal tea?" You could tell from the way he said it that he equated herbal tea with cardboard.

"Yes, herbal tea." I was getting a little put out. "Do you have a problem with that?"

"You don't strike me as the herbal-tea type," Mick said.

"Well, that's because you haven't seen the black light in my bedroom. It's right next to the pot and the bong and the Jefferson Airplane poster."

"Are you always this touchy?"

"Only when people try to make me into a type," I said.

"Sorry."

I wasn't too sure he was the one who needed to be apologizing. Maybe I was being too sensitive. "People have been making judgments about me my whole life. I guess I don't like it much,"

I sighed. "And maybe being knocked out has made me a bit irritable."

"Since you brought it up," Mick said, pulling the notepad from his back pocket. "What can you tell me about tonight?"

"Not much. I was searching Crutchfield's office for midterm papers for the class I'm teaching. I'm missing grades for two kids." I stopped, feeling the muscles bunch up in my neck and shoulders. I gently rolled my shoulders back and forth, willing them to relax. "I was about to give up when I found a closet."

"What was in there?"

"Mostly what you would expect. A coat. Umbrella. At the bottom of the closet was a box."

Mick scribbled something and mumbled incoherently to himself before nodding for me to go on.

"Anyway, I pulled out the box. There were papers. I sat down to go through the box. And . . . and I really don't remember anything until I woke up to find Crutchfield's graduate assistant and a student next to me."

"They the ones I talked to at the clinic? Tall, studious-looking black guy and a fidgety white girl with huge blue eyes that looked like they were about to cry. They were together—hugging, hand holding?"

"I don't know about 'together,' although that might explain why they were in the building together tonight. I hadn't realized they even knew each other." I shook my head. Desiree and Trevor. Go figure. Wait. That was it. The bandage. That was what was different about Trevor. The clumsily applied bandage on his right hand was gone. Why had I noticed that? Jeez, I wish my brain would start working.

Mick misinterpreted my confusion. "You think they might have hit you over the head?"

"Wouldn't it be rather stupid of them to stick around if they had hit me over the head?"

Mick shrugged. "Makes it look like they had nothing to do with it. What did you say you were looking for?"

"Midterm papers. Joe Bob and . . ." Maybe they did have something to do with it. Desiree's paper was the other one missing. And if she and Trevor were together . . . maybe the bandage on Trevor's hand was a powder burn from shooting Crutchfield through the back.

"And?"

"Hmmm?" I looked up from my tea.

"You said what you were looking for? The midterm papers and . . . ?"

I took a sip of still-hot tea and felt it go down my throat smoothly. "A manuscript Crutchfield was supposed to send to a California publisher."

"Why were you looking for that?"

"While I was in Crutchfield's office, the publisher called, said it was late. I thought it might have something to do with his murder."

"Why is that?"

"I'm not sure. I know that Zachariah Bent wasn't happy about a book being published. Said a sensationalist book like Crutchfield's would make our department look bad. Maybe there were *others* who didn't want to see the book published."

"Did you find anything in the box?"

"I didn't have time to look through it. Hey, why don't we go back over there now and look for it? It could still be behind . . ."

Mick shook his head. "I sent an officer over there. There was nothing about a box."

"You mean it's gone? That means whoever hit me on the head took it!"

Mick's mouth thinned. He closed his notebook and set it down on the table, but didn't say a word.

"So what do you think?" I urged.

"I think it's time for you to get some sleep."

"Maybe we should go over there anyway. There could be a clue or something."

"*Detective* Raven, you are suffering from a concussion. Not to mention that you don't have any business looking for clues anyway." Mick stood up, looking more like a stern father than a youthful campus cop. "Now, can you manage to put yourself to bed or am I going to have to do it?"

CHAPTER TEN

I woke to a throbbing headache. Like a super-bad hangover, but without any of the fun of the journey. I lay in bed hoping unconsciousness would consume me again, but I was one of those unfortunate people who found it impossible to go back to sleep once my eyes popped open. Giving up, I rose to sitting easily enough, yet it seemed to take forever to maneuver my legs over the side of the bed.

I understood why my head hurt, but why did the rest of my body feel as if it was caught in a battle zone? Very slowly, I put weight on my feet. With one goal achieved, I toddled off to the bathroom, taking great care not to look in the mirror over my chipped pedestal sink.

After popping a couple more Extra-Strength Tylenol, I cranked the shower to give up all the hot water it had. It took several attempts to ease my head under the showerhead. I don't know how long I stood beneath the pounding spray, but the hot water still ran out all too soon.

I grabbed the first clean clothes I could find, white cotton slacks and a navy T-shirt. Putting on a bra required more dexterity than I had at the moment. While dressing, I paused to sniff the air. Bacon. Weird. I thought I smelled bacon. I had heard of people hallucinating smells; olfactory hallucinations, they were called. Was this an effect of my head injury? And, if so, why couldn't I smell chocolate-chip cookies baking instead?

Taming my tangled mane of hair was a chore any day. Today,

it was almost impossible because of the tender lump I had acquired. I reconsidered my frequent threat to shave my head bald. I could be the bald professor of PU. But however much I might like to shock, my hair was staying attached to my head. Like Samson, I didn't want to lose whatever powers I might have.

The smell of frying bacon intensified on my way to the kitchen. Bacon and a few other odd smells identifying breakfast. I stopped when I reached the faded patchwork-pattern wallpaper that marked where my kitchen began. While cooking ranked among my least favorite domestic chores, and I admitted the list was extensive, I still loved my kitchen. Real-estate agents called it cozy. You could walk from the kitchen sink to the breakfast nook at the other side of the room without taking an extra breath. Faded walnut cabinets joined green countertops in a way that said make yourself at home.

But something was different about my kitchen today. Specifically, a man. Mick, with tousled hair looking every bit as tangled as mine, stood over the stove with a spatula in hand.

"Morning. How do you feel?"

"Uh, okay, I guess. Where did you find bacon?"

Mick grinned a lazy smile. "At the grocery story over on Main. Found coffee there, too."

Apparently, the other foreign smell emanating from my kitchen. "I don't drink coffee."

"What do you do for caffeine?"

"Coke. Pepsi. Whatever's available, although I prefer Diet Pepsi."

"But what about in the morning?"

"Like I said, diet pop."

The face might have been different, but I had been on the receiving end of that incredulous expression since reaching the decisive age of fourteen years old and concluding that cold brown carbonated beverages were great any time of day. My mother just shook her head now and sighed when I popped the top of a cola can before noon. At least Mick's expression distracted me from examining how he looked standing in my kitchen in jeans and a shirt haphazardly buttoned to mid-chest.

I went around Mr. Domestic to retrieve my trusted box of Cheerios and a bowl. Opening the fridge, I balanced a carton of skim milk in my arms and headed to the table. I poured cereal and milk into the bowl, but had to go back for a spoon. I tried to ignore the glare that I knew was aimed in my direction. After one crunchy bite of cereal, I looked up. As expected, Mick was scowling at me from the stove.

I quit crunching and laid my spoon to the side of the bowl. "Look, I really do appreciate your fixing breakfast, but my stomach can't handle more than cereal or yogurt in the morning." I elected to stay quiet about breakfast smells making me nauseous and how my kitchen would probably smell like bacon for days.

Mick shrugged and dumped a plate of bacon and eggs into a bowl. Before the bowl touched the floor, a grateful James Dean gulped it down in two swallows. And then burped. Hearing my dog belch wasn't a new experience, but I joined Mick in laughing anyway.

"How does orange juice grab you?" Mick said with an eyebrow arched.

"I would love some, thank you."

He brought my juice along with his plate of food. A big plate of food. My new cop friend had a healthy appetite that he used to inhale big bites of food in the way only men can get away with.

After finishing my Cheerios, I sipped my juice as he shoveled the remaining bites into his mouth. When he neared the end, I asked, "Did you stay here all night?"

Mick answered by turning the inside of his left arm up, continuing to eat with his right hand. Red streaks, impossible to miss, ran the length of his arm.

"I did that?" I said. "I did not!"

"I woke you up, just like the doctor ordered, every two hours. This was what you did the first time." He used the injured arm to push away his plate before reaching for a Valentine's Day mug, given to me by my nephews, full of dark steaming brew.

I had always been a heavy sleeper, and there hadn't been enough traffic in my bed lately to know how I behaved when I slept. But I could see no reason for Mick to lie. "I'm really sorry."

"It's okay. It wasn't as bad as the third time."

I winced and covered my eyes with my hand. "What did I do then?"

"You said you were going to kick the shit out of me if I woke you up one more time."

I laughed. Now *that* I believed. I used to say the same thing to my brother, Steven, when he woke me up a long time ago.

Mick laughed, too, and it all seemed quite natural. Having breakfast in my little breakfast room with the morning sun shining through the huge picture window next to shrubbery that had survived an odd winter of freezing temperatures one day and sunny days in the sixties the next.

Still laughing, I asked about the second time he woke me.

A devilish grin replaced his openly laughing face. Actually, it was more like a leer.

"What?" I said.

"Let's just say it was more enjoyable than the other two times," he said over his shoulder as he took the dishes to the sink. "Much more enjoyable."

I didn't know whether to be embarrassed or angry. I racked my brain, trying to figure out what could have happened, but my mind was a blank. What if I had thrown myself against him or something? No, surely not. I tried to tell myself it was probably nothing. Regardless, I wasn't asking again, even if not knowing drove me crazy.

"Maybe your bosses will give you combat pay for last night," I said, more for my own benefit, but Mick heard it, too.

"I thought you understood, Ronnie. I wasn't on duty last night."

I sensed Mick staring at me, willing me to lift my eyes to his. Instead, I examined the worn grooves in the table. The silence was stifling, but as my mother liked to say, I had a stubborn streak a mile long.

"Mind if I use your shower?"

"I don't mind, but the water's probably cold," I apologized, trying not to let my imagination conjure a vision of this guy in my shower. "I forgot you were here and used up all the hot water."

"That's okay. I could use a cold shower right about now."

As he walked out of the room, the air was thick with tension. Specifically my sexual tension, which I decided to drown with a Diet Pepsi. I found the last one tucked behind the eggs. After the first cold gulp traveled down my throat, I noticed Mick's notebook lying by the telephone, just begging to be read. Really.

As soon as the groan of the pipes signaled the start of the shower, I flipped the worn notebook to the first page. My name was circled. Below it, Mick had written:

hit over head = professor's murder? What's the connection?

The second page contained details I had given him, more or less. The missing midterm reports. Missing manuscript with a line pointing to Zachariah's name with a question mark. Nothing new there.

The third page was titled SUSPECTS. I took the notebook

back to my chair and sat down, very interested in whom Mick suspected. Both Trevor's and Desiree's names were listed, with a line joining them and a question mark next to the line. After that, "other students—who? ask Ronnie." Mick also mentioned Zachariah. While a logical assumption, it still seemed doubtful to me. And then, "other professors?" was written.

The next page contained only one sentence: *Check Crutchfield's background.*

Rapid, impatient peels of my doorbell startled me out of snooping. Probably a good thing, since I hadn't been aware of the shower being shut off. I quickly replaced Mick's notebook by the phone and hurried to the front door. Since I had to fight to get around James Dean, I knew a friend rather than a foe stood on the other side of the door.

Terry was preparing for another barrage of doorbell ringing when I opened the door. He looked shocked, then relieved to see me. "Are you all right? Get away from me, James Dean. What was that message about? Scared the hell out of me."

"When you heard it this morning?"

"Of course, this morning. If I had heard it last night, I would have been over here last night. I haven't even taken a shower yet," he grumbled as we moved inside to the center of the living room, looking even messier during the light of day.

"Why didn't you use Maggie's shower?"

"Because her kids were fighting about whose turn it was to be in the bathroom. Until they saw me, that is. Seemed like a good time to leave." Terry shuddered as only a man who viewed children as alien beings could. "So, what's going on?"

I sighed. There really wasn't any point in upsetting Terry now. And I might have to tell the same story to others, too, particularly if Mom's ESP was tuned to my frequency. "I met with a little accident last night and had to be taken to the campus clinic to be checked out. I called to see if you could . . .

if you could give me a ride home."

"What happened?"

"I was hit over the head."

"No shit?" His sleepy eyes sprang open. "Where?"

"In Crutchfield's office. You see, I was . . ."

"No, I mean where on your head were you hit?"

"Back here." I pointed right of center near the base of my skull. Terry was the sort of person who wanted to experience everything, which was why he proceeded to experience the size of my lump. "You see, some students found me . . . ouch! Be careful!"

"Sorry. That's quite a lump. Kind of like a plum, but not as soft."

I turned and glared at him. Plum, indeed. "Anyway, I was taken to the campus clinic, where the doctor said I had a concussion. Wouldn't let me leave unless somebody could keep an eye on me during the night and make sure I was oriented."

"So who stayed with you?"

"I did."

I winced, but had no other choice than to turn with Terry toward the voice in the doorway leading to the hall. I saw Mick through Terry's eyes—towel draped around his neck catching drops of water from glistening hair. No shirt, of course.

Terry briefly placed himself between Mick and me. Turning to face me, he silently mouthed a "yes" while bringing his fist down like he was at a sporting event. To Terry, sex *was* a sporting event, and it didn't matter what I hadn't done. The evidence was drying his hair with my towel in my house at eight in the morning.

Terry turned back around and stuck out his hand. "Hi. I don't know if you remember me. We met the other day when Ronnie and I were having lunch?"

Mick shook the hand. "Terry, right?"

"Yeah." Terry grinned. "I'm glad you were able to help Ronnie last night. I would have made an awful nurse, and it usually takes a team of wild horses to get her up in the middle of the night."

"No problem. I was happy to do it."

"You were? Hey, that's really great." Terry sounded a little amazed, but a swift elbow to his midsection helped him restrain it. Moving a few steps away from me, Terry began asking questions in a serious tone usually reserved for "who's going to win the Super Bowl" and "beer research." "So, any ideas on who whacked her?"

"No, but we're working on it."

With Mick's list of suspects reflecting mine, I wasn't feeling very hopeful.

"How about a weapon?" Terry said. "What was used to hit her over the head?"

Yeah! What had bounced off my head last night? I faced Mick, but he shook his head. "An injury to the head isn't like a bullet wound with fragments. There's no definitive evidence to say what it was."

Our disappointed faces must have been transparent because he quickly added, "It was probably something metal, but, unfortunately, the perpetrator took it with him . . ."

"Or her," I said automatically.

"Or her. There's nothing in Crutchfield's office that suggests it could have been used as a weapon."

"Premeditation?" I said, looking to Mick for confirmation and receiving a hesitant nod. I began pacing around the two men. "So, whoever did this either planned to get rid of anyone who happened to be in Crutchfield's office . . ."

"Or someone deliberately came after you," Terry interrupted.

Mick nodded grimly before turning sideways and leaning his back against the doorway frame to the hall. I stopped walking circles around my living room and swallowed with difficulty.

"Something metal. Something metal heavy enough to knock a person out would probably be conspicuous." Terry mumbled while he paced, looking at the floor. I could see him taking on a role, this time as Sherlock Holmes. "A lead pipe? How would you hide a lead pipe?"

A picture immediately came to mind. "Or a gun. A handgun is more compact. It fits in a purse, a pocket, underneath the waistband of your pants. A gun was used to kill Crutchfield, and I bet your ass it could also raise a lump on somebody's head if you whacked them with the butt of it."

Mick's lack of response told me I was probably on the right track. Although just this once, I wouldn't have minded being wrong. Perhaps I had just been in the wrong place at the wrong time.

"No, wait! The gun that killed Crutchfield was found in his hand, wasn't it? It couldn't be the same gun," Terry shouted.

Mick shook his head while I explained. "The bullet that killed Crutchfield came from a different gun."

"Not the same gun?" Terry said. "Damn. How many people are walking around with guns over at Psych?"

My thoughts exactly. I'd never been a big fan of guns anyway, and I certainly didn't like the idea of someone carrying one around Rubenstein Hall. I tried to shake away visions of Dirty Harry getting fed up with students not paying attention in class and blowing them away.

"You knew that Crutchfield's gun wasn't the murder weapon." Terry turned and accused me. "Why didn't you say anything about the gun when we were trying to figure out who the killer was at dinner last night?"

Mick also turned to me, waiting for some kind of answer. Luckily, the phone rang at that moment.

"I think I'll get that in the kitchen."

I rushed off to retrieve the phone before the answering machine picked up on the fourth ring. It garbled half my messages anyway.

"Hello?"

Silence.

"Hello?" I said a bit louder.

Still silence. Wait. Was that breathing I heard or just my imagination? Before I could decide, a soft click sounded.

I, too, hung up. I probably got hang-up calls at least once a week. Who knows why? Someone gets the wrong number and is too rude to say, "Sorry, wrong number"? It could even be a student who had nothing better to do. Or a killer checking up on my whereabouts. *Stop it!*

When I reentered the living room, I heard Terry talking about Joe Bob. Mick's gaze turned to me, glittering with irritation.

"Why didn't you tell me that you suspected Joe Bob Wayne?"

"I don't know. I guess because I don't really have proof. I just don't like the guy much."

"Well, she's not a big football fan . . ."

I glared at Terry. "And for that I'm going to accuse someone of murder?"

"Why the football player?"

"He was in Crutchfield's class. Now he's in mine. His was the other midterm paper that is missing. He and his coach came to see me, asking my cooperation in making sure Joe Bob got a decent grade."

"Really? What did you say?"

"I said I would give the kid a decent grade as long as he earned it."

"Atta' girl."

"Unfortunately, they both looked like they could kill me that day. But I guess someone would have noticed Coach Henderson hanging around the psych building."

"Probably. But I'll take a look at him and Joe Bob anyway."

Silence invaded the room. Each of us stood with our own thoughts for several minutes. Mine, of course, centered on the fact that I had been lucky only to be hit over the head with a gun. It was far better than receiving a gift from the other end of the murder weapon. I looked up to find both men looking at me, ready to jump in case I fainted or freaked out or did something girly.

"So, who was on the phone?" Mick asked.

"No one," I answered, probably too quickly.

Terry sighed. "Look, luv, Mick here will find out who did it."

"It's so ridiculous," I said. "Did the murderer not realize that the authorities would test ballistics and things like that? He . . ."

"Or she," Mick interjected.

I grinned. "Or she didn't do a very good job murdering Crutchfield. There were so many mistakes."

"But even with the mistakes, the murderer still hasn't been caught," said Terry. A big sigh. "Well, I guess I had better get going."

I nodded and walked with him to the door. "When are you going to campus today?"

"Today's my late day. Don't have a class until three, then back to back until nine o'clock. Why?"

"I need a ride to work. I left my car at Emilio's, and I don't feel like walking or biking today."

"Stay home," came a suggestion from behind me. Mick had traded in the towel for a shirt that he was now tucking it into his jeans.

"I have two classes. And office hours."

"Call in."

"Bye, kids." Terry seemed eager to leave as I squared off with Mick.

"I will not call in. I have a responsibility to my students,

137

and . . ." I put more determination into my voice than I actually felt. "And I won't let someone scare me from going to my job."

"The doctor said you need to rest for twenty-four hours."

"I'll rest just as well in my office as here," I answered.

"You are the most stubborn woman I have ever met."

We glared at each other, but I wasn't backing down. Nobody told me what to do. My mom will tell anyone who listens that I have a stubborn streak a mile long.

"I'll take you, then!" Mick said.

"Fine!"

"But . . ." Here was a man who hated losing almost as much as I did. "I want you to stay away from Crutchfield's office, *and* under no circumstances be in the building by yourself until this is over."

I nodded. The cold edge of fear dug a little deeper, and I couldn't help shivering, even though it was already a warm day. Mick saw my shiver and wrapped his arms tightly around me. I buried my face in his neck, looking for the safety I had always taken for granted.

"I'm going to catch him," Mick whispered into my hair.

"Or her."

He chuckled softly. "Or her."

I wanted to believe this man who had come into my life so recently. Kiddie cop. Who was I kidding? But trust wasn't something I gave easily, so I pushed myself away from the warm cocoon of his arms and walked out the door.

The sun shone brightly, requiring me to shield my eyes with the palm of my hand. A day for sunglasses. I hadn't the slightest idea where mine were, nor did I want to exert the brainpower trying to remember.

I opened the passenger door to Mick's police car before he could get to it. Before getting in, I looked across the roof of the car, already radiating with the heat of the sun. Mick stood across from me with questions and concern in his eyes. Places I didn't want to go. I shook my head and climbed in.

CHAPTER ELEVEN

"Really, Lisa, you're doing fine in Practical Applications of Behavioral Practice," I told the shaking girl in front of me, my last appointment for the day. I wasn't in the mood to see tears today, particularly when they might serve as a catalyst for my own. My head was killing me. In fact, the pain from the bump seemed to have spread throughout my head and radiated down to my neck and shoulders. My muscles were tight enough to bounce a quarter off of. I should have listened to Mick and stayed home, not that I would ever let him know that.

"Then, why do you want me to change my major?" Lisa said with Bambi eyes peering at me, and, jeez, was I a sucker for Bambi.

I twirled a pencil between my fingers before it flew beneath the desk. Lisa bent to pick it up, but I waved her away. "Listen. I'm not suggesting you change your psychology major, just the focus. All your papers show a talent for psychoanalytic theory. Have you taken a psychoanalytic theory course?"

She nodded stiffly. "I received a D."

"A D? I don't understand. What was the problem? Heavy class load?"

"No. The professor told me I had no grasp of psychoanalytic concepts and never would."

"Who was the professor?" My stomach knotted as I asked the question.

"Dr. Crutchfield."

I sighed. Why had that idiot told this obviously bright junior that she wasn't suited for studying psychoanalytic theory? "Why do you think he told you that?"

It took a moment for her to answer, as she apparently played out the options in her head. Finally, a stubborn chin indicated that the matter had been decided. "Because I refused to sleep with him."

I watched brown eyes glinting with anger. Jeez, even from the grave Crutchfield was screwing with people's lives. "Did you ever tell anyone?"

Lisa shook her head. "I heard that another student, a senior, blew the whistle on him last year. She was forced to drop out with only six more hours to go for her bachelor's degree. I saw her last week working at the music store over on Navajo Road."

I recalled a similar thing happening to a dorm roommate too many years ago to count. With a business-school professor. Unfortunately, she had been a business major. I think she dropped out, too. Temporarily, she told me. I wondered if she ever received her degree. I blew out the air I had been holding. It wasn't fair. Not then, not now.

"How would you feel about contesting your grade in that class and refocusing your plan of study to what you're best suited for?"

If possible, her eyes became even wider. "Dr. Raven, could I? I would even be willing to take the course again."

"It might mean talking to the dean about this."

Lisa shrugged her shoulders.

"I'll see what I can do." She stood up, looking a little too hopeful. "Lisa? Regardless of what happens, I want you to understand that in no way were you at fault here. Assholes are everywhere, even at PU."

She nodded and smiled with glistening eyes. When she left, I let my face fall into my hands and massaged my temples. The pain was like a vise, pulling tighter and tighter. I pulled my head upright with some degree of difficulty and gingerly placed myself on the window seat behind my desk before pulling at the ancient window release and pushing the window open.

Air. Wonderful fresh air. With eyes closed, I inhaled deeply. What was it about early spring air that smelled so much sweeter than regular air? It was as if I could smell every flowering plant and tree in a five-mile radius.

A barrage of sneezing took place beneath me. I smiled. Apparently, some people reacted differently to the spring air. I located the source of the violent sneezes. Justin. Even from the second-floor window, I could see red-rimmed eyes. He honked his nose into tissues. Then he snorted some nose spray, which must have helped some. Hunched shoulders straightened somewhat as he sat down on a bench overlooking the oval. It was a beautiful sight—not Justin—but the multicolored flowers in geometric patterns dotting the lush green lawn.

Justin's pose changed to one of alertness as he quickly tucked wadded up tissues and nose spray into a jacket pocket before jumping up to greet Zachariah. The two engaged in companionable conversation as they entered Psych.

The sight of Zachariah reminded me of my mission. I closed the window with some regret. The fresh air had worked as a super-strength pain reliever, removing all but the lingering tenderness on the back of my head. Even my shoulder and neck muscles had eased a notch.

As much as Crutchfield had irritated me, I was really sorry to hear about his sexually harassing Lisa. Some things were supposed to be sacred, like the professor-student relationship. In addition to acting as therapist for his graduate assistant, he sexually harassed a student. I didn't doubt Lisa's story. And I couldn't think of any reason to justify what Crutchfield had done. Trading grades for sex was wrong, no matter how you looked at it. Hadn't the jerk had any morals at all?

I left my office, wanting to catch Zachariah before he became involved with something or someone else. Just let him try to avoid me today. I passed Crutchfield's door on my way to the stairs. I had kept my promise to Mick, so far at least. It was easy to do when I stayed tucked away in my own office. But the sight of the door gave me another idea as I hurried up the stairs to the third floor, stopping off at a room next to the faculty lounge.

An assortment of secondhand desks greeted me, along with one or two familiar faces. And in the corner was the face I was looking for, his nose buried deep in a graduate-level text. I lowered myself in a wobbly chair next to his desk and waited for him to look up. I didn't wait long.

"Ronnie? Sorry, I didn't hear you come in," Trevor stuttered without the assurance he showed last night. "How's the h-h-head?"

"Fine. I want to thank you—you and Desiree, for coming to my rescue last night."

"No, no problem."

"I'm lucky you were around. What were you two doing in the building at that time of night anyway?"

He bent his head down and picked up a pencil. After tapping it against the desk a couple of times, he laid it down and picked up a legal pad. His right hand, bandaged when we first met, now showed no scars or sign of injury. How long did it take powder burns to heal?

No amount of intense staring on my part opened Trevor's mouth. I really didn't want to harass him, and I did owe him for coming to my rescue. Who knew? He and Desiree might have even scared off my attacker before more damage could be done.

"Okay, maybe you can answer another question for me," I said.

Trevor looked up and gave a nod so slight that I wasn't positive I had seen it.

"Did you know Crutchfield was working on a book?"

"Sure, everyone knew that," Trevor answered.

Well, for some reason, I hadn't known. "When was the last time you saw the manuscript?"

Trevor frowned. "I think it might have been right before spring break. He was talking about how he couldn't take a vacation because the publisher was insisting he finish it."

That fit with what Ben Calvin told me. "So, do you think he took it home to work on it?"

"Oh, no, he wouldn't have done that."

"Why not?" I said, puzzled at Trevor's certainty.

"He never took it home. Said a book about psychology had to be written in a psychologist's office."

I looked at Trevor a little more intently. He grinned and nodded. Yeah, that sounded like Crutchfield's logic. And it wasn't as if the campus closed down during spring break anyway. Obviously, someone else had been here with him.

Trevor looked about as relaxed as I had ever seen him, so I decided to spring my big question on him now. "Were you aware that Crutchfield was sexually harassing female students?"

I hoped the bluntness of the question would take him by surprise, but instead he chewed on his lip, no doubt wondering how much to tell me. "I . . . I . . . heard . . . things."

"Did you ever witness anything?"

Trevor shook his head. "When a female student entered his office, he . . . he always told me to leave."

"Did he tell you to leave when male students came to see him?"

Again, he shook his head. "The door was locked a lot, too, even when I knew he was in there."

I substituted a loud sigh for pounding my fist on Trevor's

desk. We were still talking circumstantial. Zachariah wasn't stupid. He wouldn't accept my word that Crutchfield had sexually harassed his students. Still I had to face my boss and tell him what I knew.

Before leaving the teaching assistants' office, I turned to face Trevor once more. "Was Desiree one of Crutchfield's victims?"

Trevor kept his gaze on his book. If I hadn't known better, I would have thought he hadn't heard me. I took a couple of steps toward the hallway before he called out.

"Desiree really did turn in a midterm paper."

Then where was it, and did she happen to do some extra-credit work for Crutchfield to ensure a good grade?

My steps slowed in the hall. A growing desire to procrastinate filled me. Would it hurt to wait until tomorrow before enlightening Zachariah about Crutchfield? The memory of Lisa's face proved too powerful a motivator. I also found myself deeply ashamed to have been part of the faculty for three years and totally unaware that female students were being sexually harassed. Talk about your head being buried in the sand. I owed it to both past and present students to speak up.

No one was in the outer administrative office when I arrived, which was to my advantage. Eloise had chased me off on more than one occasion when Zachariah was busy. Not only that, but catching Zachariah off guard couldn't hurt. I gave the door a few quick raps and opened it before I heard "Come in" or "Go away." In my case, it would surely have been the latter.

Zachariah frowned but didn't say anything, probably because his ear was attached to a telephone receiver at that moment. He waved his hand, which I took as an invitation to sit down. Zachariah rubbed his eyes while alternately saying, "Yes" and "No" and "I don't know."

"Yes, Mr. Calvin. I can understand why you would be upset about the manuscript, but as I told you, there is really nothing I can do about it."

Ah, talking to my old pal Ben, the publisher.

"Yes, I will tell Dr. Raven that you enjoyed talking with her," he replied through gritted teeth with a special glare for me.

I grinned. You would think Zachariah would relish the idea of playing matchmaker. After all, if Ben and I hit it off, I might move to California.

Zachariah massaged his right temple while he said his good-byes. I thought I heard him mutter "Thank God" under his breath before he turned an irritated face toward me. "Can this wait, Dr. Raven?"

"No, it can't, Dr. Bent."

"Then make it fast."

"I received a report from a student in one of my classes, a junior, about a professor giving her a poor grade because she turned him down."

Zachariah's expression looked blank. "What do you mean 'turned him down'?"

"For sex, Zachariah. She turned him down when he propositioned her."

Zachariah closed his eyes as if to make it all go away. "Who?"

"Crutchfield."

I swear I thought I saw relief wash all over him before leaving only a patronizing smile. "Ronnie, dead men can't defend themselves . . ."

"Maybe not, but is it any more fair for a student, maybe more than one, to have a blot on her academic record because of what a professor in this department did?"

"No, of course not, but it's out of my hands." Looking at his watch, he stood up to dismiss me. Probably had a power cocktail meeting somewhere.

I stood up, too, and smiled. "Fine. Maybe it's something the president of the university or the regents can take care of. Hell, maybe the best people to handle it are the media."

"You wouldn't."

"Try me."

Zachariah, his entire body rigid, sat back down, momentarily showing a rage I'm certain few people ever saw. He masked most of it before speaking again. "What do you want?"

"Let the student retake the exams for the Psychoanalytic Theory class." I placed both my hands squarely upon the desk. "Her grade from the scores on the tests will replace the D that Crutchfield gave her."

I could see Zachariah weighing this in his mind. "And that will be the end of this? I have your guarantee?"

"Zachariah, surely you realize there are no guarantees in life." I paused. "But I'm pretty sure this young woman just wants a fair grade in the course."

"And so she will have it."

"Thank you, Zachariah." I stood up and walked to the door, proud of the results.

"I heard about your accident last night."

Like I could avoid a statement like that? I turned and leaned against the glowing cherry finish of his door.

"Ronnie, you're a fine professor, but you're a troublemaker. You constantly flaunt authority and rules. And end up where you have no business being." Zachariah paused. "Obviously, someone gave you a warning. Maybe you should listen before something more serious happens."

Shock propelled me silently out of Zachariah's office. Had I just been threatened? My breath caught in my throat as I sank to the nearest chair in the outer office, my legs no longer able to hold my weight.

Zachariah and I had always had our disagreements, but they had always been laced with humor and respect before. I played the scene from his office again. That hard and glinty stare? The hostility that emanated from him when I threatened to go over his head? That had been a person who could kill. Even if Zachariah didn't bring that gun barrel down on my head, he certainly approved of it.

A round of sneezing in the small room directly across from me awoke me from my reverie, for which I was grateful. I moved to investigate the source of the sneeze and found Zachariah's secretary, complete with red nose and eyes, using the copy machine.

"Hi, Eloise."

Her greeting was tempered with a few rapid-fire sneezes.

"Sounds like you should be home in bed."

"It's just allergies. Besides, Zachariah was here late last night working like a demon on next year's budget projections. He wants copies sent to everyone who is anyone." Her nasally voice told of her misery. "And maybe I'm not the only one who should be home in bed?"

"What do you mean?"

"Honey, if someone hit me over the head, I might never enter this building again."

I smiled at the picture. "Yes, you would. And you'd find out who it was and have that person pouring out his or her soul to you."

Her only answer was a harrumph. A vague sense of suffocation grew as my breathing shifted into overdrive. It was this room. Windowless and tiny, the room was stuffed with the copy machine and five four-drawer file cabinets. Just the right kind of catalyst for a claustrophobia-prone person like me.

"What's with all these files?"

"Zachariah's a paper hound. Never throws anything away. Even prints memos from the computer. There's a file on everything and everybody in here."

"Personnel files?"

148

Eloise nodded before another fit of sneezing overtook her.

"All this paper must gather dust. That can't be good for your allergies."

Eloise gave me a "no shit" look, although she would never say that. In the three years I had known her, she was the most dignified person to walk the halls of the psych building. Never a cuss word. Not even a raised voice. Taking care of this screwy bunch for as long as she had, she should be nominated for sainthood.

"Eloise? Who is handling Crutchfield's affairs," I said, almost choking on the word *affairs*.

"Some cousin from Arkansas. Fort Smith, I think?"

"Have you spoken with him or her?"

"Her. A. G. Crutchfield. Don't know what the A.G. stands for, and she didn't tell me." Eloise began straightening and sorting through the papers she and the copy machine had created. "I'm the one who called her. Didn't seem too broken up about it. If I had to guess, I would say she sounded relieved."

"Hmmm. I wonder why," I said more to myself, but with the ears of a hawk, Eloise heard.

"Who knows? People these days aren't close to family. But still you would think as his only relative she would have come out for the memorial." Eloise shook her head.

"You would think so," I agreed. "Well, I guess I should be going. See you later."

"Bye, Ronnie. You be careful, honey."

Be careful. As I made my way back to my office, I decided that was easy advice to take. After all, someone might be trying to kill me. I tried to figure out who or why anyone would want to kill me. I might not be the most agreeable person in the world, but I found it hard to believe that someone hated me enough to kill me. I entered my office and immediately shut the door behind me. Kind of made the sibling rivalry that my brother and I shared seem like small potatoes. But maybe I was jumping the gun. Even alone, I had to groan at the expression "jumping the gun." It could just be a coincidence. Maybe I really was in the wrong place at the wrong time.

Zachariah had been in the building last night. Eloise said so. Had he hit me? Or was Mick right? Should I not dismiss Trevor or Desiree as possibilities? It seemed ridiculous to include Trevor and Desiree in my suspicions since they were my rescuers. But as Dad used to say, never overlook the obvious because it just might bite you in the ass.

The sharp shrill of the telephone jarred me from my thoughts, forcing me to reach for the receiver.

"Ronnie Raven, may I help you?"

"What's the matter?"

I grinned. "Hi, Mom. How are you?"

"I didn't call to talk about me, darling. I called to find out what's wrong with you," my mother's husky voice said.

"Why, nothing is wrong with me. What a silly idea." I tried to sound as sincere as possible. I don't know who I thought I was fooling. Apparently, neither did my mother.

"You've been eating chocolate, too, haven't you? My goodness, how bad is it?"

Maureen Raven. My mother. She had the sight when it came to her children. Said she inherited it from her Irish grandmother. Mom always knew when something was wrong. When I was at a junior-high track meet for district finals one year, I broke my ankle. No one could find her to let her know because she had been waiting at the emergency room for me.

So I knew better than to lie. But maybe I could omit the part about being a murder suspect. "Oh, nothing really. One of the other professors died, and I've taken over his introduction . . ."

"How did he die?"

"Well, that's still being investigated. So, anyway, I guess I'm feeling a little stressed, what with the additional class load and all."

"He was murdered, wasn't he?"

"No one knows yet, Mom."

"Veronica?"

"Okay. He was murdered."

"And what do you have to do with this murder?"

"Obviously, I killed the man so I could teach his introduction psychology class. It's always been a dream of mine, you know. To teach hundreds and hundreds of certifiable freshmen . . ."

"I don't know where you get such a smart mouth, young lady. Your father spoke like an angel. Never a nasty word to or about anyone. And you never hear me smart off like that," she said.

Yeah, and the Pope was a born-again Southern Baptist. But I kept that one to myself. I might be a smart ass, but Mama didn't raise no fools. "Sorry, Mom, but if you're going to have the sight and invade my privacy, you have to put up with a little attitude."

"Fine. Maybe I should just come up there and check out things myself . . ."

I sighed. I know better than to underestimate my mother. She would follow through with that threat. "Okay, I found the guy. I was pissed because he parked his monstrosity of a motorcycle at the bike rack. I had no place to park my bike. So I went to his office to give him a piece of my mind."

Maureen Raven began laughing. Not an uncommon sound. She was a woman who loved to laugh. But I failed to see the humor in what I just said. "How long did you yell at him before you realized he was dead?" my mother finally spit out.

Did my mother know me or what? I couldn't help laughing along with her.

"Jeez, I hope the cops don't have my phone bugged. That

would confirm their suspicions that I did it," I said, still chuckling while wiping away the tears that came with a hard laugh.

Mom's laughter came to an immediate stop. "You're a suspect?"

Maybe Mama did raise a fool. "Well, not really. There's just this redneck detective giving me the third degree."

"How dare he? Who the hell does he think he is, thinking my daughter would commit murder? Who is he? I'll call his superiors. Why, I know the governor. Remember, he sent that nice peace lily when your father died?"

"Mom, the redneck is just doing his job." Jeez. I couldn't believe I was defending that jerk. But somebody had to. A mother's wrath and all that. And my mother could be the mother of all mothers. Therefore, her wrath the mother of all wraths. "I can handle it, Mom."

"You're sure?"

"You'll be the first to know if I need help," I said.

"I suppose I will, but that doesn't give me much reassurance."

I could still hear a "maybe I should come up" tone to her voice. What I didn't need during all this chaos was Mom's help. "Everything's fine, don't worry. So, what's new with you?"

"What about the man you went skiing with? How are things with him?"

"We're not seeing each other anymore."

"He wasn't right for you anyway, dear. So, is there anyone else?"

"Mom, I just quit seeing Rick five days ago."

"And your point is?"

"Nothing. Gotta' go, Mom. Love you."

I rushed off the phone because standing at my door was none other than my favorite redneck cop.

CHAPTER TWELVE

Melvin blocked my doorway with a wide girth barely covered by a cheap brown suit. I flashed back to a corrupt sheriff back home who had been in office forever and a day. Hoppy Hull had been used to running things his own way and refused to change with the times. After too many illegal searches and questionable detentions, the legal watchdogs finally got rid of him. It took one hell of a fight to do it, leaving everybody questioning whether the results had been worth it. There was a saying popular around the time of Nixon's impeachment—the crook you know is better than the crook you don't. Personally, I didn't want to spend time with either.

Their appearances were similar. Melvin and Hull both had that southern middle-aged spread akin to a toy top, but their similarities didn't end there. Melvin also carried that self-assured "I'm the law" swagger that broadcast he could do anything he wanted to. He was probably just as corrupt as that county sheriff back home. It took all my self-control not to get up and slam the door in his face. Granny used to tell a rebellious teenager that she could catch more flies with honey. Without any other plan of action, it seemed like a good time to give Granny's advice a try.

"Why, Detective Melvin, what a pleasant surprise. Please have a seat." I smiled and gestured to the chair, briefly wondering if he would fit into it.

The detective's eyebrows arched as he sank into the chair

while he picked his teeth with a toothpick. His eyes never left mine. Maybe I laid the honey on a bit too thick. Melvin had already made it clear that I was his chief suspect, so I probably shouldn't give him any more reasons to suspect me.

I sighed and lost the smile. My jaw hurt anyway. "What can I do for you, Detective?"

"I know who you are, girlie."

Girlie! This guy wasn't interested in winning any popularity contests, was he? *Keep it together, Ronnie.* "And just what is it you think you know, Detective?"

"You're that Injun artist's girl. The one the governor was friends with long time ago."

Like James Dean, I felt my hackles rise. "And?"

He let out a slow smile, like our conversation was a piece of candy with several layers and he was relishing each one. "It don't matter how many high-placed friends you got or how much education you have. You're still just another Injun who got in over her head. This time, a man's dead because of it."

"Detective? Whose ass did you kiss to get this far in the police force?" I stood up, my rage exploding against this idiot. "It's quite obvious you didn't get where you are for your sensitivity. Or your brains!"

The toothpick, previously resting in the corner of his mouth, flew out and he started spitting. It took him a moment to push himself up from the leather chair, but when he did, he placed his huge meaty hands on my desk.

The putrid odor from his mouth almost knocked me over. "You think just because of who you are you can get away with abusing the police force? With murder? Well, girlie, you've got another think coming."

I should have listened to my earlier instincts and thrown him and his wrinkled brown suit out on his ass. "What planet are you from? *You* are the one who is abusing me. You could be looking for the real murderer, but instead, you're harassing me. I should bring you up on charges, you obnoxious worm!"

Everything around me faded into a blur. Everything that is, except for Melvin's face and his little wisps of hair sticking up. I tuned out what he was saying, but his large mouth kept moving and moving and moving. I felt a roaring in my ears, like the ocean at high decibel.

Eventually I became aware of hands on my shoulders and a voice in my ears. *Breathe.* I kept hearing that word repeatedly. *Breathe.* I concentrated, finally able to make my body obey the command. With each breath I took, my office gained a little more focus.

Warm hands gripped my shoulders. Long fingers. A man's hands. Mick's. I turned my head at an angle to see warning emanating from his expression. I nodded my understanding and turned back to Melvin. Behind him, a small crowd formed in the hallway. Justin. Paula. A couple of other professors and students. Trevor. Desiree. And here I was putting on quite a show. I didn't see Zachariah, but it would take only minutes before the grapevine contacted him.

Melvin ranted about how women like me thought they were better than he was. I looked him straight in the eye and when he took a breath, I jumped in.

"Detective Melvin, do you have proof that I murdered Weldon Crutchfield?" I said.

"Your fingerprints are on the telephone."

"As they should be, since I told you I notified the police from that phone. My guess is that you'll also find some of *their* fingerprints"—I gestured at the small crowd that had gathered—"in his office." When Melvin turned, most of the audience scattered. I didn't have the luxury of seeing who was most uncomfortable at being pointed out.

Melvin looked back at me and answered in a low voice. "All

fingerprints will be identified, even though it's a waste of my time and taxpayer money."

"Do you have enough proof to arrest me?" Melvin started to say something, but I didn't want to hear any more speculation. "To arrest me here and now for the murder of Weldon Crutchfield?"

"I have witnesses that will attest to the fact that you and the victim were involved in a long-standing feud," said Melvin.

"I've made no secret of the fact that Crutchfield and I didn't get along. That doesn't mean I killed him." I almost lost it again, but was able to pull back when Mick's hands touched me on the shoulders again. "I repeat, do you have enough evidence to arrest me this minute?"

"No, but it's just a matter of time before . . ."

"Then I suggest you get the hell out of my office. Come back when you're willing to ask reasonable questions pertaining to the murder or to arrest me. Not to cast aspersions on me or my family," I said.

"This is how it happened, isn't it, Raven?" Melvin spat out.

"What do you mean?"

"Somehow Weldon Crutchfield made you mad, real mad, and you lost control, like you did just now. Then you killed him."

Mick's hands, still on my shoulders, kept me grounded. Which I suppose was a good thing, because I kept seeing myself leaping across my desk and throttling that thick neck. I forced myself to remain silent, nonreactive.

Melvin finally stood up straight, removing his hands from my desk. Beady little eyes tried to stare me down but never had a chance.

Minutes passed with Melvin's raspy breathing the only sound. Finally, he shoved both hands into low-lying pants pockets. "I've got better things to do with my time."

"Why don't you go ahead and go, Detective Melvin," said

Mick behind me. "I'll take care of things here."

"I just bet you will, boy." Melvin took out another toothpick and stuck it into his mouth. "I just bet you will."

I heard Melvin cough his way down the hall. When I was pretty sure Melvin was truly gone, I turned. Mick watched me carefully.

"I had to say it," Mick said.

"Say what?"

"That thing about taking care of things here. It was the only way to make him leave."

I nodded. It had been rather a high-handed thing to say, but I couldn't argue with the results. Melvin was gone. No, what nagged at me more was Mick's coming in my office and interfering in the first place. What would have happened if he hadn't?

I ran the index finger of my left hand around the perimeter of my desk, stopping when I saw the sweaty imprint of Melvin's hands on the vinyl desktop. I jerked my hand up and brought both hands close in to my body in an effort to drive the shakes away.

"Do you want to go someplace else?" Mick said.

It disturbed me how easily he read my thoughts. "Actually I want to fumigate my office, but I'll settle for a walk."

"Mind if I join you?"

I shook my head and started out the door with Mick behind me. I kept my head down, not ready to invite questions from anyone who had witnessed the incident with Melvin. I practically flew down the staircase to the first floor. A gaggle of students, a minute late for class by my watch, almost ran me down, but Mick pulled me out of the way before I got lost amid the backpacks and chatter.

As we approached the double doors of the front entrance, I looked at Mick's hand still on my upper arm. Not tightly, but possessively. He noticed and removed his hands to the pockets of crisp, clean uniform pants. Beige, a color meant to make you invisible, couldn't managed to hide this campus cop who was quickly becoming an important fixture in my life.

The temperature immediately dropped ten degrees as I walked among the vivid colors of the landscaped oval. Who knew flowers came in such a variety? Granny would have known the names of every one of these gifts of nature. If nothing else, PU looked good. I shook my head and turned my attention to the fresh air, inhaling deeply of it.

I took off at my usual long-legged pace. I sensed Mick with me as I circled the oval, the student union, taking any path not crowded with passersby. Once some of my anger burnt off, I located a bench hidden by shrubbery so dark that it appeared more black than green. Pointy leaves stretched toward an empty cement fountain adorned by an aging cherub posed in the middle. It wasn't the best view. An empty fountain was as depressing as a tree without leaves.

But I couldn't think about that; it was time to analyze my situation. I wish I had brought paper and pen. Things looked more logical when spelled out on paper. I sat on the cold, hard, ornate bench, grateful for the endorphins starting to pump through my veins. Mick sat next to me, neither winded nor red-faced, just quietly watching me.

"Are you keeping me under surveillance?"

"Why would I do that?" He grinned.

"Well, I am obviously a suspect."

"Actually, Melvin considers you a suspect, not me."

"Can't you talk some sense into him?" I said, hating the fact that I sounded so whiny. "Convince him I didn't do it?"

Mick shook his head. "I've tried. He won't listen. And Ronnie, there's something else you should know."

His tone sounded ominous. He hunched over, staring at the drought-affected fountain. Mick knew something. Something bad for me? That was ridiculous. There couldn't be proof against me because I didn't do it.

"I have absolutely no authority in this case. Our charter says that felony crimes are handled exclusively by the city police department," Mick said. "I've offered Detective Melvin my assistance so that I can stay involved. But he can kick me off the case at any time."

"I see." Actually I didn't.

"I'm trying to tell you I can't protect you when you go off on Melvin like you just did."

I jumped up and away from a hand reaching for my shoulder. "Excuse me, but who decided I needed protection? And even if I did, I don't recall appointing you for the job."

Mick looked exasperated and just a little irritated himself. "I don't know how to make this any clearer, Ronnie. A professor was murdered in your department. Not only do we not know who did it, but we don't even know why he was murdered."

"You don't need to talk to me like that. I'm not a child . . ."

"And," he interrupted in a louder voice, "according to Melvin, you're the number-one suspect."

"This means I'm the number-one person to find out who killed Crutchfield. If only I could get into Crutchfield's house."

"Crutchfield's home has already been searched and the contents donated to Goodwill," Mick said. "The house is now empty and on the market."

My heart sank. How was I supposed to find anything now? A clue? "That was awfully quick. Who made that decision?"

"Donating to Goodwill? The Arkansas cousin. His only relative and a distant relative at that. She said she hadn't even seen Crutchfield in more than ten years."

"Did Crutchfield have a will?"

Mick shook his head. "Apparently he didn't plan on dying."

"People who think they're God rarely do. But there must

have been a life-insurance beneficiary?"

"The university will receive ten thousand dollars from the life insurance now that suicide has been ruled out," Mick said.

"Is that legal?"

Mick shrugged. "No one seems to be fighting over it. It's not much life insurance anyway."

"Damn. Then there has to be another reason someone wanted Crutchfield dead. Maybe it does have something to do with that manuscript," I muttered more to myself than him, although it was obvious that Mick heard me. "I hate to say this, but maybe Melvin was right, at least in part. Maybe Crutchfield made someone mad enough to kill him. That wouldn't be hard to imagine."

Mick's hands clenched before he stood up and circled the fountain, as if studying it closely. I knew he was trying to find a way to convince me to butt out and behave myself, but I wasn't about to just sit back and turn my life over to someone else. Mick LeGrand had better learn that right now. Especially since he was so intent on hanging around.

A piercing beep interrupted the tension. Mick looked at his beeper, then at me, then at the beeper again.

"Go on," I said. "I just want to sit and relax for a while anyway."

He moved close enough that I had to crane my neck to see his face. But with the sun behind his head, he was just one big shadow. "I'd like to talk more about this. Are you free for dinner tonight?"

"How old are you, anyway?"

"What does that have to do with anything?" Mick said, stepping back so I had a better view of his clenched chin.

"I want to know."

Mick looked like he was trying to figure something out. I knew it couldn't be his age. He wasn't old enough to need time to calculate it. "Twenty-six."

Twenty-six! Twelve years. "I'm thirty-eight."

"Congratulations. Now about tonight?"

"I have plans," I said, not bothering to mention that my plans were to go home and share a pizza with James Dean.

Mick's hands moved to his hips. As he started tapping his foot, I noticed his furrowed forehead. "Then, can I have your promise that you'll quit asking questions and stay away from Detective Melvin until we finish this discussion?"

"I promise you I will go out of my way to avoid Melvin."

"Ronnie . . . ," Mick said in a warning tone.

"Look, you've got a choice here. If you want me to lie to you and say that I'll be a good little girl and obey you, I will. But it will be a lie. I guarantee it." Mick started to say something, but I wasn't finished. "And nothing you say will change my mind."

Oddly enough, the sight of Mick's retreating back disappointed me. I was honestly flattered by his interest and more than a little attracted to him. But the whole idea of Mick. And me. I shook my head. That was one new experience that I didn't feel up to taking.

CHAPTER THIRTEEN

When I arrived at my office the next day, I rummaged through my backpack and found it splitting at the seams. I groaned, knowing that I could barely thread a needle, must less fix a split seam. That's what came from overloading a lightweight denim backpack. I needed one of those heavy canvas packs able to withstand a ton of books. The problem was that I hated how they felt. If the day were halfway warm, it wouldn't take long for little rivulets of sweat to slide down my back. Drove me crazy. An Oklahoma version of Chinese water torture.

Digging through the pack resulted in half a dozen wadded-up pieces of paper. Jeez. The first one was the phone number for Rick, the broken-legged skier, which I quickly tossed in the trash can. The rest were about as useless. Grocery lists. To-do lists. Library book call numbers. All hit the trash can with varying accuracy. I unfolded the last wad. My notes from Crutchfield's office. Why was it that what you looked for was always the last thing you found?

I glanced through notes that looked as though a doctor drinking moonshine wrote them. I stopped when I found something about the manuscript. No manuscript had been mailed to the publisher in California. And I knew for a fact that there wasn't a manuscript in Crutchfield's office, unless it had been in that box that someone had wanted so badly that they beaned me in the head for it. I touched my head, reassured that the bump was indeed going down.

Also possible was that the manuscript had been at Crutch-field's home, regardless of what Trevor said about Crutchfield's compulsion to work on campus. But Mick said the house had already been emptied out to the . . . the Arkansas cousin!

Grabbing the phone, I asked for Fort Smith information and was quickly rewarded with a recording of a phone number for A. G. Crutchfield. And now, if only A. G. Crutchfield would answer the phone. I closed my eyes and crossed my fingers when the ringing started.

"Hello?"

I paused, taken back when a young, bubbly female voice answered.

"Hello?" she said again.

"Yes, I'm sorry," I hurriedly answered. "I'm trying to reach A. G. Crutchfield."

"Speaking."

"Maybe I don't have the right A. G. Crutchfield. This one is a cousin to Weldon Crutchfield."

After a period of silence, a decidedly colder voice with less of a twang answered. "You've reached the right Crutchfield. Who's calling and what do you want?"

"I'm Ronnie Raven, I'm a colleague, or rather, I was a colleague of Weldon's. I'm sorry for your loss, Ms. Crutchfield . . ."

"Save it."

"Excuse me?"

"I don't need any condolences from anyone regarding Weldon. He was a sorry excuse for a human being when he was alive, and I don't understand what else PU needs from me. Just because his ex-wife had the good sense to leave his sorry ass, I'm stuck with arranging for the burial and receiving his belongings. Signed the release so the university would receive the ten-thousand-dollar life insurance . . ."

"Look, I really don't mean to bother you. I myself was not on the best terms with Weldon. The reason I'm calling is that I'm trying to track down a manuscript that may have been inadvertently sent to you. The publisher reached me and is demanding to know where it is."

"Hey, I'm sorry." Her voice softened a little. "I'm afraid Weldon's name brings out the worst in me. He used to torture me when I was a kid."

"You don't sound old enough to have been one of his victims."

She laughed. "Victims, huh? Yeah, you knew Weldon. I was five; he was nineteen. He teased me unmercifully. I don't mean kid stuff. I mean he was old enough to know better, right?"

"Um, probably, I guess." A long silent pause stretched on while I told myself it was none of my business. Finally, I blurted, "What happened?"

"Oh, many things that I would like to keep forever submerged in my subconscious. But off the top of my head, he used to tickle me." A. G's voice oozed anger. "I don't mean a light-hearted tickling. I mean tickling that went on and on. Tickling that hurt. I guess that sounds silly, huh. That tickling can hurt."

"Actually, no. Tickling that goes on against someone's wishes is abuse."

"Abuse. Yes, it is." She paused. "I'm sorry. You said something about a manuscript?"

"Yes. Have you seen it?"

"No, I'm sorry. Most of the stuff was just clothing that I dropped off at the Veteran's Hospital."

"Well, thanks anyway, A. G. By the way, what does A. G. stand for?"

"Agnes Gertrude. Can you friggin' believe it?"

Could Veronica Kay Raven believe having a name that didn't fit you? You bet your ass I could. But instead, I just said good-bye and hung up the phone.

Well, that was a waste of half an hour. I was no closer to

figuring out why or who killed Weldon Crutchfield than the day I stormed into his office and found his body.

A Coke run is always a good idea when you don't know what else to do. The faculty lounge was empty except for Paula, sitting alone with a cup of coffee. No books, no papers to read. Just staring into space. Even my can bursting through the soft-drink machine didn't stir her. I thought of joining her, but she'd been so unpredictable lately.

What the hell? After what I had been through, I could handle anything. And maybe I could pick up some helpful information. I was scraping the bottom of the *what to check out* barrel anyway. Tapping the top of the can, I approached the table.

"Mind if I join you?"

Paula shook her head. "Please make yourself comfortable."

"Thanks." I opened my can and took a big swallow. "So, how's your day going?"

"Pretty good, really. My students actually asked intelligent questions in research class." Her laugh sounded like the tinkling of Christmas bells. Soft. Musical. And fake. "How about you?"

"I've had better. In fact, I thought maybe you could help me."

Surprise washed over her features. "Certainly. That is, if I'm able."

"I'm having a lot of trouble with Weldon Crutchfield's introduction class." I paused, noting her face tense up at the mention of Crutchfield. "It seems he approached Intro differently than I do. And I hate for the students to pay for having to adjust to a new professor halfway through the semester."

Paula nodded slightly. She began chipping at the Styrofoam of the now-empty coffee cup. I once heard that tearing up Styrofoam released harmful toxins in the air. Even if it's not true, Styrofoam should be outlawed, if only for the mess it caused when people reduced it to pieces too tiny to pick up. Something people did when they were bored or nervous. And Paula didn't look bored.

"I guess where I'm trying to go with this is that if I understood Weldon a little better, maybe I could get a feel for how he would teach the class," I said.

"What does this have to do with me?"

"I had the impression that you knew him. Better than I did anyway."

Paula shrugged, apparently not willing to volunteer details about their relationship.

I decided to start with an innocuous question. "What was his teaching style like?"

I wasn't sure she would answer, but after a moment, she sighed. "Impatient. Frustrated. Brilliant."

"How do you mean?"

Paula turned clouded eyes toward me for only a minute before looking down. "Weldon had a picture in his mind of how he thought things should be. When things didn't go according to plan, which was often, he could be short-tempered. And he always blamed someone else when things didn't go his way."

I nodded, searching for another question to keep her talking without frightening her off. "So he wasn't good at teaching?"

"In the old days, he was wonderful. Very inspiring. It's just . . ." Paula paused, going back to some long-ago moment. "He just couldn't make his vision match reality."

"His vision?"

Paula smiled a sad smile. "Beloved professor and scholar. Respected by students, peers, the world."

"That's a tall order."

"Yes, it is."

"Paula? What were you and Weldon to each other? Were you romantically involved?"

"I don't know what you mean." She hastily stood, but not

before I saw the terror in her eyes.

"I'm sorry if I said something I shouldn't have. Please stay."

Paula shook her head. "I don't think I can help you understand Weldon anyway. I certainly failed at it."

"Then who can help me?"

The question hung in the air as she rushed from the room. I couldn't quite see prim, proper Paula aiming the butt of a gun at my head, but something wasn't right. I shook my head. Paula Burke had just joined my list of suspects.

I walked down the sidewalk along the campus district shops and restaurants, Terry at my side. Although sunlight still radiated from the western horizon, faux-antique streetlights began to glow. A blanket of cool air made me glad I had grabbed a sweater at the last minute.

"I think Kung Fu's has a new cook." Terry's baritone startled me out of my meditation with the red brick sidewalk.

"Wong Fu's."

"Just wanted to make sure you were listening. You didn't say anything in the restaurant when I told you there were eels in the chow mein."

We stopped at the corner with a decision to make. We could cross the street onto campus or continue around the corner to see what unique entertainment the campus district had to offer tonight. Countless beer bars sat between trendy boutiques and sports-nut stores. Stores came and went at the district; the only thing that remained constant was the type of establishment.

I looked up at Terry. "I'm not sure I'm in the mood to share space with drunken college students tonight."

"I'm not sure you're in the mood to share space with the human race tonight."

"I'm sorry if I'm not very good company." I gritted my teeth, oddly hurt by Terry's comment.

"Look, luv. There's a lot of craziness going on in your life right now. You come back to work after yet another failed relationship only to find a dead man. You have two cops hanging around. One wants to hang you for murder, the other is falling in love with you—"

"I really don't think . . . ," I interrupted.

Terry put his hand up to halt my conversation.

"And the one who thinks you're a murderer seems oblivious to the fact that someone—probably the killer—is also after *you*. You're more than a little attracted to the cop who has a thing for you, but can't get over a twelve-year age difference. Which is kind of hypocritical, seeing as that musician you lived with for two years was fifteen years older than you."

I wrapped my arms around the lamppost, soothed by the cool metal at my cheek. "God, my life sounds even worse when you sum it up."

My friend chuckled and gave me a squeeze around the shoulders. "Reality sucks, doesn't it?"

"Yeah, it does. So, got any advice you would like to impart?"

"Actually, I do."

I straightened up, letting my hands fall from the lamppost. Terry grabbed my hand and pulled me across the street toward campus, oblivious to the cars braking all around us.

"Where are we going?"

"You'll see."

My fast, long-legged pace still had to do double time to keep up with Terry's larger gait. By the time I began to feel a little winded, Terry slowed down, and then stopped.

I looked around. We were poised at the crossroads of sidewalks offering as many options as a Dallas interstate exchange.

"Terry, I don't understand."

"You decide where we go now, Ronnie. Listen, feel, trust yourself."

I muttered. "When did you decide to go all New Agey on me?"

Terry laughed. "Not a chance. But all this craziness is taking its toll. You don't know which way to turn. Close your eyes. Which way do we go?"

Wondering if Terry had adopted yet another peculiarity, I obeyed and closed my eyes, feeling a little ridiculous. But as I stood there, still and listening, I began to hear something. A heartbeat. Vibrating and freeing. Faint voices in song. Before I realized it, my feet itched to join the music. And I open my eyes and grinned.

"Let's go, oh wise one." I hooked my arm through Terry's and took the path leading to the armory.

As we got closer, I felt the vibrations of drumming, strong and steady as a heartbeat. The singers chanting what I recognized as a Kiowa song. We passed others coming and going, many of them familiar faces sending a smile and a nod in our direction.

When we entered the armory, I stopped and took it all in. Right now, a fancy dance was in progress with men of all ages attired in the spectacular dress of their ancestors. Bells and turtle-shell rattles joined in rhythm each time a dancer's foot hit the floor. Dancing continued at a fevered pitch with younger men dropping to their knees and getting back up again. Feathers, beads, and painted faces flashed before my eyes in frenzy. I spotted the thick gray hair of Dave Lonewolf, an Apache professor in the education department, as he danced by.

I stood on my toes and loudly spoke in Terry's ear so he could hear me. "I didn't know there was a powwow tonight."

"I know," Terry said just as loudly. "That's another sign that things are out of whack in your life. Ronnie Raven does not miss powwows."

I laughed. Just entering the powwow had lifted the weight of worries from me. I was still smiling as Dave approached us, the dance apparently over. I nodded.

"It's good to see you, Ronnie." He draped a shawl around my shoulders. "It's intertribal. Go dance."

I touched the shawl, woven in yellows and blues with a sunny fringe along its edges, and delighted in its weight. As the drumming began again, I approached the circle. Nodding at three women, all sisters, I stepped in behind them. I took small quick steps, a dancer's steps.

The armory walls fell away and the cement floors turned to dirt beneath my feet as a fragrant spring breeze washed over me. The men in the circle sang while my heart kept time to the drum. I opened my heart and soul to the healing magic of a powwow. All around me, people of the past danced alongside people of the present.

James Dean and I sat on my front stoop the next morning to greet the sun. With a cup of tea warming my hands, I marveled at the colors of the sky. Shades of pink, purple, and blue turned the sky into a tie-dyed shirt. Soon, the traffic of an entire neighborhood with places to be drove me back inside. Showering, dressing, and washing my cereal bowl and mug took little time.

Since I had no classes until afternoon, I strolled to campus while planning my own murder investigation. Eloise had mentioned Zachariah's need to save paper in the file cabinets on the third floor. Somehow I had to get into those files and hope that Crutchfield's file hadn't been removed yet. Yet even if I chanced a visit to the file room during Eloise's lunch, Zachariah might still be lurking around.

My conversation with Paula had been a bust, but what about

the other professors? Maybe they knew something I didn't about Crutchfield. I grinned. Chances were they did. Maybe Justin, who coveted Crutchfield's office, had spent some kiss-up time with him. Then there was the always elusive Trevor. Perhaps the way to Trevor was through Desiree?

I arrived at Psych all too soon and tried to ignore the butterflies bungee jumping in my stomach as I entered the building. I paused outside Crutchfield's door on the way to my office. What had been so important that someone would knock me out? And did they get what they wanted?

A crash sounded behind the door, quickly followed by muffled oaths. I swung the door open quickly with the telltale squeak announcing me. I don't know who was more surprised, Joe Bob or me. The latter was picking up psychological tomes that had most recently resided in Crutchfield's bookcase.

"I guess you're wondering what I'm doing here."

"The thought crossed my mind." I folded my arms and leaned against the wall near the open doorway. No way was I closing the door while confronting this kid.

"I was looking around to see if my midterm paper was here."

"Find anything?"

Joe Bob shook his head. "Heard you got attacked in here the other night."

"Out of curiosity, where were you when I was having all that fun?"

"I was with a couple of foxy ladies who know how to appreciate football players." His leer was almost too much. "Your cop boyfriend already checked it out."

Jeez, there was that wonderful small-town atmosphere that was partly responsible for me leaving my own small town in the first place. Mick had been designated my boyfriend. "Doesn't your coach have rules about your use of time and energy?"

Joe Bob approached slowly, his tight blue jeans rubbing

together in time with the clacking of some rather worn cowboy boots. Although he seemed to walk in slow motion, Joe Bob was violating my personal space within seconds. Hands as big as dinner plates landed on either side of my head, effectively trapping me. With his breath in my face, it took all my control not to flinch. There was nowhere to look but at his eyes. Bloodshot. The red all the more obvious because of the contrast with the light blue of his eyes. I willed my own face not to betray any nervousness.

"Coach understands that what he doesn't know won't hurt him. Maybe you should take a lesson from that book, too, Teach. Crutchfield had to."

Joe Bob lifted his hands from the wall and grinned before leisurely swaggering out into the hallway. I placed my hand over the heavy pounding of my heart until it slowed down.

I busied myself by pushing desk drawers back in and replacing books onto the bookcase. Straightening up Joe Bob's mess. Had he really been looking for his midterm paper? Something else? My gaze fell to the makeshift closet. After checking around the room and finding it empty, I felt compelled to open the closet door. There, at the bottom, was the box. Mick said his cops had checked out the office and couldn't find the box, which meant that whoever knocked me unconscious brought the box back later. Was that why Joe Bob had been here, to return the box? If so, then why was he standing next to the bookcase when I walked in? Did the box not have what he was looking for?

I tugged on the box while facing the open doorway. I doubted anyone would attack me in the light of day in a building full of people, but I wasn't taking any chances. I wanted to see anyone coming at me. Once I had tugged the box from its cramped confines, I was able to get my hands underneath the bottom and achieve a wobbly standing position. I used my back to close the closet door. Out in the hall, I glanced at Crutchfield's door, unsure of how to close it while holding onto the box. The hell with it. With all the traffic in and out Crutchfield's office, why not just leave the door open? Give the door a rest, not to mention my ears against that annoying squeak.

I lumbered down the hall with the box, grateful that I didn't see anyone. I didn't want to answer any questions right now. Especially when I no longer knew who my enemies were. I held my breath until I was in my office with the door closed.

I dropped the box on my desk, causing a few papers to float up. And then . . . then I heard a very distinctive sound. A sound I hadn't heard since my brother and I used to tramp around the woods surrounded Granny's house. I heard rattling.

CHAPTER FOURTEEN

I froze. I had a good idea who my unexpected visitor was and felt it wise not to make any sudden movements. I also happened to be scared. Okay, my inability to move was ninety-nine percent due to being scared shitless. A strand of hair had found its way to my mouth when I carried the box to my office. As irritating as feasting on hair was, I wasn't even brave enough to risk removing it from my mouth. After what seemed hours, I finally summoned the courage to look down at my feet. To my delight, nothing was wrapped around them.

By only moving my eyes, I checked the perimeter around me. Still nothing. Had I imagined the rattling? Another side effect of the concussion? Not yet ready to give up on reality, I slowly moved to where I could see the left side of my desk. A single piece of paper—if I had to guess, one of Zachariah's memos—lay on the floor. It probably flew off when I dropped the box on the desk. No matter, it was too flat to hide anything.

The right side of the desk. That's where I found him. Squirming out from under the desk—a place I would never again be able to put my feet without looking first. A nice-sized rattlesnake, very active, lots of writhing, which I assumed had something to do with it being angry. Too angry for me to stick around.

As quietly as possible, I backed up to give my desk a wide berth. Keeping the snake's diamond markings and multiple hues of brown in sight, I continued stepping backward toward the door, praying that my usual clumsiness wasn't going to make its customary appearance. It didn't, and I shut my door quietly before rushing next door to Justin's office. I grabbed the phone, ignoring the fact that his office was occupied.

"Ronnie! I'm meeting with a student right now."

"Where's your campus phone book?"

"Later, when we're finished," Justin said.

"Your campus phone book!"

"I'm not sure I remember . . ."

"*Campus phone book! Now!*"

As if by magic, the phone book appeared in front of me. I thumbed to the end of the department listings and punched out four magic numbers while praying someone would answer.

"Hello, zoology department?" I said after hearing a click and a mumble. "This is Ronnie over at Psych. Second floor. Are you guys missing a reptile?"

"I'm pretty sure they're all accounted for," a bored voice replied.

"I was afraid of that. How would you like a donation?"

"Whatcha got?"

"Rattlesnake." Out of the corner of my eye, I saw Justin lift his feet off the floor.

"Really?" The zoologist's interest seemed to perk up. "It's kind of early yet. Most rattlers are just now coming out of hibernation. How big is he?"

"Well, we didn't really have time to size each other up, but I would say he's about as big around as my wrist and at least three feet long."

"We're on our way."

My smile to Justin and the student was a little shaky, but they paid more attention to the floor beneath their feet anyway. "Thank you for the use of your phone, and I'm sorry for the interruption."

Who said I didn't have manners? Back in the hall, I stood

against the wall directly across from my closed door, guarding it from unsuspecting souls who might enter to visit me. I wouldn't wish a rattlesnake on anyone I knew, with the possible exception of Detective Melvin.

I also wanted to make sure the snake stayed put and didn't start wandering the halls. I wasn't sure if he could flatten himself to fit underneath the door or not. And if he was really determined to leave, God knew I wasn't going to stop him. But I wanted to know where that sucker was every minute until his capture so that we never crossed paths again.

I kept my arms tightly wound around my middle, trying to hold my panic at bay. I felt the shakes start. I tried to contain them before they grew as large as a California tremor, but I hated snakes. I mean, I really hated snakes. If snakes could sense fear like dogs, I was in big trouble. I kept telling myself everything was okay; in fact, it became my mantra until help arrived.

It was probably only minutes, but it seemed like forever until a shaggy young man and woman approached with smiles of anticipation similar to the ones I see on my nephews' faces after Santa dropped the loot down the chimney.

The kids carried a cloth sack and some kind of grabber tool in their hands. I pointed to my door. They entered quietly, although I didn't know how, what with all that enthusiasm bubbling over. Before I could find a new vantage point, they closed the door.

As much as I didn't want to see that thing again, I needed proof it was out of my office. And there was always the chance I would need to barge in on Justin again and call somebody in case one of the students was bit.

"What's going on?" said a voice in my ear.

I smiled gratefully at Mick and would have hugged him if it weren't for the fact that a crowd was forming. You could tell by their questioning faces that they didn't know why they were gathering, but people at the university could sniff out a potential disaster scene with one nostril closed.

The zoology students came out of my office with even bigger smiles on their faces and a large bag. A very large bag. A very large bag that moved. The crowd gasped and moved back.

"I think you underestimated. It's at least a four-footer. A western diamondback," the young woman said with all the enthusiasm that other women used in talking about jewelry. "An old guy, by the looks of him. He has more than twenty sections on his rattle."

I smiled weakly. "Congratulations. Could you double-check and make sure he didn't leave any family or friends?"

"Well, snakes don't usually travel together . . ."

"Please do as the professor asked," said Mick, out of uniform but still carrying a sense of authority with him that didn't require a badge.

It didn't take more than a couple of minutes to get the all clear.

"Show's over, folks." Mick gently pushed me toward my office, having to give me a shove in order to close the door behind us. He leaned against the door, preventing me from running out into the hallway screaming.

But, since I was there, it was like that "falling off the bike" analogy. The sooner I got back on, the better off I would be. Although the snake-loving students had checked my office, I searched again. And it made me mad. This was my office, a haven of sorts; I shouldn't have to be scared. Snakes—creepy things I had feared since a bull snake had visited my tree house when I was six.

Suddenly my breathing became more rapid. When I couldn't slow it, Mick moved in. His plan was to comfort me, I guess, but I batted his hands away and started pacing, not easy with

177

Mick standing in the middle of my cracker-box office.

The spiral of panic spun faster until I was afraid I might spin out of orbit. Words, always my anchor in times of craziness, vanished. Finally, I focused on the window, prepared to break it if it hesitated in opening. It protested noisily, but it opened.

Pure cool air entered my lungs as I closed my eyes and made myself breathe slowly through my nose. Finally, I felt control returning; shaky, but returning. I kept my location at the window by hopping up to sit on the wide windowsill.

"Sorry about that."

Mick was suddenly next to me, but not touching. "Don't be. You ready to tell me what happened?"

"I think they call them panic attacks." I knew I sounded flippant, but truthfully, I was embarrassed for Mick to have seen the episode.

"That's not what I meant," he murmured, his fingers lightly touching my arm.

"Well, you'll have to be clearer. I'm not a frigging mind reader."

He removed his hand from my arm. "What about the snake?"

Deciding a long explanation wasn't necessary, I told him that someone had obviously left a gift for me.

"You don't think someone put it in here, do you?"

I raised an eyebrow. "No, I believe a rattlesnake—a snake that should have just started coming out of hibernation— navigated a flight of stairs, and out of all the places it could visit, decided to slither under a closed door into my office."

"Where was it?"

I stifled the shiver that threatened to erupt. I pointed behind him. "There, under my desk."

"And it made noise?"

"Yeah, and lots of squirming, like it was mad or something."

"I wonder what disturbed it."

"Other than whoever brought it in, I don't know," I sighed before my eyes focused on the box. "Oh, yeah, I found that box I was telling you about, and instead of hanging around Crutchfield's office again, I brought it back here and dropped it on my desk. I guess the noise startled the snake."

"I told you to stay away from his office, Ronnie." Mick gave me a warning look.

"Well, I think I'm damned lucky I didn't listen to you. Otherwise my first indication of the snake would have been when it latched onto my ankle."

I jumped off the windowsill and started rummaging through the contents of the box. "How about that? Joe Bob's paper is the second from the top. I wonder how it got there. And there's Desiree's paper right there in the middle. Well, golly gee, I guess Crutchfield overlooked them."

I threw the papers down on the desk. Would students actually go to all this trouble over a midterm paper? Hitting a professor over the head? Putting a rattlesnake in an office? It was hard to believe. Joe Bob worried that his psychology grade would keep him from playing ball. Desiree might have slept with Crutchfield for a good grade. And then there was Trevor, Crutchfield's graduate assistant, who, as far as I could tell, was a classic abuse victim. Sometimes victims fight back. And none of these speculations included the faculty who wanted Crutchfield dead.

"Let's change the subject," Mick suggested.

"Fine by me, but I'm fresh out of ideas. The floor's yours."

"Okay, how about dinner and a movie tonight?"

I groaned. "That's not fair, and you know it."

"What do you mean?"

"I've had an emotionally charged day, my defenses are down—"

"Are you saying you don't want to go on a date with me?" His voice sounded oddly hurt.

I really wasn't in the mood to repair a shattered male ego when my own was so precarious. "I'm saying I don't think it's a good idea while all this is going on."

"Why not? At least I can keep an eye on you that way."

"I don't want to date someone so he can keep an eye on me!"

Luckily at that moment, Mick's beeper sounded. He pulled it out of his pocket and glanced at it before shutting it off and giving a wave good-bye. Before he shut the door, he slipped his head back in.

"Regardless, I will be keeping an eye on you. I don't want anything happening to you before we go on that date."

After another day of activity limited by my head injury, I was going stir crazy. Enough. Since I was pain free and felt more like myself, I chanced biking to work again. Mick was calling me two and three times a day. Nothing more was said about a date, but then I tried hard to keep conversations at a professional level. He didn't say much when I asked about leads in Crutchfield's murder. Mick was holding out on me, and it pissed me off.

But today nothing was going to get me down. Literally and figuratively. The world had shaken off that last vestige of winter, making it official: spring had arrived in all its colorful glory. Morning introduced itself in the high fifties with the promise of higher temperatures to come. A few brave souls, students mainly, walked along the oval in shorts. I even noticed my old zoology professor in some wild-looking Bermuda shorts. By afternoon, when the temperature climbed past eighty degrees, more young people would be in various states of undress as they tried to catch some rays, ignoring all warnings of skin cancer.

The bike rack outside the psych building held just that,

bicycles. No enormous motorcycles. It was fascinating how the single act of choosing transportation could have such an impact on a life. It was enough to make one believe in fate.

A slower pace replaced my usually quick one as I entered Rubenstein Hall. I would be lying if I said I didn't feel some residual fear upon entering my office. The first thing I did was check under my desk. It was clear, but then I bumped my head on the underside of the drawer when the phone rang.

"Damn, I'm going to lose my head yet," I muttered. Rubbing the sharp sting away, I reached for the phone with my other hand.

"Ronnie Raven. May I help you?"

"That's exactly what I was going to say to you," said the voice.

"That you're Ronnie Raven? Impossible. They broke the mold when they made me."

The laugh lifted from the receiver and surrounded me with love. "Don't I know it."

"Hi, Mom."

"Hello, sweetheart. So, how can I help you?"

"By taking care of yourself and having a good time." Luckily, I had remembered to pack a Diet Pepsi before leaving the house this morning. I pulled it from my backpack and opened it. There was no such thing as a brief conversation with my mother.

"Veronica, I'm serious. Things aren't right. I just know it."

"Disturbances in the force, huh?"

"Exactly. Tell me what's going on."

"Nothing much. I just got to work. James Dean, of course, sends his love . . ."

"And the murder investigation?"

I sighed. "It's still going on."

"Are you still a suspect?"

"I guess it depends on who you talk to." I decided to be honest about that part. "The city detective would like to arrest me, but he doesn't have any proof. However, the investigating campus police officer is certain I'm innocent."

"Is he cute?"

I choked on my cola. "What do you mean, is he cute?"

"The one who knows you're innocent. Is he cute?"

"What does that have to do with anything?"

"Well, if everyone else thinks you committed a murder—"

"Wait a minute. Who said everyone thinks I'm a murderer?"

"Why you did, sweetheart."

"No, I didn't. I said . . ." I stopped for a second, noticing that my voice was getting too loud for paper-thin walls. Hadn't I learned my lesson from Melvin's last visit? "I said that the city detective in charge of the investigation thinks I did it."

"You're missing the point, dear."

I buried my head in my hand and reached for the mantra from my teenage years: *I will not let her make me crazy. I will not let her make me crazy.* I took a deep breath and exhaled. "What is the point, Mother?"

"This other policeman."

"Police officer."

"Police officer. Is he cute?"

"I guess so."

"Good, then—"

"He's also twelve years younger than I am."

I smiled at the silence at the other end. Finally. Now maybe we could get off this matchmaking obsession of hers. At least until she located another victim.

"That's nice. As I was about to say. He's cute, you like him, he likes you."

I conceded defeat. While my mother made plans for my love life, I consoled myself that at least she didn't know about my reptilian visitor. That would have her up here standing guard with her trusty hoe, used for chopping the heads off deadly copperheads that traveled too close to her home and family. Me, I don't get that close to snakes. Give me a shotgun, and I'll obliterate the sucker from as far away as possible. It was also some consolation that she didn't know about my head meeting with a blunt object. But, then again, she probably would have been ecstatic that Mick spent the night with me.

"So, I guess this young man is keeping an eye on you? I don't need to come up there?" my mother said.

"What? No. Everything's fine, Mom." I jumped at the chance to reassure her, even willingly letting her think I had a boyfriend taking care of me. "Besides Joey and Jamie have school."

"True. But they'd love to see their Auntie Ronnie."

"Maybe next month, when this blows over, they can come and stay for a long weekend."

"They'd like that. Well, I guess I'll let you go."

"Okay, thanks for calling, Mom."

"Bye, then. Oh, and Ronnie? Don't think you've fooled me. I know something is going on that you're not telling me. It's only a matter of time before I figure it out."

"Bye, Mom."

"Bye, dear."

I smiled grimly. And if things didn't get resolved quickly, she would. Another reason for getting the situation figured out as soon as possible. My glance fell to Crutchfield's cardboard box. I reached for the two midterm papers that had earned me my conk on the head.

After laying them side by side in front of me, I started reading the paper to my right, but was wincing before I finished with the introduction. Lots of BS without ever making a point. Typical blow-off paper. The rest of the paper wasn't much different. Oh, the right terms were there, regurgitated from the text. Obviously, the writer thought to fool the professor by changing a word here and there so that it wasn't verbatim from the text. I glanced at the name in the left-hand corner of the paper. Joe Bob. Past experience with plagiarism? I had to give him some credit. He obviously knew what a thesaurus was.

Knowing that anything would be an improvement, I turned to Desiree's paper. After skimming over the first page, I found myself returning to the first paragraph and reading more slowly. Good, logical sequence. An actual introduction. The rest of the paper followed the sequence laid out in the introduction. Clear language made actual points. They weren't points I necessarily agreed with, but she had said that she wrote it to please Crutchfield. Why had she been so worried about my reaction to this paper?

Would someone who wrote such a brilliant paper still feel obligated to sleep with the professor? Had she? Slept with Crutchfield, that is? Or was the reason a grade hadn't been written down for her was because Crutchfield had been expecting to grade another performance? Was murder the only way that Desiree could get out of sleeping with the professor?

CHAPTER FIFTEEN

We had settled down to a routine of sorts in Crutchfield's Introduction to Psychology class. It was basically like any other intro class I'd ever taught with the material imbedded in my brain. Sometimes I liked to shake things up a bit, but today I was content to lecture from memory and observe.

Joe Bob was in his usual center spot where everyone could see him. He was oblivious to my lecture, intent instead on the giggling blondes seated on either side of him. Guys like him had irritated me when I was a college student. Frat boys. Jocks. The guys who thought they were the center of the universe and the rest of us didn't exist. I would like to think I had matured over the past twenty years, but to be honest, I felt my irritation grow every time I looked at Joe Bob. I solved that easily enough by not looking at him anymore.

Desiree was practically in my lap, scribbling down every word I said. A few times her eyes glanced to my right. Looking for Trevor? Her waif-like appearance suggested a fragility I doubted existed. I had seen her dig her heels in the first time I met her. But, Lord, this child needed some sun. Her skin was more than white; it was ghostly pale. She might want to change her hair conditioner, too; that strawberry-blonde hair looked like straw getting ready to break.

Class passed quickly. Before I knew it, it was twenty after the hour and the kids were squirming in their seats. After I dismissed class, I gathered my untouched notes. I looked up to the expected, however unpleasant, sight of Joe Bob Wayne.

"Yes?"

"Did you find my paper?" he demanded.

I studied his face, trying to decipher what he knew. "Yes."

"And . . ."

"And what?"

"I want to know my grade."

I looked him straight in the eye, not allowing our last encounter to intimidate me. I was in charge here. "Your grade is barely a C. The paper is garbage. So listen up, Romeo, because this is the deal."

The smirk disappeared. With blue eyes narrowed, Joe Bob looked like a football player ready to tackle his opponent. I tried not to think about the opponent being me. "Your final grade, and therefore your future in collegiate football, depends on your grade on the final. A closed-book, multiple-choice-and-essay exam, on all material covered this semester. Some of it will be from the text. Some will only be from lectures."

The young fullback moved his mouth, but nothing came out. I hoped he was thinking about his class performance during the semester. If he had taken any notes in class, I was Miss America.

"I suggest you ask one of your smarter classmates—very nicely—if you can copy their notes up to this point." I finished packing up my belongings before looking up at him again. "Your future is in your hands, Joe Bob."

Speechless, he walked away without his usual self-assurance. I either just scared someone into taking his studies seriously or invited another mishap. I hoped it was the former.

"Dr. Raven?"

I looked up to a body swaying a little faster than the pendulum from a grandfather clock. "Yes, Desiree?"

"About my paper?" She twirled stringy hair around her finger.

"Desiree? Have you decided on your major?"

She gave a slight nod and looked down at her feet.

"What have you decided?"

"Psychology," she whispered.

I waited for her to drag her gaze from the floor. "I think you made the right choice. That was the best freshman paper I've read in a very long time. Definite A."

Like Joe Bob, Desiree was speechless.

What can I say? Brain-numbing "professor work," it wasn't. But I enjoyed the change of putting my feet up and looking out the window. Except for an occasional buttoned-up-to-the-neck, pasty-faced kid probably on his way to the library, students had adopted the easier pace of spring. For most of the kids, midterms were over, and they had another six weeks before finals. They deserved a little breather. So did I.

People watching was a hobby from my younger days. I couldn't remember the last time I had engaged in it. I enjoyed making up stories about the people who caught my eye. My mind drifted to the nagging question of my future. Maybe I just wasn't cut out for academic life. And at my alma mater, of all places. What had I been thinking?

I had wanted to be closer to Mom and the nephews, especially since my brother went AWOL from his paternal responsibilities. PU had seemed like the best place to do that. Close enough in case my family needed me, but far enough away to make dropping by a rarity. Now I didn't know if I had made the right choice.

Perhaps my wanderlust was returning. After all, three years in one place was a long time. For me, anyway. I'm not sure where my need to move around came from. It might have started as a way to assert my independence. Getting away from my loving but meddlesome family was a bonus.

I hesitated to define my family as dysfunctional since

"dysfunctional" along with "codependency" were just excuses, the way I saw it. Words that gave us someone or something to blame for our screwed-up state of mind. The world might be better off if we just accepted that we're all codependent personalities from dysfunctional families. That makes all excuses null and void, leaving us with the novel idea of taking responsibility for our own actions.

Still, moving around a lot provided me with an excuse to avoid dealing with the alcoholism and borderline personalities in my family. Escaping might have been healthy at one time, but now it was too easy. Feelings get a little hairy, and I was outta' there. I tried to ignore a little voice that asked whether I was running from a cute cop or a murder charge. Did it really matter? They both scared the hell out of me.

While contemplating my place in the universe, a knock sounded at my door. Not the timid knock of a student. A knock of authority rattled my door. I tensed for battle as I called for my visitor to enter. I expected the football coach or Detective Melvin. Instead, Zachariah stood in the doorway.

I'm sure my jaw dropped open. I couldn't remember the last time Zachariah entered my office, if ever. We exchanged social niceties before Zachariah turned his attention to the walls of my office. Prints of Dad's work couldn't hide all the water stains from leaky pipes. Stains remarkably like Rorschach inkblots.

"Heard anything about Crutchfield's book?" he finally asked, still checking out my office decor. I knew Zachariah, and he never engaged in idle chitchat. Every conversation had a purpose, a reason for being.

"Like what?"

"Oh, whether anyone's located it."

"Why would I know anything?" I said.

"I thought you might have heard something from that publisher you talked to."

I frowned. Why would the publisher contact me, a colleague who just happened to answer Crutchfield's phone one day? The fateful day, I reminded myself, of my concussion.

Zachariah must have realized how flimsy his words had sounded. "When I talked with him, he said something about giving you a call."

"Well, you know Ben," I said, hoping that I remembered the name correctly. "He did tell me he thought it was possible that Crutchfield mailed the manuscript over the weekend. He was going to let me know if it didn't arrive so that I could look for it. Since I haven't heard from him, maybe he received the manuscript."

I told myself it was more of a beige lie than a white lie. But it was enough to send Zachariah into a cold sweat. He gripped the back of the leather chair, his fingers digging into the upholstery.

"Have you read the book, Zachariah?"

He nodded. "Parts of it."

"What is it about the book that upsets you so much?"

"It's trash!" Eyes flashing, he approached my desk like a locomotive, only to be interrupted by another knock at the door.

Zachariah struggled to pull himself together while I grudgingly told the interruption to come in. Before Crutchfield's murder, I might get the occasional student knocking at my door. Now I was Ms. Popularity. I quickly forgave my visitor when I saw who it was. Paula. My, what a day of surprises. Did everyone assume that I knew something?

Paula stopped cold when she saw Zachariah. An interesting display of emotions crossed her face. Anger. Fear. Hostility. I half expected her to retreat, but Zachariah took action first.

"Please keep me informed if you hear anything on the matter we discussed, Dr. Raven." He turned to Paula and nodded.

"Dr. Burke."

After the door closed, she sat down in front of me, muttering something. I raised my eyebrows and cocked my head when she looked up. Again, she studied me. This woman didn't trust me. Why? Was it me personally? Or everyone?

"The air seems a little fraught with tension," I said.

"Dr. Bent has seen fit to inform me that I may not receive tenure."

"Oh." I didn't know what else to say. Tenure. The big T. More than job security, it was also a measure of our worth as professors. Tenure was everything. Still, I was surprised at Paula, the teacher's pet, not receiving tenure.

"He says he needs a department of go-getters." She sneered. "Publishing. Serving on committees. People making their mark in the professional community or some rubbish like that. If he only knew what I've done."

I tried my best imitation of Rogers's client-centered therapy by staying in a neutral pose, nodding my head and not saying anything. My imitation said a lot about why I didn't make my living as a therapist. I wanted to ask questions. Hell, sometimes I wanted to answer them, too. It takes great effort not to butt into other people's lives with advice. To try and fix things. I shivered a little. Not unlike my mother.

"Why not tell Zachariah what you've done, Paula? Or I can tell him if you would like?"

"He doesn't understand. None of you understand." Paula's voice dropped to a whisper as her eyes darted nervously around the room. "He wouldn't let me."

I leaned forward. Panic was unmistakable, reminding me of a cornered animal. The only time I had ever seen a look like this was when I volunteered at the local women's shelter.

"Who wouldn't let you, Paula?"

"And now things should be different. They're supposed to be

different. But he's still standing over me. *He* still won't let me."

She finally looked up, clearly uncomfortable with the conversation. The glaze in her eyes faded, and she became Dr. Burke once more. Prim, proper, and not the slightest bit scary. I wished I could get her to trust me, open up. *Even if she's the one who tried to stop me from snooping? Even if she's the killer?*

"Have you discussed tenure with your family? Husband, kids, siblings?" Unless I missed my guess, somebody close to Paula was abusing her.

"I don't have a family. I wanted kids, but . . ." She stopped cold and looked at me suspiciously. "My job is my family. I have to get tenure, don't you understand? It's the only thing I have left."

Before I could fish for more information, she was gone. Really, how did all those fictional detectives do it? Sharon McCone. Kinsey Millhone. V.I. Warshawski. Miss Marple. I always went a step too far and frightened someone into silence.

What were the real-life detectives finding out? Was Detective Melvin about to arrest me on circumstantial or manufactured evidence? And Mick. I know he wanted to help me, but he didn't have any more experience solving murders than I did.

Deciding a jolt of caffeine and sugar-free chemicals might help the thinking process, I made my regular journey to the Coke machines. On my way, I saw Desiree and called out to her, but she hurried away. Had she not heard me, or was she purposely ignoring me?

Intent on finding out, I followed her into the women's restroom and was greeted by the sound of vomiting. Had I been mistaken? Did Desiree go through another door? I was about to retrace my steps when it occurred to me that there was something odd about the sounds I heard. It wasn't just the vomiting, there was a gagging noise, too. I ducked into a nearby stall when I heard a flush.

The view from the crack in a bathroom-stall door wasn't ideal for spying, but Desiree seemed oblivious to the fact that anyone was in the bathroom with her. She smeared lipstick on her lips, a raspberry color that intensified the gauntness of her face. Straightening up from the sink, she looked at herself and smiled. A confident smile. Running her hands through strawberry-blonde hair that hung lifelessly on her shoulders, she picked up her backpack and left. Now I knew what Desiree's problem was and that she needed help. Unfortunately, I still didn't know if she was a murderer or not.

The dimly lit top floor protested with every step I took, broadcasting my approach to the entire building. If I was lucky, no one was around to hear the creaks and squeaks. I tried the door in the middle of the hall and was rewarded when it opened effortlessly.

Good. Eloise remembered to leave the door open. I wasn't sure she believed my tale about needing to do some late-night copying. Her office was dark, but I didn't want to risk attracting any unnecessary attention. I moved in the direction of the copy room, bumping into the wall with my knee before finding the doorway.

I flipped the light switch in the smaller room, flooding it with a yellow artificial sheen. No windows, so no one could see the light from outside. And it would be next to impossible for anyone from the hallway to see the light. I shook off the closed-in feeling that threatened to creep over me. Then I walked over to the copy machine.

I laid some lesson plans and test questions on top of the copy machine and turned it on. I wasn't taking any chances. If someone came by, I was going to be copying. While the machine warmed up, I took the opportunity to check the outer office once more. A couple of dark corners held nothing but dust. Zachariah's door was locked.

I returned to the copy room and made a couple of copies of the first paper. I put another sheet on top of the glass and pulled the cover down on it. The room was so small that if I heard a sound, I could be back at the machine in half a second punching that little green button.

Moving to the personnel files, I first checked for Zachariah's records on a lark. With his compulsiveness, you never knew. This afternoon's discussion about Crutchfield's book still made me uneasy. But, of course, there was nothing. If you were head of the department, would you leave your personnel file in a place where cretins like me could get their grimy little hands on it?

I hoped Eloise had been too busy to clear out files of the recently deceased. My throat caught when I didn't see Weldon Crutchfield behind Carter. Instinct made me look through all the C's, finally locating it after Curtis.

I inhaled deeply before skimming over the cover sheet. Weldon Arnold Crutchfield. Date of birth 10/27/45. Birthplace: Fayetteville, Arkansas. Divorced. Hadn't A.G. said something about her cousin's ex-wife? The divorce didn't surprise me as much as the fact that someone had once been married to Crutchfield.

The next page detailed his academic career, first in Arkansas, then in Oklahoma. Mediocre. Certainly jumped around a lot, though. Almost as much as I did. PU was by far the most prestigious university he had been affiliated with.

The last three pages in Crutchfield's file were reports of verbal disciplinary action taken against Weldon Crutchfield for alleged sexual harassment of female students. Every one signed by Zachariah.

Zachariah couldn't have been that surprised when I told him about Lisa's harassment by Crutchfield. The question was why

Zachariah had let Crutchfield get away with it. Our department head ran too tight a ship. He wouldn't let Crutchfield get away with sexual harassment, a death sentence for his department.

A thump sounded nearby. I hurriedly pushed Crutchfield's file back and shut the drawer, and leaped for the copier and pushed start. I looked around as a ray of light passed beneath my fingertips.

No one appeared. Since snakes didn't thump, I assumed the noise must be some sort of rodent. Preferably a squirrel instead of a rat, but the only thing that mattered was checking two more files.

Albertson, Justin. Graduated from a college in the East. His record was like his personality. Nothing stood out. Average grades. Pursley was his second job since gaining his PhD; his first position had been with a small Maine college that I had never heard of. I wrote down the phone number for a McIntosh College.

Hurriedly I looked for Burke, Paula—easy to find. I started at the back of the file, where the good stuff seemed to be. But Paula's file only consisted of two sheets of paper. Identifying information on one and academic information on the other. She shared a similarity with Crutchfield: birthplace. What were the chances of two professors in the same department being born in the same small town in another state? Had Paula known Crutchfield before she came to PU?

There was also a copy of a published paper from several years back, before she started working at PU. Interesting. If Paula published before, what had stopped her from continuing? I hurriedly folded the paper in quarters and stuffed it down the front of my jeans.

It was then that I heard a definite thud. In the next office. I shut the file drawer, but didn't make it back to the copy machine before Detective Melvin entered the room.

CHAPTER SIXTEEN

Anger soon wiped out any embarrassment at being dragged down to the police station. Melvin refused to listen to any explanation, and I soon quit trying to give him one. Luckily, midnight on a weekday in a small college town meant that the police station was close to empty.

The redneck detective disappeared behind a door with the papers he'd confiscated from me. No doubt eager to detect a criminal plot with his great detection skills. Or maybe he hoped I had been photocopying my private parts so he could hit me with a lewd conduct charge.

I dreaded having to call someone to bail me out, but the call after that should go to the attorney Terry had recommended. Anger pumped adrenaline through my body. I wasn't taking any more harassment from Melvin.

Sitting in the chair that Melvin assigned became impossible. I stood up to stretch, drawing the attention of two uniformed cops at opposite ends of the age spectrum. The young one watched me warily, but the older one smiled and winked. His lustrous silver hair reminded me of my dad, although this man didn't wear a ponytail.

"Would you please sit back down, miss?" the young one said.

"My butt's numb. I need to move around." He looked stumped. I mean, how do you make anyone over the age of two sit down without the use of physical force? "Look, you have my permission to shoot me if I try to escape, okay?"

The old guy laughed and told the other one to lighten up. I liked him immediately. Before long, we stood around chatting like old friends. Even the young guy thawed a little when I told a humorous version of the snake story.

That's how Melvin found me—shooting the breeze with the other cops. And it griped him. You could tell. His lips all but disappeared in his full face, and he looked like a red balloon ready to pop.

"Raven!"

"Yes, Melvin?" I said as sweetly as possible.

He sputtered for a couple of minutes. There were probably many things he wanted to say, but no coherent words escaped from his mouth. Finally he moved aside and jerked his arm in a gesture that I assumed meant I was to go through the door.

I slid off the desk I had been perched on and smiled at the two uniforms before following the direction of Melvin's arm. Light spilled out from an open doorway at the end of a long, dismal-looking hallway. I tried to ignore the feeling that I was walking to my doom. Let him try to question me. I was demanding a lawyer before I said another word.

I entered a room decorated in early police style. No artwork on the walls. Not much color at all, just a gray sheen to everything. Even the floor. Much to my joy, Mick sat at the rectangular table that filled up the room. He seemed pretty happy to see me, too, even though his dark eyes shouted warnings.

I sat across from Mick and winked, leaving the head of the table for Melvin, whose cheeks bulged like a chipmunk storing his dinner. He sat down and muttered something.

"I'm sorry. I cannot understand you with that stuff in your mouth."

You could see him turn the tobacco around a few times, squeezing all the juice he could from it before he deposited the wad in a Styrofoam cup. I looked away, hoping my nausea would disappear as easily.

"What are these papers I confiscated from you?" he finally said.

"Excuse me, but aren't you supposed to read me my rights and let me call an attorney?"

Mick kicked me underneath the table and shook his head. I glared back. Since when did asking for your constitutional rights turn into a crime? I sighed. This was Mick's territory, not mine, and I would have to trust him. Again.

"These papers contain information about different behavioral studies I will be using in an upcoming lecture. I was making copies of them." I reached for the papers, but Melvin pushed them out of my reach. Obviously, he hadn't ruled out some kind of plot written in secret code.

"All I was going to do was explain the content of the papers to you."

"Then why did I find you by the file cabinets?"

"Because I was looking for the earring I lost." I pulled both sides of my hair back to show that I only had one earring on.

You could tell he didn't buy it, or didn't want to. "Where is the other earring now?"

"I'm assuming somewhere in the copy room. You didn't give me a chance to find it."

"I ought to charge you with trespassing," he muttered.

"Are you that stupid?" I saw Mick shake his head out of the corner of my eye. "How the hell can I trespass at my place of work? I'm a psychology professor. I was making copies on the copy machine in the psychology building, for Christ's sake!"

Melvin stood up and leaned over me. "I know you were up to something, and if I find out what it was, I'll throw your butt in jail so fast, it will make your head spin."

"And, in the meantime, my attorney will be contacting your

supervisor and filing charges of harassment and false arrest."

Melvin threw my papers at me and bellowed at Mick. "Get her out of my sight!"

Mick wasted no time grabbing my upper arm and pulling me out of the room. He seriously looked like he would throw me across his shoulder if I resisted. I squeaked out good-byes to my new cop friends before Mick maneuvered me into the night air. Instead of lingering, he propelled me into his black Range Rover.

Mick glanced in the rearview mirror a few times after leaving the parking lot. He didn't say a word until we pulled up outside my house. Before I could undo my seat belt, he had my door open.

"Well, thanks for the ride . . ."

"We're going to talk." He walked to the front door and turned to wait for me.

Obviously, I didn't have a choice. I quickly unlocked the door before he could kick it in, getting as far as the living room when Mick began talking. Rather loudly, too.

"What the hell are you trying to do?"

"Let's see. What am I doing? Oh, yes, could it be doing my job in the place where I work?" I sat on the couch and kicked off my Reeboks. God, that felt good. I settled comfortably in the couch before catching Mick's glare.

I sighed. "The city police come into Psych to drag out a psych professor for being there? How much sense does that make? You know, I'm serious about pressing charges. That man has got to get off my back."

"That man wants to pin a murder on you."

"He's an asshole. You know I didn't do it."

"Ronnie, he may be an asshole, but he's a dangerous asshole. If there isn't evidence, he might just decide to conjure some up."

"But that's illegal. He wouldn't do that." I caught sight of

Mick's grim expression. "Would he?" Only a desperate man would manufacture evidence, but what if Melvin were desperate for this case to be concluded? I could just see the good old boy network of which our illustrious university president was a member clamping down on the local police force to solve the crime. Letting an unknown murderer hang around a college campus was bad for business.

Mick shook his head. "I really don't know what Melvin might do, but you can't keep antagonizing him, Ronnie."

James Dean decided we had ignored him long enough and hopped onto the couch. It felt like riding a small tidal wave until the black lab settled down. I folded my feet underneath me and concentrated on rubbing the fur on his ebony head resting on my knees.

Mick sighed and sat down at the other end, adding his hand to the task of petting black, tangled fur.

"What were you doing in there anyway?"

"Didn't you listen, I was copying—"

"The truth, Ronnie."

I knew Mick was on my side, that I should trust him. But trust could be so one-sided. I took the lost earring out of my front jeans pocket and put it back on.

"Let me guess," Mick said. "You were going through the personnel files. Didn't find anything on Bent, but you did find information in Weldon Crutchfield's record that indicated he was probably sexually harassing female students from the day he set foot on the PU campus."

The campus cop knocked me over with a feather. "How did you know that?"

"I've already checked the records."

"You could have told me."

"I shouldn't have to. I'm the cop here. I'm the one who is supposed to be investigating, not you."

"And it's my goddamned life here, LeGrand!"

I don't know how long we sat there staring. Granny used to tell me not to look at someone directly. Looking people in the eye was the height of rudeness, but it was something the white man did all the time.

But, right now, my white blood was showing. I did look Mick in the eye and told him in the best way I could that he wasn't going to stop me.

Mick finally closed his eyes and rubbed the bridge of his nose. After a minute, he looked back at me and smiled. James Dean suddenly disappeared and the space between Mick and me grew smaller.

Warm fingers touched my face and very slowly moved strands of hair away from my eyes. Then those same fingers, feathery soft in spite of the heat they radiated, traveled down my cheek to my mouth, sending a charge that turned my insides upside down.

I leapt from the couch with my heart pounding so loudly, I wanted to put my hands over it before it jumped out of my chest. I glanced back at Mick. Watching me closely. I saw curiosity, disappointment, and, of course, passion in his eyes. Mirroring my own eyes.

A barely audible whine sounded. On automatic pilot, I walked through the kitchen to the back door and let James Dean out to chase things—real and imaginary. Leaning against the door frame, I let the night air wash over me and concentrated on slowing my breathing.

I sensed rather than heard him approach. I pushed the door shut and walked around him, careful to keep some distance between us.

"Want something to drink? Pop? Iced tea?" I made a pretense of sticking my head in the refrigerator before looking at him again. "Beer? I have beer if you're not on duty?"

"I'm not on duty. I haven't been on duty all night."

Like that was supposed to reassure me that his motives were honorable or something. If only he knew that honorable motives send me screaming in the other direction.

I set out two bottles of Coors Light on the table, before rummaging through a junk drawer beneath the telephone. It took a minute to locate a legal pad and a badly chewed-up but still-functional pen.

"Okay." I sat beside him, noticing that he had opened both beers and that his was already half gone. "Let's start with something that's been nagging me. Why was Melvin in Psych in the first place? It's not like it's on his rounds or anything."

Mick sighed and took another drink. "Said he got a call about a prowler."

"But that doesn't make sense. If someone thought there was a break-in, wouldn't they call the campus cops? Did you . . ."

He shook his head. "No calls reporting anything suspicious."

"Then either he lied or someone called him and set me up. Somebody wanted me arrested."

"We don't know that," Mick started to say, then stopped. "All right. Who knew you would be in the building tonight?"

I stopped and chewed on the pen. "No one really. Eloise, of course. I had to ask Eloise to leave the door unlocked so I could use the copy machine."

"Eloise is . . ."

"Zachariah's secretary. Actually, she runs the place. Without her . . ."

"How do you two get along?"

"Fine, but . . . wait a minute. You don't think Eloise set me up, do you?"

Mick gave me a look.

"All right, I know. Everyone is a suspect. But what's her motive?"

"Did she know Weldon Crutchfield?"

"Of course she did, she knows all the staff. The kids, too."

Mick took the pen and paper from me and started writing. I watched the muscles in his jaw move as he wrote, before looking over his arm to read:

ELOISE—connection to Crutchfield or protecting someone?

"Zachariah!" I said a bit too loudly, and then lowered my voice. "What if she's protecting Zachariah?"

Mick nodded. "Or maybe she and Crutchfield were romantically involved?"

I cringed at that thought, but who knew what drew someone to another—really? Look at my parents. A traditional full-blood Cherokee artist and a little redheaded Irish woman who never stopped talking. And, as I found out tonight, someone had once married Weldon Crutchfield.

"Mick? Do you really think that whoever has been doing these things to me—the snake, hitting me over the head, and now calling the police—is the same person who murdered Crutchfield?"

He laid down the pen, drained the remaining drops of beer, and walked to the refrigerator. He lifted another beer in my direction. After I shook my head, he opened it for himself.

"It's a good possibility, Ronnie."

I couldn't stop the chill that passed over me. This wasn't a practical joker with bad taste. It wasn't simply a case of someone not liking me. The person harassing me was a murderer.

"Are you all right?" Mick said.

I knew if I asked, hell, if I even *looked* like I needed comforting, his arms would swallow me up in an instant. If I allowed that, I would lose all reason. And I needed reason if I was going to figure out who murdered Crutchfield, and who also might be plotting my own demise.

"So we need to look at people with a motive to kill Crutchfield *and* at people who may not be fond of me."

Mick nodded. "There might be a motive for killing Crutch-field that we don't know about."

"Okay, there's Zachariah, of course. And my favorite suspect, Joe Bob Wayne."

Mick wrote down "Joe Bob" with a question mark. "I didn't learn anything when I talked to him a couple of days ago. Did something else happen?"

I thought back to the incident in Crutchfield's office. Had he really threatened me, or was he just playing around?

"Ronnie? What are you not telling me?"

I sighed. "It's not a big deal, not really, but you remember when I went back to Crutchfield's office for the box?"

"After the concussion? When you promised not to go back to Crutchfield's office?"

I nodded, ignoring the sarcasm. "Well, Joe Bob was there looking for something, or maybe he was putting something back. And he tried to intimidate me. At least that's what I think he was doing."

"How?"

"He had me pressed against the wall where I couldn't move. Towering over me. Breathing on me."

"Definitely on the list." I watched Mick's hand clench into a fist before taking up the pen again. "Ronnie, stay away from him from now on."

I nodded. No problem there. It wasn't like I was going to go party with the guy.

"Then there's Justin, office next to mine, whose last name I keep forgetting."

"Albertson? Justin Albertson?"

"That's him. How do you know his name?"

"I questioned him."

I shrugged. "And I'm the one who dated him."

"When?"

"About six months ago, just once." I smiled. "I remember your last name, and I haven't been on a date with you."

"Yet." Mick smiled back. "Okay, motive for Justin?"

"Nothing much, really. He wants Crutchfield's office. It's bigger. Probably means status and prestige to Justin. He's into that kind of thing."

"What about the two of you? Anything else there?"

"Just that one date."

More writing. Obviously, Justin was a suspect, too.

"Who else?"

"Trevor, the graduate assistant. And, I guess, Desiree. They might have a thing going. Maybe they joined forces to kill Crutchfield." I tapped my fingers against the brown bottle in front of me. "Or one could have acted alone and is protecting the other."

"Motives."

"Let's see," I sighed. "Crutchfield treated Trevor like shit. Like a slave, really. But there's something else." Something Trevor said. I snapped my fingers. "Oh, yeah. Trevor indicated lots of people came out of Crutchfield's office mad enough to kill."

Mick interrupted. "He give you any names?"

"No. Even if he didn't kill Crutchfield, Trevor's hiding something. Maybe something to do with Desiree."

"How so?"

"Well, you read Crutchfield's file, so you know about the sexual harassment. I think Desiree might have been one of his victims."

Mick nodded. "We have a file on him at the office, too. Pretty much the same thing."

"Except for?"

"One domestic-abuse call, from a Mrs. Weldon Crutchfield."

"Really? When was this?"

"Ten, maybe fifteen years ago. Probably happened soon after he moved here. Mrs. Crutchfield withdrew the complaint."

"That's odd. His personnel file said he was divorced, and it wasn't scratched out or whited out. I don't suppose Mrs. Crutchfield had another name?"

Mick shook his head. "I'll do some more digging. I have a friend over at the clinic. Maybe she can check the files for injuries to a Mrs. Crutchfield. If we locate the former Mrs. Crutchfield, she might be able to tell us about enemies her ex-husband had."

It was on the tip of my tongue to ask further about the friend, but I didn't want Kiddie Cop thinking I was jealous or something. "Check your records on Paula Burke, too."

"Professor? Student?"

"Professor. She's from the same small Arkansas town as Crutchfield. You can tell she had some kind of connection with him."

Thinking of Paula made me remember the paper I had stuffed in my pants. I pulled it out and begin skimming it.

"What do you have there?"

"A copy of a paper Paula published in a journal before she came to PU. What's interesting is that just earlier today she was telling me that she was going to be denied tenure because she hadn't published."

Mick sighed. "I supposed this is something you stole from her personnel file?"

I ignored him. Like I was going to admit to stealing. There was something so familiar about this style. I went over to the coffee table and the pile of magazines and journals waiting to be read. I found one from the American Psychological Association from three months back. Obviously, I was a little behind in my reading.

I checked the contents then quickly turned to an article about research analysis in the academic community. By none other than Weldon Crutchfield.

I looked up at Mick. "She was writing his papers."

He sat down on the couch next to me. "Who was writing whose papers?"

"Paula. Paula was ghostwriting Weldon Crutchfield's professional papers." I winced at the knot forming in my neck. Did Paula writing for Crutchfield really have anything to do with his murder? Probably not, but who was to say?

"Why?"

"I wish I knew," I muttered. "But if she wrote his papers, who's to say she didn't write his upcoming book? But then for some reason she didn't want it published?"

"Or maybe she wanted credit for it."

"Maybe," I admitted. "Maybe Crutchfield was blackmailing a couple of people."

"Why do you say that?" Mick pushed his chair back and moved behind me to apply his fingers to the knot in my neck.

"How else would he get one professor to do his writing for him and the department head to cover for him on sexual-harassment charges?" Warmth invaded my shoulders. It was as if the sun grew fingers to give me a massage.

"Okay. That makes sense." Mick's hands worked their magic on my neck. "So what do you think Crutchfield had on them?"

"I don't know. I can't think when you're doing that," I said with some irritation, even as I felt my body melting into his hands.

"Not thinking might be good for a change," Mick said in a low voice close to my ear.

"Mick."

"Okay. Okay." He removed his hands from my neck and pulled me up.

I walked him to the door, grateful yet sorry he didn't insist on spending the night again.

"Ronnie, call me if you need anything."

I nodded.

"And be careful."

"Always," I smiled.

I thought he was going to stand there and revisit his lecture about all the possible dangers that awaited me. Instead, he kissed me.

CHAPTER SEVENTEEN

A restless night found me in the kitchen the next morning with a Diet Pepsi in hand and an eye on the microwave clock. It seemed to stay forever in the seven-fifties. By seven-fifty-nine, the cola had traveled to my bladder and sent me on a mad dash to the bathroom. I was rewarded by a red boxy 8:00 when I returned. Grabbing the phone, I dialed the number from a worn scrap of paper.

"Errrrr!" I slammed the phone down with unnecessary force as if it were the phone's fault for giving me a busy signal.

I walked over to the bay window to gaze out at the backyard greenery turning into a forest. Watching James Dean frolic with a butterfly in the yard helped me calm down. The way the butterfly dipped up and down made it look like it enjoyed teasing canines.

Back at the telephone, I told myself it didn't matter that I had been waiting for over thirty minutes for it to be eight A.M. in Oklahoma so that it would be nine A.M. in Maine. Nine o'clock, the official opening time for administrative offices all over the country. Either McIntosh College in Maine was the exception or someone beat me to the punch.

No matter. I would stay here all day if necessary, dialing the phone. I wasn't leaving the house until I obtained more information about Justin. My determination was rewarded by the sound of ringing, followed by a nasally hello on the other end.

"Yes, this is Maureen Paul from the University of Texas," I

208

said in my best administrative tone, praying that McIntosh College either didn't have caller ID or didn't notice I was in the wrong area code. "I'm following up on a résumé on a former professor of yours, Justin Albertson . . ."

"I'll put you through to the college president," she interrupted.

I was so taken back that I got through so easily that I missed the college president's name when he picked up the line. No matter. I identified myself again and explained my purpose, and received a long pause in return.

"Hello? Are you still there?"

"Yes, I'm sorry, Ms. Paul, you just took me a little by surprise. Are you saying that Justin Albertson applied for a position at your university?"

"Well, yes. In the psychology department, of course."

"And you're considering hiring him?"

At this point, I could have shared countless Aggie jokes I had heard through the years about the intelligence of people from the University of Texas. They told similar jokes about us at PU, often about the stench.

"Is there a reason we shouldn't consider Dr. Albertson for this position?"

"Look, I just assumed the University of Texas had higher standards. Aren't you a Big Eight school or something?"

"Actually, it's Big Twelve now."

"Yeah, well, McIntosh is a very small community college. I mean very small. We only have one session of introductory psychology, an evening course that Justin taught. If I remember correctly, he never had more than eight students in the class."

I had assumed McIntosh College was an exclusive four-year college in Maine that only accepted the collegiate elite. This opinion had been helped by Justin's résumé, which had described McIntosh as one of Maine's oldest and most exclusive liberal-arts schools. Additionally, Justin's résumé had indicated that Justin was the head of the psychology department. Not exactly a lie, of course; he had been the entire psychology department.

"And how was he as a professor?"

"Ambitious, but mediocre."

I thanked the man for his time and hung up. Obviously, someone hadn't done a very good job checking Justin's credentials. While Justin hadn't out and out lied, he had been misleading. Ambitious, as the college professor said, but did that make him a killer? Not necessarily, I told myself.

When I had seen Justin coming out of Crutchfield's office, I had assumed he was trying the office for size. Nobody killed for office space, but maybe that hadn't been Justin's purpose for visiting. Had Crutchfield known about Justin's background? That PU was Justin's first university post? If so, I could see Crutchfield using the information. But for what purpose? I couldn't think of anything Justin had that Crutchfield might want. If not, that would leave Crutchfield using the information only for his own sadistic pleasure. Not outside the realm of possibilities.

My head began to hurt from hypothesizing. Time to check on another suspect. I stuffed my house key in my jeans pocket, not wanting the burden of a backpack or purse during the brief trip I planned to make on foot to the brain of PU—the library.

I loved the smell of libraries. Freshly printed material. Dog-eared pages of favorite books. The aromas that came from housing a warehouse of books. Although the Internet had its place, I hoped libraries and books with actual pages continued for some time to come.

Sometimes I regretted not majoring in library science. The idea of hiding myself away amongst books sounded romantic, but a brief stint as a researcher right out of college didn't measure up to my expectations. It had taken a journey of jobs to find what I had thought was my element—teaching. Until recently, I had been happy with my choice. Now I wasn't so sure. While reinventing my life was nothing new, being the subject of a murder investigation was.

So when I entered the university library, I felt more comfortable than I had in recent days. I was among friends—books. No one threatening me, hitting me over the head, or leaving reptilian surprises. I wandered over to the computer search terminal, parked next to dust-covered card catalogs. I preferred the antiquated card catalog, but it would contain little, if anything, on my subject.

While I waited for eating disorders to appear on the screen, I glanced up to see a woman rush by swathed in a long coat, hat, and sunglasses. No clouds in the sky, and the temperature was sixty-nine degrees and rising when I left the house. But there was something very familiar . . .

Paula! Paula in disguise? A clandestine meeting? I thought about following her out of curiosity, but she disappeared too quickly.

I glanced back at the terminal. Eating disorders easily took up several screens. I wrote down the call numbers that sounded the most promising and rushed up two short flights of steps to familiar surroundings—the third floor.

While eating disorders wasn't my area of expertise, the third floor was definitely my domain. It housed all the psychological and social-science texts you could ever desire to see, and then some. It took all of my willpower not to browse.

I quickly located the books I needed and took a seat at the vacant, mile-long table, its smooth finish marred by the hands of students who must have believed they were still in junior high as they etched their names and objects of desire into the table. I bet I could find the same names on the bathroom stalls.

Bulimia. An eating disorder often seen in young women from middle-class families. Perfectionism and a need to control . . . Desiree's obsession with grades? Unlike the better-known anorexia, bulimics often ate normally, but expelled the food. Typically by vomiting, but also through laxative use, and increasing numbers of people were exercising to death. Lovely. If you ever needed an excuse to stop exercising, that was it.

I skimmed through the rest of the books. Like everything else in the behavioral sciences, there seemed to be some disagreement on the best treatment. Inpatient psychiatric admissions. Medically focused admissions. Psychoanalysis. Group therapy was mentioned a few times.

I closed the last book, wondering what to do with the information I'd gleaned. When I glanced up, I noticed Trevor sitting two tables over. Since he had been so adept at hiding from me, I took the opportunity to corner him while I could.

He looked up as I approached, and his mouth opened and closed a couple of times before resignation reached his dark, troubled eyes.

"How are you, Trevor?"

"Fine, Dr. Raven." He looked down at the table. "I mean, Ronnie."

"Hitting the library kind of early, aren't you?"

"I come here every morning. It's quieter than the graduate residence hall."

I'm sure it was. Graduate students could be a rowdy bunch when they needed to blow off steam. "Even the morning Crutchfield was murdered?"

Trevor hesitated before nodding.

I gestured toward a rapidly approaching young woman. "What about Desiree?"

"She was studying with me in the library that morning."

212

I smiled hello to Desiree and received a restrained grimace in return. "Whatever are you doing here, Professor Raven?" Desiree said, setting down a stack of books.

I laughed. "Even professors come to the library on occasion. You don't think we know everything, do you?"

"Um, I need to look for a book," Trevor stammered as he rose, simultaneously hitting the table and chair to send a muffled bang throughout the room.

Desiree smiled after the lanky body, a smile both shy and sophisticated in scope, before sitting.

"You like him a lot, don't you?"

"Yes, I do, Professor Raven." She lifted her chin a little higher.

"Trevor's a nice guy. Your family met him?"

She gave an angry chuckle. "Are you kidding? They would eat him up and spit him out."

"Because he's African-American and you're white?"

"Because Trevor can't live up to my stepfather's expectations. Nobody can."

"Is that why you're forcing yourself to vomit up your food?"

Desiree knocked over her books, sending them scattering to the edges of the table. She didn't answer, but looked at me with fear and a little bit of anger. I should tread carefully. I didn't want to be classed with her father and send her to the john with her finger down her throat. But, as a professor, maybe I already represented an authority figure—like her father. Like Crutchfield.

"How long have you been bulimic, Desiree?"

"You know, my mother married my stepfather when I was a year old." Desiree sighed as I sat down. I forced myself to remain quiet until she was ready to continue. "My stepdad was always cold, demanding. I figured my own dad would be different, you know?"

I nodded, dating myself with a vision of Fred MacMurray in

My Three Sons.

Desiree smiled harshly. "I met dear old dad recently. He was a drunk. A wife beater. My mom tried to tell me, but . . ."

"You didn't want to listen."

"I guess not."

"Have you thought about getting help for your eating disorder?"

"You can't make me get help," she answered with all the defiance of a two-year-old.

"No, I can't, but I don't want to see you waste away, either." The glint in her eyes didn't waver. "And it would devastate Trevor to find out that you're slowly killing yourself, don't you think?"

At this, her pouty lower lip began to quiver, her fondness for Trevor obviously real. I saw the object of her desire slowly approaching, no doubt disappointed that I was still there.

"Desiree? Where were you the morning Crutchfield was killed?"

She paused, looking happy to change the subject. "I think I was studying in my room that morning."

"Alone?"

"Yes. Wait, no. Trevor was with me." She nodded her head emphatically. "Yes, Trevor was with me."

When Trevor reached the table, the two locked gazes. I pushed myself from the table without saying a word. Young love. Special even to an ancient relic like me. This, of course, got me thinking about Mick. Again.

What was I going to do about him? The age thing didn't even seem as important now, although the first time we ran into a young ex-girlfriend might leave me with an overwhelming desire to yank out all my gray hairs.

No, what put me off was that I sensed this guy was different from the other guys I had been with. He could easily have power over me. I'd seen it happen too many times. Intelligent women. Women you'd think would know better. Men weren't immune, either. There was always a point where one half of a couple started acting like an idiot and the other moved on. Well, I was always the one who moved on, and I planned to keep it that way.

I shook all thoughts of Mick out of my head and rushed down the stairs to the basement. I still had one more book to find, a book covering early research in eating disorders, and it was located in the Tombs. Then I had to decide what I was going to do with Trevor and Desiree's conflicting stories.

Once upon a time, PU's library was housed in a beautiful, ornate building with stone carvings of mythical creatures standing guard. When the university's library needs outgrew the space, they simply built a large glass-and-cement structure that merged with the old library. Much of the old library was now closed off and used for storage, but two floors contained bookshelves of mostly out-of-print books.

The most interesting path to the Tombs was the long, scenic route through a small doorway in the library basement. A dingy hall opened into a magnificent three-story entry that was like a step back in time. Giant heavy oak doors had long since been barricaded. But what commanded your attention was the colossal staircase. My hand caressed the rich mahogany banister that took me to the second floor.

Directly in front of me was a magnificent room with thirty-foot ceilings. I frequently studied in this out-of-the-way location when I was a Pursley undergraduate. It was a room steeped in so much atmosphere that, as a student, I used to wait in reverence for the ghost of the Tombs to appear.

Supposedly, a young student poet in the earliest days of the university—the latter 1800s—spent time here. Like many artists, he had trouble transferring what was in his heart to paper.

He met another student, a young Seminole woman, and they fell in love. Times being what they were, people had trouble accepting the idea of any nonwhite person attending the university and falling in love with a white man, so the young woman was forced from the university.

Many versions of the story existed at this point. Some say she returned to her Seminole family; others say she left for the white foster family who had sponsored her education. Another rumor was that a group of students who had too much to drink killed her. After the disappearance of his beloved, the poet came to this room and wrote a poem, a poem that made people weep for its raw beauty. After the poet finished the poem, he jumped to his death from the roof, which he reached from a window in this room. Windows that were now painted shut to prevent a repeat performance from another brokenhearted college student.

The story had been told so many times and in so many ways that it qualified as a legend, as no one knew the true story anymore. But since discovering the room at the tender age of eighteen, I always expected to see the young poet at work at the table in front of the huge stained-glass window. The window now adorned with pigeon droppings.

The poem, if it ever existed, was lost long ago.

On the far side of the room, a doorway led to the old books. I had to duck my head to pass through to a room in remarkable contrast to the ornateness of the study room. I could touch the ceilings with the flat of my hand as I weaved through a maze of books placed side-by-side on utility bookshelves. I inhaled an almost-overpowering mustiness.

I enjoyed the solitude of my own footsteps walking over the squeaky floors. Hardly anyone journeyed into the Tombs anymore. It was probably just a matter of time before they sold the books at a book sale and closed the area completely.

I found my book in a corner, far from any desks or tables. It was almost time for me to go to Rubenstein Hall, so I perched the book on an empty space on the shelf in front of me and started perusing. Unfortunately, the book was little help. Most of the books in the Tombs were only helpful for establishing history on a subject. And the book I read recommended shock treatment. The theory was that eating disorders stemmed from depression, and at the time the best cure for depression was believed to be electroconvulsive therapy. While I knew some private psychiatric hospitals still engaged in the practice, I didn't think shock was the answer for Desiree.

Two squeaks followed a creak in another part of the Tombs, alerting me to the fact that I had company. Because of the echoes in the Tombs, my fellow bookworm could have been in the next row of books or on the other side of the room.

I closed the book, laying it on the shelf in front of me. Suddenly, as if hit by an Oklahoma blast of air, the book flew off the bookshelf and clattered to the floor. As I bent to pick up the book, a loud explosion sounded as something whizzed over my head.

CHAPTER EIGHTEEN

Sharp pain radiated through my lower body as I dove for the floor. I had grown up in a place that considered Thanksgiving just another day in the week because it fell during deer-hunting season, so I knew a gunshot when I heard one. And I had just heard one. Not a paper bag exploding. Not a balloon popping. A gunshot.

Clattering footsteps echoed in the distance, going away from me or coming toward me. I couldn't be sure. As I lay frozen on the cold cement floor, prayers flooded my brain. Prayers from hundreds of Sundays when Granny forced me to church.

As the only other occupant in the stacks, I could only assume the shot was intended for me. Fleeting thoughts of Mick wagging his finger in my face and admonishing me for taking chances came and went. Was that what they meant by your life passing before your eyes?

My ears, cocked for further sounds, competed with the bass drum in my heart. Finally, I pushed myself to my knees, remaining in that position for several long minutes.

I laid a hand on the nearest bookshelf to steady myself as I rose to my feet, but my throbbing left foot had to take second place to the scene before my eyes. Directly in my line of vision was a book. With a hole big enough to stick my pinky through.

Breathe! I told myself as quakes threatened to sink me back to the floor. I sent silent thanks to the haunted poet of the Tombs for sending the book on bulimia to the floor at the right moment. I grabbed the newly pierced book and grimaced my way to a less scenic but shorter route to the fourth floor of the main library.

Never was I so happy to be blinded by florescent lights. It finally occurred to me to check myself out. Warily I let my gaze touch on each part of my body. No blood. The knees of my jeans were a little dusty. And a rapidly swelling left ankle promised to make each step a living hell.

It took forever and a day to reach the telephone near the information desk, a mere twenty feet away. I picked up the receiver before turning around and letting the wall take the weight of my body instead of my foot. Without thinking, I dialed Mick's number, unaware until that moment that I had committed it to memory. Right now, his lectures about personal safety were nothing compared to getting me the hell out of the library. I wanted to cry when I heard a click after the fourth ring.

"I'm not home right now, but I really want to hear from you . . . ," said his irritatingly sexy voice. Probably already left for work, but I decided against the campus police station in favor of Terry, who, if I was lucky, was home in his own bed and not in someone else's bed this time. With each successive ring, my heart drooped. I waited for the click of another machine.

"This better be important," came a familiar growl.

"Oh! Terry? Terry. Thank God you're there."

"Ronnie?" His sleepy voice immediately went into alert mode. "What is it? What happened now?"

"I'm at the library." I breathed a sigh of relief. "By the time you're dressed and here, I should be able to make it to the first floor, but I may have to lean on you in getting to the car."

There was a moment of silence before a suspicious voice responded. "Ronnie? What's going on?"

"I'll tell you when you get here, but"—I paused—"it looks like I need to go to the clinic again."

"Did you get smashed over the head again? I swear, Ronnie . . ."

"I was shot at." My whispered answer stopped Terry's tirade. "Please hurry."

With that plea, I hung up, certain my friend would soon arrive at the library. The next order of business was getting to the first floor. Obviously, the stairs I usually traveled were out of the question. I fixed my sights on the elevator across the reading room. I've crossed the Sangre de Cristo Mountains on foot, yet I dreaded making this particular hike.

I scanned the room. Trevor and Desiree sat at their table. No sign of Paula, but was that Joe Bob over there in the seating pit, exchanging laughs with other athletic types? He looked up. Yes, it was him. I would know that smirk anywhere. Might Justin be nearby? What about Zachariah?

There was no way to reach the elevator without going through this room. This room that very possibly held a killer. Surely, the killer wouldn't shoot me in front of an audience. *Unless he or she is already too far gone,* taunted an inner voice. I told the voice to shut up. I tried to draw up inside myself as I had during junior high when I carried around an awkward rail-thin body with no shape to it. I hadn't wanted to attract anyone's attention back then. I had just wanted to disappear. Like now.

I discovered that by walking between empty rows of chairs bordering the mile-long tables, I could brace myself on the backs of the chairs without putting much weight on my foot. I almost succeeded in getting to the end when I encountered a throat, decorated with a silk tie. I raised my eyes to Justin's grin and wanted to take that tie and strangle him with it.

He held his hands in the air. "Want to dance?"

I was tempted to tell him that I knew what a fake he was. But who said a fake couldn't be a murderer, too? I bit my lip to contain my suspicions and my pain, moving to one side to pass him, keeping all screams of pain buried within me. Hah, wait until I told Terry about my great acting ability.

I made it! The elevator doors closed around me, leaving me within its small cocoon. No claustrophobia. I was alone—and safe. I might not ever leave this elevator. I slumped against the faux-wood paneling until the doors opened to a most welcome sight—Terry.

"Okay, I've got it, Ronnie, although I'm still not sure it's such a good idea." Terry's gaze moved from the road to my now-swaddled foot.

"Terry, I have to draw the killer out. I refuse to be a sitting duck like this any longer." I paused. "Either my health-insurance rates are going to skyrocket, or next time I open my office, I'll find a rhinoceros in there."

"Maybe next time the killer can do something about that thing you call a sense of humor."

"You mean like a humor transplant? I wonder if that's covered by our health insurance."

That was enough to get Terry started on a round of corny jokes that drew my attention from my still-throbbing foot, but it only lasted a few minutes. Luckily, I only had a mild sprain, but it hurt like a bitch.

"I still don't understand why we can't tell Mick." Terry turned his worried face to mine. I was worried, too, but now was the time to take action; otherwise, fear was going to swallow me up.

"Because Mick will try to stop me."

"Speak of the devil," Terry murmured as we pulled into my driveway directly behind a campus police car.

I actually hoped it was police business with another cop, but one look at the head popping out of the driver's side of the car told me what I already knew. This wasn't my lucky day.

I glanced at the crutches beside me, a dead giveaway, even if my foot hadn't looked like a mummy's body part.

Mick came to my side of the car as I opened the door and struggled to get all of me plus the crutches out, leaving Terry casting worried looks at the upholstery of his vintage Jaguar.

I managed to get the crutches underneath my arms before looking up to Mick's questioning face. "I sprained my ankle."

"When? Where? I've been here for over an hour."

"That would explain why you weren't at your house when I called," I snapped before regretting it. I tried to replace my irritation with a smile. "I'm okay. It's no big deal."

Unfortunately, Terry chose that exact moment to toss the newly pierced library book in Mick's direction. Easily catching it with one hand, Mick looked at the hole, even sniffing at it before looking at Terry and me.

"The library. Can you believe it's even open at such an ungodly hour?" Terry said before heading to the house, his copy of my house key poised and ready.

Mick didn't look like he was going to let either of us budge until I told him my life story. I sighed. "Look, do you think we can do this sitting down? My ankle is starting to hurt, and I still have to maneuver crutches through a yard filled with holes dug by moles and by James Dean trying to find the moles."

After tucking the book between the front of his shirt and his pants, Mick swung me up in his arms, leaving the crutches clattering in the drive.

CHAPTER NINETEEN

Terry's vivid flyers lined the walls of Rubenstein Hall. He had really outdone himself this time. Hypnotizing graphics featured a crazed figure centered on the poster with both hands raised high, one holding a gun, the other, a knife. Underneath the figure, some bold, skewed lettering shouted, "The Psychology of the Criminal Mind. Come see what turns a person into a murderer!"

I only hoped it drew the attention I wanted. So far, most of the interest was from former students and nonmajors asking if they could come hear the special lecture.

To say I was nervous was like saying Oklahoma summers were a little on the warm side. With the walls of my office closing in on me, I left, not certain where I was going, just out of my box. But when I rounded a corner and saw Mick, my reflexes kicked in. He hadn't seen me, but there was anger in those steps, which, unless I missed my guess, were headed for my office.

I made time turning and heading in the opposite direction until I reached the staircase. My ankle felt almost normal after I'd spent several days of being good. Up, I decided. Time for a diet pop in the faculty lounge. Luckily, I had change rattling in my pocket for the machine.

The first gulp might as well have been laced with rum because I could feel my muscles unbunching as the brown liquid flowed through my veins. People say caffeine makes you jittery, but I think some of it's psychological. Tobacco is a known stimulant, but smokers say that cigarettes calm them down all the time. For me, it's Diet Pepsi.

After that first drink went down, I looked around. I was alone. All except for those dratted aluminum cans overflowing in the corner. Damn. Zachariah had been after me for weeks to recycle those cans. If I didn't take care of them, somebody was going to waste valuable land dump space for a perfectly recyclable product.

Now or never. I finished my Diet Coke before walking over to the box. If I tried to carry the box downstairs in this condition, I was sure to draw attention when the cans clattered in my footsteps. I shook the top layer of cans out and began stomping them into misshapen circles of metal. After I reduced enough cans to make the load more manageable, I started returning them to their home. It was then that I noticed something white in the box. My first thought was that someone got lazy and decided the box was as good a place as any to put their trash.

But as my hand made contact with the rather thick bundle of paper, my fingers tingled. *The Myth of Marriage,* by Weldon Crutchfield, PhD, decorated with drops of cola.

I looked over my shoulder, thankful to still be alone. The faculty lounge suddenly seemed like a dark and sinister place. A place where a murderer might walk in any second. A murderer who wanted a certain manuscript, might perhaps even be willing to kill for it. Zachariah had made no bones about wanting to see the death of the book before publication. Then there was Paula, ghostwriting for Crutchfield. Perhaps she had written *The Myth of Marriage*? What part did the mysterious ex–Mrs. Crutchfield play?

I tried to place the manuscript down the front of my pants, but it was too thick. Obviously the best place for it was with the aluminum cans, so I shoved it back into the bottom of the box.

I picked up the box and walked out of the room, straight into Eloise.

"Oh, Ronnie!" She struggled to regain her balance. With both hands occupied with the box, I couldn't help her. It took a moment before her body stopped weaving.

"Excuse me, Eloise. I'm afraid I wasn't watching where I was going."

"Well, it's no wonder with that big box of cans. Why don't you let me call one of the students to help you with . . ."

I backed toward the stairs as I spoke. "No. No, that's okay. Really, I've got it."

I took the stairs as quickly as I could and still keep the box and myself upright. Luckily, the second-floor hall was deserted, as was my office. Mick obviously got tired of waiting.

I closed the door and set the box down behind my desk. With my heart hammering, I pulled the manuscript back out. Until I knew what I should do with it, I needed a good hiding place. Both Zachariah and Paula would be looking for it. And who knew who else might want it? Be willing to kill for it.

I scanned my office before I settled on Taos. I perched the manuscript behind Dad's painting, balanced in the frame. As long as no one touched the painting, the manuscript was safe. My eyes glanced at my Timex. Shit. Time to go.

When I rounded the corner to the classroom, even I was amazed at the number of people filling the hall. Why, the pope wouldn't draw this many people, not in Oklahoma, anyway. Even with the size of the crowd, it was impossible to ignore my number-one fan waiting outside the door.

I nodded. "Detective Melvin."

"You think you can tell me something I don't already know about criminals, Doctor Raven?" He sneered, as usual saving most of the sarcasm for my title.

"I just might." Before he could respond, I added, "If you can keep an open mind. Personally I don't think you can." I entered the hall, knowing ego and curiosity would demand he follow.

Maneuvering around clusters of people gathered in the aisles, I almost made it to the podium when my upper arm was grabbed with definite force. I was pulled off to the side of the room, attracting a bit of attention in the process.

"Are you out of your freaking mind?" Mick whispered harshly in my ear.

"It's been suggested before."

"You practically sent a handwritten invitation to the killer."

I nodded. "Mick, please. I have to do this. Now let me do my lecture before the whole place wonders what we're up to."

He dropped my arm and walked over to lean against the wall, clearly not happy. I knew he wouldn't be, which was why I had avoided him since Terry and I hammered out the plan while I recovered from my sprained ankle. If he had known about the lecture, he would have tried to stop me. And I didn't have the energy to fight Mick and a killer.

Left of center near the front was Terry, toasting me with a Dr. Pepper. My two protectors, one on each side. I smiled.

"Time to get started. Everybody take a seat." I looked around and to my amazement, every seat was filled. It was standing-room only. "Well, take a seat somewhere if you can find one."

My jaw threatened to drop at the sight of all these people. It was enough to send the most seasoned speaker into stage fright. Suddenly I realized the killer was out there, in the audience, and my throat went dry. Who was I kidding? What if the killer had some kind of super-duper laser weapon and shot me during the lecture? No one would be able to figure out who the killer was, not in an audience of this size.

After days of me planning and plotting for this moment, doubt seeped in, leaving me to question my wisdom. Then I saw Zachariah against the back wall, arms folded across his

226

chest and not looking any happier than Mick. No doubt a disciplinary letter rested in his pocket, chastising me from swaying from my filed class plan. Next to Zachariah stood Justin, wearing that dumb smile he pasted on every morning when he got out of bed.

I looked for Paula and found her seated at the end of a row directly behind Eloise and her reassuring smile. I scanned the crowd for other suspects. Joe Bob, in his usual classroom seat, still surrounded by a bevy of beauties, but not appearing to enjoy the company as much as usual. And was that Coach Henderson in the back corner? Whatever was he doing here?

Desiree in front, paler than usual, avoided my gaze. Unlike the last time I saw her in the library, Trevor wasn't glued to her side. I finally located him in the middle of the crowd, slumped down. Hiding? From me? The police? Or Desiree?

The gang was all there. I took a deep breath and began.

"After, see, after we'd taped them, Dick and I went off in a corner. To talk it over . . . He was holding the knife. I asked him for it, and he gave it to me, and I said, 'All right, Dick. Here goes.' But I didn't mean it. I meant to call his bluff, make him argue me out of it, make him admit he was a phony and a coward. See, it was something between Dick and me. I knelt down beside Mr. Clutter, and the pain of kneeling—I thought of that goddamn dollar. Silver dollar. The shame. Disgust. And they'd told me never to come back to Kansas. But I didn't realize what I'd done till I heard the sound. Like somebody drowning. Screaming under water . . . but I couldn't leave him like he was. I told Dick to hold the flashlight, focus it. Then I aimed the gun. The room just exploded. Went blue. Just blazed up."
(*In Cold Blood*, Truman Capote; Original copyright, 1965; Renewed copyright, 1993; page 244)

An appreciative audience did wonders for my confidence. Hundreds of shiny eyes watched me. "Truman Capote's account of the infamous Clutter-family murders in Kansas thirty years ago can be understood by behaviorism. Many murders can be explained by behaviorism, because behaviorism is the science that says all mammals have an identifiable way of behaving under certain conditions, a conditioned reflex.

"Actually, the murders documented by *In Cold Blood* aren't the norm. Many murders take place between people who know each other, some intimately, not from evil people with an insatiable need to kill. Not gang killings, but people who kill someone they know, someone close. Why?

"Sometimes it's a means of self-defense. Someone repeatedly threatened with physical or sexual abuse might be driven to violence in order to stop that abuse. Not as easy to understand is emotional abuse. Emotional abuse leaves scars also, internal scars, and it can take many forms—humiliation, loss of self-esteem.

"When we as individuals perceive a threat, whether imagined or real, we react. We cry. Maybe we run away. Smoke a cigarette. Have a bad case of butterflies. Get drunk. If the threat continues, we take further action. We must take action. A person can only tolerate so much before fighting back.

"Murder can be the result of someone threatening to take away our way of life—recognition, fame, fortune. When your identity is taken away, stolen, you too can be driven to murder.

"Then there are the motives that movies of the week are made from. Blackmail. Power. What would you do if someone were blackmailing you? Threatening to expose you? What if there was a roadblock to your success? Would you get rid of the roadblock?"

For the first time in my life, I felt like people—lots of people— were interested in what I had to say. It was a heady sense of power, and I finally got a glimpse at what attracted Terry to acting. This was magic. I glanced at my watch, seeing the need to start wrapping things up.

"Often we have two victims in a crime. The person who dies and the person who feels he or she has no choice but to kill." Before anyone felt that I was advocating justifiable homicide, I hurried along. "But we do have choices. We have the choice to kill or not to kill. Anyone who chooses murder must take responsibility for his or her actions. It's the law.

"None of us believes we can murder another human being. But we can. I can. You can." I pointed to a nodding young woman near the front.

"So can you." I pointed to Desiree, whose dear father perhaps shared too many disturbing similarities to Crutchfield.

"And you," I moved my pointed finger to Joe Bob, Trevor, then Paula. "Any of you, even you standing against the back wall, can murder.

"Any of us can be driven to commit murder. Against a psychology professor. Especially a psychology professor who, let's face it, wasn't a very nice man. Through promises, threats, and blackmail, Weldon Crutchfield forced people to do what he wanted them to do. And then he ridiculed everyone around him, blaming them for his lack of success.

"We have one million, six hundred thirty thousand, nine hundred forty people in our prisons and our jails. About the same number of graduate students in the United States. College campuses tend to be relatively peaceful places. Only fifteen murders were reported at American universities last year. Most of the murderers weren't part of the university, neither staff nor students. Unfortunately, PU can't make the same boast about the death of Professor Crutchfield. He was killed, murdered, by someone he knew well, somebody who is very much a part of the university community.

"Who killed Weldon Crutchfield? Behaviorism clearly points to the murderer. It even tells us why the murderer had to take action. The murderer believed it had to be done."

I stopped my lecture and walked back to the podium to gather up my things. After several seconds, the audience broke out into applause. What was even more startling was that some people were standing, too!

"Don't get too much of a big head," Mick murmured in my ear. "Right now, I think you've driven me to murder. Let's try to get you out of here in one piece."

We slipped through a side exit, taking the concrete steps at such a pace that I was out of breath by the time we got to the second floor, but that didn't keep me from smiling, nor did it keep Mick's hand from being permanently attached to the small of my back.

When we reached the sanctity of my office and the door closed, steam began pouring from his ears and nose. "Damn it, Ronnie. I can't believe you did that!"

Mick began pacing the boundaries of my small office, showing all the anxiety that I had been feeling since I found Crutchfield dead. Oddly enough, his anxiety calmed me.

"You told the murderer you knew who he was!"

"Or she."

The man actually growled at me. His hands reached for my neck as his face turned various shades of red. Finally, he dropped into the chair, sighed and covered his face with those same hands.

After a couple of minutes, he looked up, recovered somewhat, but with worry remaining in his eyes. I reached for one of his hands. A surprise to both of us.

"What's going to happen now?" he said quietly.

"Well, I expect that Crutchfield's killer will try to kill me. At least I hope so."

"You hope so?"

"Mick, this is the only way I could think of to draw the killer out. I'm the bait."

"There has to be some other way."

"What? Keep waiting for snakes, bumps on the head, and being shot at?" And then a bitterness crept into my voice that I couldn't keep out. "Or should I just let myself be charged with murder?"

"It's better than being a murder victim."

"No, it's not. I can't have everyone looking at me like I'm a killer. It will destroy my reputation as a professor. I'd have to go into hiding or something."

"But at least you'd be alive."

"Alive, not living."

Mick and I were at a standoff, so whoever knocked on my door at that moment had great timing. As I started to walk around Mick, he put his arm out to prevent me from getting to the door.

"Okay, just stop with this macho bullshit. Our killer's not stupid enough to kill me in a building full of people right after I addressed the building full of people. Get a grip."

In order to avoid getting hit by the door, Mick had to move behind it as I reached for the doorknob. Probably a good thing or he might have scared off my visitor.

"P-p-p-professor Raven? Can I speak with you a moment?" he stuttered.

"Certainly, Joe Bob. Have a seat."

In moving to the comfy chair, Joe Bob had failed to see Mick, and Mick seemed content to leave it that way for the moment. I resumed my seat and settled my forearms on my desk. "What can I do for you?"

"First of all, I want to apologize for trying to scare you that day in Crutchfield's office," he stammered.

"Was that the day that you claimed to be looking for your paper?"

Joe Bob's eyes grew larger. "I *was* looking for my paper, I swear."

Behind Joe Bob, I watched Mick get into ready mode. His body was tense and ready to spring into action. His pose made me braver . . . or a little reckless. "You mean you weren't putting a paper back in a box so that I would find it?"

Confusion rained down on Joe Bob's face. "Why would I do that? I just . . ."

"Or had I interrupted you from finding your paper a couple of nights before that? The night you hit me over the head?"

If I thought that I would make Joe Bob mad enough to spill something, I was wrong.

"Professor, I swear I didn't do any of those things. Honest!"

Out of all my suspects, Joe Bob had probably been the most likely, because frankly, I just didn't like the kid. But I'm usually a pretty good judge of character and unless this kid was Oscar material, he was telling me the truth.

"What about a snake? Know anything about rattlesnakes, Joe Bob?"

A pink tinge soon covered his face as he looked away. "It wasn't me."

Mick spoke up. "Who was it, then?"

Joe Bob jumped out of his seat, his eyes moving back and forth between Mick and me. He mumbled.

"I'm sorry, I didn't quite make that out," I said.

Moving toward the door, Joe Bob said, "Look, I've said enough. I'm just going to . . ."

"Think again, Mr. Football," Mick said quietly, blocking Joe Bob's escape.

Joe Bob sized up Mick, slightly smaller and much skinnier than himself. He sighed and returned to my desk. "I think it might have been Coach."

"What?" I'm sure I looked like I could have swallowed a fish.

"Why do you think that?" Mick asked.

"Because I met him on the stairs that day I saw you in Crutchfield's office. I told him about not being able to find my midterm paper and not having a grade." Joe Bob began rhythmically tapping his hands on his lap. "He said I shouldn't have gone into Crutchfield's office, and that he had already checked it out."

Mick and I looked at each other at the same time. Could Coach Henderson have gifted me with a lump on the skull?

Joe Bob continued. "Coach said that he'd taken care of the situation already. That he had left a present for you. I had thought he meant some kind of bribe, but then I heard people at the lecture talking about a rattlesnake being in your office."

I nodded. Since no one had slipped me an envelope filled with cash, Joe Bob's guess was probably right on target.

"I swear to you I didn't know about that. I wouldn't do something like leave a snake to bite you. And I'm not getting anywhere near a rattlesnake without a shotgun."

A man after my own heart. "Thanks for enlightening us, Joe Bob. I appreciate it. In the next two months, if you continue to make intelligent decisions like this, then passing psychology shouldn't be a problem."

Joe Bob nodded and walked to the door, keeping an eye on Mick all the way. After he left, I blew out a gust of air. "I believe him."

"Me, too."

"Do you think Coach Henderson is the one who took a shot at me in the library?"

Mick didn't speak for a moment as he mulled around the possibilities. Finally, he straightened up. "I don't know, but it sounds like we need to question Coach Henderson. I'm going to update Melvin with all of this."

I snorted. Like that would do any good. You could serve the

good detective the killer's head on a platter and it wouldn't do any good.

"I guess it's pointless to tell you to stay out of trouble while I'm gone."

I smiled. The man was starting to understand me after all.

CHAPTER TWENTY

The murder lecture had ended at two-twenty. I knew it would be some time before the killer made his or her next move. Probably after the building cleared. One thing, perhaps the only thing, I knew without a doubt, was that the killer wasn't stupid. Crutchfield had been murdered in the early-morning hours. It had been late evening when I was attacked in Crutchfield's office. No one saw anyone enter my office, much less walk down the halls with a snake in tow in the middle of the day. And, of course, the library—also in the early-morning hours. The killer didn't like an audience.

Mick had thankfully been called away from my office before he could shackle himself to me. But he wanted a promise that I would stay put. I told him I would be exactly where I was supposed to be. I only hoped that he returned to the building in time.

Several congratulatory visits came from students and professors alike about the lecture. But hours passed with no visits from any of my suspects. It crossed my mind that I could be totally off base. What if the killer wasn't one of the people I suspected? I mean, wasn't the murderer usually the person you least expected? If that was true . . .

My reveries were interrupted by a strong, solid knock that made my knees so weak that I had to sit. I managed a hoarse "Enter" and sat on my shaky hands.

Zachariah. With an unidentifiable expression on his face.

Determination. Determined to do what? To fire me or kill me? He closed the door behind him. No audience.

"Two visits in a week." I forced a smile. "I'm honored."

"That was some lecture you gave today. The phones haven't stopped ringing."

Commenting about the phones told me nothing. Zachariah was funny about attention. He wanted the department to have attention, but only the right kind. My eyes strayed to midway up his suit, where the white shirt rose from the V made by his jacket. I couldn't look him in the eyes, not yet. If I could only work up the nerve to . . .

"Do you think you might be interested in doing a criminal-behavior course next year?" he said, sitting down.

"Me?" My voice came out as a squeak, probably because all the oxygen was directed toward containing my rapid heartbeat. My eyes connected with his. He was serious.

"You presented the material very well. And I have to admit"—he paused—"well, there does seem to be a morbid curiosity about criminals. All those crime shows on television."

I nodded, my only thought that Zachariah couldn't be the killer. Why would he be making plans for next semester if he was about to kill me?

"You seem surprised, Ronnie."

"To be honest, I wasn't sure how you would react. And you looked so solemn when you came in."

"That's because I've finally reached a decision." Zachariah sighed, suddenly looking more human. More like the Zachariah who hired me three years ago. "Regardless of what that oaf Melvin says, I know you didn't kill Weldon. In fact, I had more reason to kill him, which you probably suspected."

What could I say? The man was looking me directly in the face. To deny that I suspected him would have been an obvious lie.

Zachariah stood, shoving his hands into his pants pockets. "I certainly wanted to kill him."

"If it's any consolation, I believe a lot of people did." I paused for a minute—about as long as I could contain my curiosity. "What did Crutchfield have on you, Zachariah?"

"You are intelligent, Ronnie. I always knew that, even with your . . . your unorthodox ways." Zachariah smiled, but the smile didn't reach his eyes. "I just finished sending a letter to the regents and the president of the university."

To say I was at the edge of my seat wouldn't have been an exaggeration. It took all my willpower to not jump on top of Zachariah and demand he satisfy my curiosity immediately. I watched him walk over to the bookcase, making a pretense of perusing my books. He came dangerously close to the manuscript hiding behind the Taos print.

"Before I came to PU, I had a brilliant paper published on cognitive conditioning. It received a lot of attention. And I believe it was why I was considered for the position as head of this department."

Zachariah turned back to my expectant pose. "The paper was a lie. I changed some statistics to make it look good. I felt that at the time . . ." Zachariah sighed. "That the actual results wouldn't make a publishable paper."

"And Crutchfield found out," I said softly, understanding sending me reeling back in my chair.

Zachariah nodded. "And whenever I called him on anything . . ."

"Like sexually harassing female students."

"Yes, like sexually harassing female students," Zachariah answered curtly. "Crutchfield threatened to blow the whistle. Then he showed me his book."

Zachariah moved closer, placing his hands on my desk, for emphasis or support, I wasn't sure which. "It was trash, Ronnie, pure trash. Just one of the many psychobabble books out there that the public gobbles up. He laughed when I told him he couldn't publish it as a member of Pursley's faculty."

Pausing for a moment, with trouble etched on his face, Zachariah turned from me. "Weldon said that if I tried to stop his book from being published, he would tell everybody—the academic community, the regents, everyone—about my being a fraud."

"What did you do?"

"Nothing at first, but finally I realized my tolerance had gone on long enough. I had to blow the whistle first and remove Weldon's power over me."

I took a wild guess. "But then he wound up dead."

"Yes. I admit I was relieved. I thought all my problems were solved. Then a funny thing happened."

"What was that?"

"I had trouble eating, sleeping."

"Your conscience kicked in. Congratulations, Zachariah."

He smiled, really smiled, and looked like he was about to say more when the phone rang.

"Hello?"

"Ronnie? Terry."

"Uh, hi." I hesitated, but Zachariah was already heading out the door with a wave of his hand.

"Everything's ready."

I breathed in deeply. "Good."

"Ronnie, are you sure you want to do this? You can always bail out."

"After all your hard work?" I teased.

"I wouldn't mind."

For Terry to not respond to teasing meant he was really worried. And our friendship was too important to me to give him false hope, so I settled for honesty.

"It's gone too far already, Terry. At least this way I have some control. Remember, if you haven't heard from me—Mick or me—by eight P.M. . . ."

"I know. I call the cops. Be careful." He paused. "Where else would I find a best friend who thinks I'm so brilliant?"

"Ditto."

After hanging up the phone, I glanced at my watch: almost seven P.M. The building was probably clearing out. It was time. I moved to my window, startled by the nearness of the moon. Swollen with anticipation, it looked ready to burst. I had always felt an affinity with the moon. Crazies came out when the moon was full.

I pulled a manila envelope out of my desk and walked over to Taos to retrieve the manuscript. After sticking it in the envelope, I sealed it and wrote Zachariah Bent's name on it. Before stepping out in the hallway, I put a note on my door, one written days ago when my hands weren't shaking. The note told visitors they could find me in my new office, formerly Crutchfield's office.

Desiree stepped around the corner, placing herself in my path. Her sudden appearance caught me so off guard that I couldn't keep a brief squeal from escaping and my hand reaching up to clutch my chest.

"Desiree, you startled me."

"We need to talk, Professor Raven."

Gone was the eager-to-please student. Gone was the rocking motion from side to side. I didn't know this Desiree, and I wasn't sure I wanted to.

"Well, I'm on my way to another appointment right now . . ."

"It's very important. Can we go into your office, please?"

It was at that moment that I saw a bulge in her front pants pocket. Hysterically, it reminded me of the old phrase "is that a gun or are you just happy to see me?" Technically, it wouldn't work in this situation as Desiree was female, but there was obviously something in her pocket. Something that could very well be a gun.

"Can't—can't we just talk in the hall? I really am in a hurry."

"Please, Dr. Raven. This is something private. Something between you and me."

I looked up and down the hall. Shit. Not a soul in sight. Where are people when you need them? I shrugged. If no one was around, what was the difference if I got shot in my office or out in the hall?

I walked back inside the office, keeping my back toward Desiree even as I heard her quietly shut the door. Maybe I could talk her out of it.

"Look, Desiree, you really don't want to . . ." I turned and stopped short while I watched her right hand reaching into a pocket in her floral skirt. Reaching toward a definite bulge. I'd like to say I started praying at that moment. But I didn't.

"Oh shit, oh shit, oh shit," I muttered, wanting to close my eyes, but unable to.

When Desiree withdrew a tape recorder from that pocket, I didn't know whether to laugh, cry, or scream. Before my shocked brain could make a decision, Desiree pushed a button.

A squeal emitted before a faint voice I recognized as Desiree's filled the office. "P-p-professor Cr-cr-crutchfield?"

There was a sound of a door closing. "Yes, my dear, what can I do for you?"

Death usually softens our opinions of others, but even knowing that Weldon Crutchfield died violently didn't change the fact that he sounded like a slug.

"I'd like to talk to you about my grade," Desiree said on tape, her voice shaking. "I'd like you to reconsider and give me the A I believe I deserve."

Weldon's laugh boomed across the tape player. "Does that

mean you're willing to make time for the personal instruction I offered you?"

"Please, Professor, I just want my grade based on my paper. If you'll at least tell me what's wrong with my midterm paper, I'll be glad to fix it . . ."

"My dear, I haven't even looked at your midterm paper, and stop that infernal swinging back and forth. It's giving me a headache."

"But you said . . . you said I was going to flunk your course unless . . . unless I slept with you!"

"I don't believe I ever used the word 'slept,' dear Desiree. It's so archaic. A euphemism. I talk about euphemisms extensively in my book. You'll have to buy it. I'll even autograph it for you. But I digress. I believe you could learn a lot from me and, in turn, earn that A you covet so much. Come, why don't you sit down here next to me. You don't look well and . . ."

I couldn't make out the rest of what he was saying because it became muffled, but the look on the face in front of me, Desiree's face, told the story. Anger. Frustration. Tears.

The tape quality dramatically improved when I again heard the taped voice of Desiree. "Do you see this, Professor Crutchfield? I've been taping you. What you're doing is wrong. It's illegal. You can't make me have sex with you in exchange for an A."

"Give me that tape, you little bitch." Crutchfield's voice rang out loud and very angry.

"N-n-no."

"You can't fight me, you know. But I've gotten tired of this little tirade. You'll get your A and not because you deserve it, but because I'm tired of your childish antics. Now get out!"

Desiree turned off the tape recorder, and we were both quiet for several minutes.

I leaned against the front of my desk. "That was a very brave thing you did, Desiree, but why are you telling it all to me?"

"What you said in your lecture. About people having reason to kill Crutchfield. I had a reason to kill him. That's why I made this tape. If I hadn't had the proof, I think I would have been the one to kill him."

"What about Trevor?"

Desiree shook her head vehemently. "He wouldn't harm a fly."

I wasn't sure it made a difference one way or another, but I wondered how much he knew. "Has he heard this tape?"

She shook her long strawberry hair from side to side. "He got so upset about Crutchfield coming on to me."

I interrupted. "Sexually harassing you."

Desiree's back straightened and her voice became stronger as she echoed me. "Yes, sexually harassing me. Trevor thinks he should have been able to stop it. But it really didn't have anything to do with him. Anyway, I just wanted you to know."

She ejected the tape and turned it over to me before turning around to open the door. Smiling, Desiree waved before leaving.

I wasn't as sure as Desiree that Trevor had nothing to do with Crutchfield's murder. He, like others, had much to gain by Crutchfield's death. I ran up the stairs to Zachariah's suite of offices. All was dark and locked, so I stuck the envelope and the tape in the mail slot in the door before returning to the second floor, this time to Crutchfield's office. I steeled myself not to jump at every noise. I didn't know who might be watching, and I wanted the killer to feel at ease with the idea that I didn't suspect anything.

It took every ounce of strength I had to open Crutchfield's door instead of running all the way home to James Dean. As usual, the door squeaked in greeting. The glow from the desk lamp threw off eerie shadows that would be to my advantage as

I took a quick glance at Crutchfield's desk. Everything was in place.

I didn't know how much time I had so I assumed my position, squeezing my body into the small closet. Even if I could have, there was no way to relax in such cramped quarters. The speaker chip that Terry left for me was quickly bathed in sweat. Surely it wouldn't short circuit or, worse, electrocute me.

A long drawn-out squeak interrupted my paranoia. In one brief moment, I relived all the times I had heard that door's irritating squeal. Every time but once. My breath caught as I realized who the killer was. The killer who must have been hiding in the bathroom when I discovered Crutchfield's body. I wasn't as surprised as I thought I would be. Perhaps I had known all along.

"What can I do for you?" I tensed, hoping my voice really sounded like it was coming from behind the desk. Otherwise, I was dead meat.

"Interesting lecture today."

"Thanks."

"I especially enjoyed the part at the end where you brought up possible motives for killing Weldon."

"And did one of them apply to you?"

"You know it did. Do you have any idea what it was like? He was brilliant, and I loved him."

"But he hurt you, Paula."

"I have more broken bones than you'll ever know. Bruises. Injuries people couldn't see. But that wasn't the worst of it." She sobbed, pulling something out of her pocket I couldn't quite make out.

"He had this power over me. Even after we got divorced, he still had power over me and wouldn't let me go," she sobbed. The ex–Mrs. Crutchfield hadn't strayed very far from her husband.

"His research papers. You wrote them, didn't you?"

"That's why I couldn't submit anything under my own name. The styles would be too similar. Somebody would have suspected, and he would have killed me."

"What about the book?"

Paula laughed in that near-hysterical way that somebody at the end of her rope has. "That piece of trash? He tried to force me, threaten me, but I finally stood my ground. No, the book was all Weldon, thank God."

"Paula, listen to me . . ."

"Don't you understand? I had to destroy his power over me. It was my only chance for a life. And now you want to take that away from me! I don't understand how I missed you in the library. I always hit what I aim at. I learned from Weldon."

Paula was so wrapped up in her pain that she didn't notice that the body at the desk, the one she thought was me, didn't move. Didn't move even when she straightened her arms and aimed a gun at the head. What could have been my head.

I tried to push against the closet door, sure that I could stop her. "Paula, no, you don't want to do this!" Instead, the door stuck.

Flickers of light surrounded me, and I heard whispering. I couldn't make out the words, but I had heard this sound once before. These whispers, these flickers of light, had been in the woods with me behind Granny's house when I was seven. They had led me back to her house when I got lost. The Little People had protected me.

My guardian angels said good-bye immediately before the blast of a gunshot. The closet door swung open easily as a bewildered Mick burst into the office with Melvin right behind him. Paula screamed.

And a storm of foam pieces danced in the air before raining down on the desk.

CHAPTER TWENTY-ONE

"So, this professor of yours was a real shit who probably deserved to be killed," Terry said, before stuffing half a slice of garbage can pizza in his mouth.

Before I could answer, Terry jumped up, fanning his mouth. "Shit, Ronnie, why didn't you tell me this had jalapeños on it!"

I watched him pour half a bottle of Coors Light on top of the fire. "I told you it had everything on it."

"Everything doesn't mean jalapeños, you sadistic woman."

I laughed. It felt good to laugh. Really laugh, without having to look over my shoulder. It was over. Finally over. I knew it for certain when Detective Melvin gave me a forced—but possibly sincere—apology.

"Yeah. Crutchfield was screwing everyone in one way or another. Paula put up with his cruelty the longest. Apparently, she still had bruises up and down her arm. Some of them were in the shape of fingers. She just couldn't take any more. I hope she doesn't end up going to prison, though. I'm not even sure she can emotionally handle a trial."

"How come?"

"When she killed him, I think she hoped to break all ties with him, but apparently she still felt bound to him. Still heard his voice berating her all the time. And I don't think my foam rubber remains did anything to help her flimsy hold on reality."

I still regretted that part. If I had known for sure that Paula was the killer, maybe I would have done things differently. At least, I hoped so. She had already been through so much, that thinking she was shooting me and seeing foam . . . well, suffice to say that Mick had no difficulty taking the gun from her hand.

"Better than your remains, love."

"I suppose so. You did a great job on my dummy, by the way."

"I was inspired. So, what was the deal with Crutchfield and everyone else?"

"Well, I already told you about his blackmailing Zachariah. Justin is just what he appears to be—an ambitious, although inadequate, professor." I shook my head. Because everything made so much sense now, it was difficult to understand why I suspected some of these people. "And, of course, Crutchfield was trying to force Desiree into having sex with him in exchange for an A. Grades were so important to her that the anxiety sent her bulimia into full throttle."

"Please," said Terry. "Not while I'm eating."

I grinned. "She's back in a support group. And she's going to try to get a B this semester. Break that perfectionism habit."

"And the boyfriend?"

"Trevor? He's doing okay. Lies were his way of protecting Desiree. Both were afraid the other had killed Crutchfield."

"Are you disappointed that it wasn't the football player?"

"No. Not now, anyway. Joe Bob is actually working very hard. I think he really has a brain. He just didn't know it."

Terry finally tossed a half-eaten piece of pizza back in the box, groaned and fell over on my floor, which James Dean took as an invitation to lick the remaining crumbs and pizza sauce from Terry's face.

"Away, you mongrel! You're not my type!"

Terry rolled away, leaving James Dean looking at Terry with such heartbroken eyes that Terry reached for the half-eaten slice and tossed it in the air. James Dean gratefully caught it and went to the corner to do his chewing.

The phone started to ring. I pushed my own rather stuffed self off the couch to reach for it.

"Hi, Mom."

"How did you know it was me?" Maureen Raven exclaimed. "Maybe you're developing the sight, too!"

"Maybe." I didn't have the heart to tell her that it was her predictability that told me who the caller was. I knew my mother would sense that all was right in my universe and call.

"So, everything is okay now? I've had really strong feelings about you during the last day or so."

"Everything's fine." I saw no reason to burden her with the more harrowing points of my week. "I think I need another spring break, though."

"Why don't you come see us?"

Something in her tone of voice made me think the invitation wasn't exactly innocent. "Mom," I warned.

"He's just gorgeous, Veronica. He's an attorney, but that can't be helped. He works in the tribal office, and I've told him all about you, and . . ."

James Dean started yipping and yapping at the front door. Terry was passed out on the floor with only enough energy to zap the TV with the remote changer every fifteen seconds.

I said a couple of *uh-huhs* to my mother and walked over to the picture window. Through a jungle of houseplants, I watched Mick get out of his car. The Range Rover. Wearing a civilian uniform of blue jeans and T-shirt. And walking up the sidewalk to my house.

ABOUT THE AUTHOR

K. B. Gibson has more than twenty years of experience as a freelance writer for magazines, business, curriculum, nonfiction books, and the Internet. This is her first mystery. She resides with her family in Oklahoma and looks for any excuse to travel in the Southwest.